DISTANT
FINISH

A NOVEL

Steven Decker

Praise for *Distant Finish*

A relentless and poignant narrative of the challenges we face, not only in sports, but in relationships, parenting, and life. Anyone who enjoys strong, well-defined characters, intense action scenes, and finding a way to carry on will love this book. Packed with powerful truths that resonate deeply. A great read for fiction and non-fiction readers alike!
—Joanne Frantzis, Endurance Triathlete, Connecticut

Through Distant Finish I relived the roller coaster of emotions that comes from racing in triathlon. I loved this book because it covers so many of the internal personal battles one faces in the sport. It also motivated me to compete again soon, and I'm looking forward to the next book!
—Jake Baily, Endurance Triathlete, Lafayette, California

An excellent story! So many different kinds of competitions—swimming, running, open water, even football, and of course, triathlons! I'm amazed that a book like this wasn't written sooner!
—Casey Conlon, Endurance Triathlete, Marathon Runner, Texas

A fun and action-packed portrayal of how people become involved in triathlon, how they train, and what it means to become the best you can be. The Iconic Triathlon intrigued me because as an athlete with his strength in swimming, the long swim and shorter bike (with drafting!) would change my training plan for the event, and would give strong swimmers a legitimate chance of winning the race. An inspiring story of attaining your goals.
—Scott Berlinger, Founder /Head Coach, Full Throttle Endurance Racing, New York, and Former American Gladiator "Viper"

Printed in the United States of America
Published in Hellertown, PA
Cover and interior design and illustrations by Leanne Coppola
Library of Congress Control Number 2021911836
ISBN 978-1-952481-45-1
2 4 6 8 10 9 7 5 3 1 paperback

For more information or to place bulk orders, contact the publisher at Jennifer@BrightCommunications.net.
BrightCommunications.net

For my daughter, Paige, whose competitive spirit surpasses that of a normal human being, and whose keen insights helped me write a story worth telling. And for my sons, Cam and Colin, two great swimmers who taught me all I know about that wonderful sport, and much more. Family is a gift to be cherished and nurtured, our natural defense against life's relentless challenges.

PROLOGUE

2026 Iconic Triathlon World Championships—
Montreal, Canada
10K Swim, 100K Bike, 42.2K Run

Pro Women Leaders After T2 (Bike to Run transition)
1. Allie West
2. Liza Whitlock

There were 14 kilometers (8.7 miles) left in the race, and Liza was catching Allie. Suddenly, Allie had an idea. She would keep her pace right where it was. She knew what this meant, and sure enough, after about 5 kilometers (3.1 miles), Liza came up beside her. Allie glanced at Liza to gauge her condition and was both stunned and elated by what she saw. Liza looked horrible. Her face was red, and her breath was labored. She looked nothing like the beautiful, elegant woman that Allie knew. She appeared to be on the verge of collapse. But the ugly snarl on Liza's face resembled that of a rabid animal, and *that* is what caused Allie to consider that Liza might actually be able to continue on at this pace. She didn't turn her head to look at Allie. She just kept running, staring out into the distance, drawing in ragged breath after ragged breath, obviously deep inside her own mind, concentrating, as if she meant to do what had to be done, no matter what the cost. This frightened Allie, for herself *and* for Liza.

Allie increased her speed to stay beside her rival. That seemed to be the best plan. Just stay with her, if she could. They continued on this way for another 5 kilometers (3.1 miles). It was a brutal battle of wills, neither athlete giving an inch. The two women were virtually the same height, and while Liza's bright red aerosuit was easily distinguishable from Allie's black and white suit, their legs moved in unison. Relentlessly, side by side, mile after mile, they duplicated each other's stride and pace. There were now only 4 kilometers (2.5 miles) left in the race, and they were still together.

Allie was feeling the pain of the accelerated pace now. It was faster than she'd ever run in a marathon, and it was taking its toll on her. But she stayed with Liza, even though Liza showed no sign of slowing down. The pain and exhaustion were overwhelming, but as she thought about it, Allie realized that Liza had to be feeling just as bad as her, maybe even worse. Knowing this, she refused to back down.

Pro Men Leaders After T2 (Bike to Run transition)
1. Michael Stevens
2. Billy Dexter

When Michael completed the second loop of three in the marathon, Ziggy updated him, speaking rapidly as he ran along beside the road.

"Your lead is down to 3 minutes. If he catches you, it's gonna be in the final 5K. The 'stay calm' mantra goes out the window at that point, dude!"

"*You're telling me that now?*" thought Michael, too exhausted to speak as he streaked past Ziggy.

"Better late than never!" screamed Ziggy, as if reading Michael's mind.

Michael understood Ziggy's logic. If Billy caught him with such a short distance remaining in the marathon, Michael would have to stay with him, and that might mean running even faster than he was running at that moment, which didn't seem possible. A more realistic outcome was that he simply couldn't win the race—unless Billy somehow faltered. Unfortunately, Billy always won when it mattered most. He'd been doing that to Michael ever since they were 10 years old.

All I can do is give it my best, Michael thought. *That's all I could ever do, and that's what I'm going to do now.* He considered trying to increase his speed to compensate for Billy's relentless eradication of the time gap between them, but then he decided his best option, perhaps his *only* option, was to stay calm and see what happened. If Billy could catch him, he definitely was Superman. If Billy didn't catch him, then the "stay calm" mantra would prove to be Billy's kryptonite.

Michael continued running strong for another 5K (3.1 miles), but then his legs began to tighten up. His pace slowed dramatically to 3:55/K (6:18/mile) and continued to slip. With only 8K (5 miles) to go in the race, the cramps in Michael's legs worsened, and his pace slowed further to 4:00/K (6:26/mile). He checked his heart rate and saw it was redlining, meaning he dare not try to speed up until his heart rate came down, which would happen with his slower pace. But slowing down was exactly the opposite of what he needed if he was to have any hope of winning the race. Michael feared this predicament would cause him to succumb, once again, to Billy's extraordinary talent and indomitable will, and when he turned his head to look behind him, he saw the inevitable. Superman was on his tail, less than half a kilometer (0.3 mile) back and closing in.

PART ONE

CHAPTER 1

Late Summer 2005

"Swimmers, take your mark," came the starter's voice over the amplified start system.

The crowd fell silent. Ten-year-old Michael Stevens crouched into the start position on the starting block in lane 3, gripping the front of the block tightly. His best friend, Billy Dexter, did the same in lane 2. The predominant thought in Michael's mind at that moment was, *Why me?*

This was the Northern Virginia Tri-County All-Star Championship, the culmination of the summer season for the year 2005. Swimmers from more than 100 teams had competed in 15 Divisional Championship meets the week before, for a divisional championship title, and also for one of the coveted 18 spots in each event at the All-Star meet. Three heats of six swimmers gave it everything they had to become the best of the best in northern Virginia.

This was the final heat of the 10 and Under Boys 100-meter IM (Individual Medley). The six swimmers with the fastest seed times from the past week's competitions were in this heat. Michael had beaten Billy by more than a full body length in the IM at the Division I Championships last weekend. Nevertheless, Billy's time was fast enough to give him the third seed, behind Michael and the boy from Division II, who was swimming in lane 4.

In the regular season meets, Michael normally swam freestyle and backstroke, which suited his tall, slender frame, while Billy, being stockier and more powerful, specialized in butterfly and breaststroke. Both of them had already won their respective events earlier that morning. Now they had to battle against each other. For Billy, it was no problem. For Michael, it was gut-wrenching. He knew Billy would swim faster this week than he did last week. A lot faster. Billy did not like to lose.

Michael had been a year-round swimmer since he was six years old. Billy never swam in the winter. His parents couldn't afford it, and he really didn't care about swimming the way Michael did. What Billy liked was competing. Billy loved playing tackle football in the fall more than any other sport, although he also excelled at club wrestling in the winter. Michael, on the other hand, was not a naturally competitive person. He was simply an extremely good athlete who had been pushed by his parents to excel. He liked winning, but he cared more about friendship than championships. Yet he felt the pressure from his parents to train and win, train and win. Michael dreaded their disappointment on those rare occasions when he didn't win.

The horn went off, and the six swimmers hurled themselves forward. The water was warmer than it had been at the beginning of the summer. It was mid-August, and the hot summer sun had done its job for several months. Michael took an early lead due to his long underwater at the start, but Billy's powerful arms and legs pulled him into a lead of half a body length over Michael at the end of the butterfly lap. But now it was the backstroke leg. Michael got a great push off the wall. With his back now turned toward the bottom of the pool, he extended his long arms out in front of himself, staying underwater for nearly a third of a pool length, dolphin kicking for propulsion. He'd been taught that you could gain more speed underwater than on top of the water, and he took full advantage of it.

Billy had been taught this as well, but he believed his strength and intensity were more critical to victory than perfect technique. He came up off the wall much sooner than Michael, resuming his relentless battle with the water, furiously thrashing his powerful arms in a rapid-fire cadence. Billy's intensity wasn't enough to overcome Michael's skill, however. The lap ended with Michael a full body length ahead of Billy going into the breaststroke leg of the race.

Michael pushed off and got a good pull and kick underwater, maintaining his lead, while Billy, impatient for air, didn't stay under as long as would be ideal. But when the pulling and kicking began, Billy's abnormally strong arms and legs did their work, and he began to cut into Michael's lead. Michael didn't succumb to the temptation of looking back, first because it was poor technique, and second, because he caught a glimpse of the horrified looks on his parents' faces as he came up for air. This told him that Billy was catching him. Their expressions clearly demonstrated their utter disbelief that a poor, summer-only swimmer with less-than-ideal technique could challenge their well-to-do, highly trained, year-round champion of a son.

Billy pulled up beside Michael as the breaststroke leg came to a close. They touched the wall at almost exactly the same time, both of them more than a body length ahead of the swimmer in third place. The crowd let out a deafening roar as they made the turn for the final leg—freestyle. Michael was tired, but he knew Billy had to be even more tired, because Billy didn't train like Michael did. But things like being tired or winded just didn't seem to matter to Billy when winning or losing was at stake. Billy would either win, or he would die trying. Michael knew this, and even though he was a freestyler and Billy wasn't, he was certain that he was in for the race of his life in this last 25 meters.

Because Michael was in lane 3 and breathed to his left side on sprints, he had a good view of Billy in lane 2. Billy also breathed to the left side, so his view of Michael was restricted to the moments when his head was down in the water. But Michael strongly suspected that Billy wasn't looking at him, not at all. Billy was undoubtedly focusing on going so fast that no one could hold him off, not even a more experienced swimmer like Michael.

Michael once again used his skill underwater, along with a dolphin kick, to pull ahead off the turn. But each time he rotated his head up to breathe, he saw Billy thrashing the water like an out-of-control jackhammer. And with each breath he took, he saw Billy gaining on him. Michael pulled harder, concentrated harder, and worried more. It seemed that no matter how hard he pulled, no matter how much he increased his stroke count, he couldn't fight Billy off.

Billy pulled even with Michael with 10 meters to go. The crowd was going crazy. This was the kind of race that got the adrenaline going. Billy was inching ahead. Michael knew he had to get a good touch on the wall. He whipped his right arm into the water, stretched and rotated simultaneously, keeping his eyes down. He knew Billy would just slap his fingers against the touchpad that would record his time, as he always did, but Michael was also aware that Billy went into the finish about a foot ahead of him. In most races, Billy's poor technique didn't matter because he was so far ahead at the end of the race that a smooth finish was unnecessary. But Michael hoped this time it *would* matter. They hit their touchpads at virtually the same instant.

Both boys jerked their heads up to look at the electronic scoreboard. There it was. Billy had defeated Michael by two 100ths of a second, setting a new meet record of 1:12.87. The boys shook hands and got out of the water, both panting hard. Michael would soon face the hardest part—his parents.

CHAPTER 2

The drive home in the Mercedes sedan did nothing but delay the inevitable. No one spoke. Neither Michael's father nor his mother congratulated him for winning the 50-freestyle. His second-place finish in the 100 Individual Medley, with the second fastest time ever swum at the All-Star meet, did not merit even a "nice try" from either of them.

The unspoken, yet clearly understood, motto of the Stevens family was "Winning Is Everything." Michael remembered a documentary the family had watched one evening about the great Vince Lombardi, when the narrator with the deep voice had recited one of Lombardi's favorite quotes: "Winning isn't everything, but making the effort to win is." Michael also remembered his father's casual comment at the conclusion of this recitation. His father had simply said, "Wrong."

When the family arrived at their estate in the heart of McLean, Virginia, the electric gate that blocked the back driveway entrance slid open. Michael's father drove slowly up the winding drive and pulled into the detached four-car garage behind the massive home. The home was old, having originally been built in the late 1700s by ancestors from his mother's side of the family, but it had been renovated, expanded, and modernized many times. The estate sat on a beautiful 10-acre plot of land, which by itself was worth well over $10 million.

The family could easily afford to hire a driver and live-in servants, but they elected not to do so, for the same reason they insisted that their only child attend public school. They wanted him to experience the "tougher" side of life. This, however, did not prevent them from having a housekeeper clean the house twice a week, a laundress, a shopping service, a gardener, and a chef who cooked dinner for them five days a week. The other two evenings, they dined at the country club.

When they got into the house, Michael's father said, "Go and take a shower and meet us in the dining room for lunch—and a conversation."

Michael knew what that meant. He quickly went to his room, showered, and got dressed, then went to the dining room for his lecture, anxious for all of this to be over. His mother had put sandwiches on the table, prepared the evening before by Chef Thomas. Michael took a ham and cheese, filled his glass with iced tea, and sat down.

Branford Stevens was already sitting at the head of the long oak table that seated 16. Even sitting, he towered over his wife, who was just around the corner from her husband. He was a large man, around 40 years old, and quite fit. He worked out seven days a week at the club. Branford owned several construction companies, including the one he had inherited from his father, Alexandria Asphalt Company. He was an imposing presence.

Michael sat down directly across from his mother, although he would have preferred to be at the other end of the table, or not in the room at all. Michael's father gave him time to take a bite of his sandwich, then initiated what he intended to be a life lesson for Michael.

"Michael, what do you think you could have done differently to ensure your victory in the 100 IM?" he asked pointedly.

Michael waited until he was finished chewing the bite from his sandwich, buying time while he tried to come up with an idea.

"Well, the first thing is I could have done more work in the fly and breast throughout the season," he said. He waited for a response. Nothing was forthcoming. His mother, sitting directly across from him, simply raised her eyebrows, suggesting he look for another answer.

"And I could have held my underwaters coming off the start and out of the turns just a little longer," he suggested, almost as a question. This elicited more raised eyebrows from his mother and a stoic poker face from his father.

"But more than anything," said Michael, "I could have swam harder." That seemed to get them going.

"Yes," opined his father. "That seems to be what was missing."

"Billy is half a foot shorter than you, Michael!" exclaimed his mother. "And he doesn't even swim year-round! His technique is horrid. I don't see how this could've happened." She collapsed her head into her hand, ashamed that her privileged son had lost to an impoverished boy from the other side of town. She appeared to be on the verge of tears.

"I don't know either, Mom. I'm sorry."

Christina Stevens was a confident woman. She dressed with confidence, not always wearing what might be expected by others in her social class. Today she sported simple jeans and a light blue short-sleeve cotton blouse. She was of medium height and fit, a few years younger than her husband. She kept her blonde hair short because longer hair bothered her when she was at the gym or working in the garden. She worked out five days a week at the club.

Unlike Branford, whose father was a self-made immigrant from England, Christina came from many generations of wealth. She'd grown up on this estate, which had been gifted to her in a trust from her parents, who were long since retired to the south of France. Christina had grown up never wanting for anything, to the point where it was virtually impossible for her to comprehend that she could actually want something, only to have it withheld from her. In this case, she had wanted very much for her son to win that race, and he had failed to do so.

"I love you, Michael," she said, almost weeping. "But you *must* do better."

"I will. I promise."

"Good," said his father. "Now finish your lunch and go do your homework."

"Can I go to the pool after that?" asked Michael.

"I suppose so," said his father. "You could work on your underwaters in the lap lane. As you said, you could do better in that area. But never forget, supreme effort does not come without extreme pain."

CHAPTER 3

Later that day, Billy Dexter slipped quietly out of the gate at the Endless Woods Swim Club. In northern Virginia, many families belonged to private summer swim clubs. There were dozens and dozens of them throughout the area, and most of them were very reasonably priced. Even though money was always tight in the Dexter household, the dues at Endless Woods were within reach, especially because Billy's mom worked at the front desk and got a discount.

Billy's mom was working inside the pool house that day, but because she was nine months pregnant, she wouldn't be working there much longer. No one knew it at the time, but after she was rushed to the hospital a week later to deliver her second child, she would never return to the Endless Woods Swim Club.

That day, however, Jean Dexter was working tirelessly and couldn't keep a close eye on Billy. The truth was that Jean didn't feel she needed to watch over Billy; after all, he was 10 years old, and he had good judgment. She trusted him not to do anything foolish. It was indeed true that Billy could be trusted, but it was also true that he was a 10-year-old boy, and even good little boys love fun and freedom in the woods.

So, as Billy did on most afternoons at the pool, he snuck away from Endless Woods and darted into the forest behind the club. While the woods were not endless, they *did* cover enough acreage to provide several hiding places for clever, adventurous little boys. But Billy fully intended to be careful and not get into any kind of trouble. The place where he was going was very safe—once you got there. It was so safe, in fact, that he had named it The Fort.

The woods were full of tall, spooky oak trees, with a sprinkling of maples and walnuts, and even a few pines. Billy liked the pines best because they were very thick, making it difficult for people to see into them. The pines also dropped a blanket of soft brown needles to sit on. Even when it rained, Billy could stay pretty dry beneath them because he was protected by a thick canopy of green needles above and was sitting on a cushion of brown needles from seasons past.

Billy was headed toward his favorite stand of pines, the ones no one thought were of any use. These six pines were completely surrounded by a wide, circular field of threatening, prickly briars. Some kids said they'd seen copperhead snakes slithering into them, but Billy knew how to keep the snakes at bay if they really were around, and he'd taught his friend Michael how to as well. Billy knew that if you were determined, brave, and careful, you could overcome most obstacles. It seemed he'd known this his whole life, certainly he'd known this a long time before he turned 10. And he'd been trying to teach this to Michael for a while.

Billy and Michael had met in kindergarten and would go

on to spend 12 more years together in elementary school, junior high, and high school. And they saw each other all summer long at swim practice and played together at the pool in the afternoons. But with all of this in common, Billy and Michael were from very different worlds. Michael had the look of the "beautiful people." He was blond, blue-eyed, tall, and slender, with perfect teeth. His only physical flaw was a scar about two inches long that ran across his chin. He'd been pushed into an empty swimming pool when he was four and had landed on his face. The scar would probably be with him forever, but Michael seemed to like it. He'd told Billy the scar made him more of a "normal" person.

Billy had the dark hair and muscular physique of his father. His facial features were angular, tougher looking than Michael's. His nose was wider. He was quite a bit shorter than Michael, but he weighed more due to a higher density of bone and muscle. Michael had well-developed muscles too, although he wasn't nearly as strong as Billy. But what made Billy distinctly different from Michael, and also from almost everyone else, were his eyes. One was cobalt blue, and the other was emerald green. Billy's green eye looked like it had been forged over the eons, deep within the Earth, and his blue eye seemed to have been spawned by the everlasting strength of the sea.

McLean was an affluent suburb of Washington, D.C., full of politicians, professional athletes, and many other wealthy, famous people. Even the CIA headquarters was in McLean, over in the exclusive Langley section of town. While McLean was affluent overall, like most towns, it *did* have its less desirable areas. Billy lived in one of those neighborhoods—small, ranch-style, two-bedroom houses, often in disrepair, with postage stamp, mostly unkempt, yards.

Michael's family's estate sat on the highest hill in McLean. The view from there turned everything in the distance, including Billy's neighborhood, into something not quite in focus. But the boys cared little for their differences. Their friendship was strong and enduring.

Billy veered off the thin path that went through the woods and made his way toward the briar patch. He pushed past a stand of oaks that gave way to the briars and then raised his hand to his forehead in a kind of salute, shielding his eyes from the hot August sun that penetrated the forest canopy. Billy surveyed his surroundings and confirmed that he hadn't been followed. He dropped down to his hands and knees, crawling around the circumference of the briar patch until he reached a small opening in the branches.

The first time Billy had gone into this opening, it hadn't been quite so big. Now it was bigger—maybe a couple of feet wide and a foot and a half high—because he and Michael had used it many times over the past five summers. Billy went down to his belly and low-crawled into the little tunnel of briars using his elbows, keeping his head low. He took his time. His dad had taught him that the best way to avoid a snake is to let it know you're coming. And the best way to do that was to go slow and make some noise along the way. His dad had told him that a snake didn't want to run into a person any more than a person wanted to run into a snake, so if a snake felt you coming, he'd head the other way.

Billy wriggled forward a few pulls, then stopped and beat his hand on the ground. His dad had told him that a snake could feel the vibrations of the ground much better than he could hear a sound. This was the perfect solution in this situation because Billy didn't want to be heard by people, only by snakes. The place he was going was a secret. Only he and Michael knew about it.

Billy wriggled forward a few more pulls and beat his hand on the ground again. He continued this regimen as he curled his way through the briars. Billy's T-shirt got caught a few times by the briars, but he patiently freed it without ripping it. There was no reason to ruin a good T-shirt, especially if it might lead to questions Billy didn't want to answer. The trip through the briars took about five minutes. It was only 30 feet or so to the stand of pines, but it took time to do it right.

Billy emerged from the briar tunnel directly under the branches of one of the pines. The two different species of plant life touched each other as if they were kindred spirits, mutual guardians of a great treasure. Billy crawled under the branches of the pine toward the center of the circle the pine helped to create, along with its five compatriots. He came out from under the pine into an open space that was about six feet in diameter. Michael was sitting on the far side of the circle.

"I beat you," said Michael, smiling.

"Ah don't think so," Billy retorted, his Southern accent contrasting markedly with Michael's perfect diction.

"I'm here, aren't I?" asked Michael.

"Ah mean this mornin'." Of course, Billy was referring to the 100 IM from earlier that day. Billy's tart reminder brought the taste of defeat back into Michael's mouth, if only for an instant. He rubbed the index finger of his right hand over the scar on his chin, something he always did when he felt emotional distress. In this case, he was reliving the unpleasantness of his parents' rebuke more than the actual loss itself.

"Yes, you had an awesome swim," Michael said, a little stiffly. "Nice job."

"Thanks," said Billy, feeling guilty about bringing it up. He hadn't meant to hurt his best friend, and he silently chastised himself for it. He felt guilty, but he also knew that he had no choice in the matter. He simply had to win. "My dad always taught me I should play by the rules, which I did. But he also taught me to play to win. And it don't matter what he says 'cause I can't help myself. When I'm competin', it's like I'm not a person anymore. I'm some kind of monster, I guess."

"I don't think you're a monster, bud, but whatever it is you have that drives you, my parents sure wish I had it."

"They were upset?" Billy asked.

"More than I was. I really feel like I gave it my best, but that doesn't seem to be good enough for them."

"Well, at least your parents show up at the meets," said Billy, somewhat despondently. Even though Billy knew both of his parents worked on Saturdays, his mom at the pool, and his dad on the asphalt crew, it still hurt that he had no one other than Michael to share his success with, and in this case, sharing his success with Michael was a sore spot Billy should probably have avoided. Yet the boys' friendship was so strong they could even talk about a situation like this, helping each other to get through it.

"You know they can't help that," said Michael. "I bet the first thing your mom asked when you showed up at the pool was how you did, and I bet she was so happy for you, and I bet she would have been happy for you no matter whether you won or not. Am I right?"

Billy pondered this. "You know, you're right. And my dad called my mom at the pool to find out how I did. When I think about it, I bet they both really would have wanted to be there."

"For sure they would have. My only regret is that my parents *were* there, and they didn't approve of my performance."

"Well, they're just trying to help. You know they love you, right?"

"I guess so," said Michael, feeling a little guilty about his negative feelings toward his parents.

"Hey," said Billy, "why don't we go for a bike ride down to the creek? Maybe we can catch something!"

"Like Grandaddy Pimmit maybe?" said Michael, referring to the legendary snapping turtle that was rumored to live in a deep hole down at Pimmit Run—a snapper that had never been seen by either of the boys in spite of years of hunting for him.

"Let's go!" said Billy. "Bet I can beat you out of here!" He disappeared into the tunnel, with Michael right behind him.

CHAPTER 4

Billy's mom died at night, 10 days after giving birth to her second child, Richard Wallace Dexter.

Wallace had been Jean Dexter's father's first name. Jean hoped Richie wouldn't grow up to be the unemployed alcoholic Wallace had been, but like most children, she had loved her father. It was important to her to keep his name alive, although a middle name was as far as she would go.

Jean Dexter, formerly Jean Jones, was born and raised in Madison County, North Carolina, the poorest county in the state. Madison County is in the northwest corner of North Carolina in the Appalachian Mountains and butts up against Tennessee. When Jean was growing up there, Madison County was dry, meaning it was illegal to sell or buy alcoholic beverages in the county. As a result, Madison had the highest percentage of alcoholics in the state. Moonshine was readily available, and it did the job quicker than the retail beer, wine, and liquor available just on the other side of the county line.

Jean left home at the age of 17, soon after her father accidentally killed himself, passing out at the wheel while driving drunk, the car careening off the road and cascading down a steep ridge. In spite of Jean's father's troubles with alcohol, he was always kind to her, and she appreciated that. But when he died, she saw her mother's burden alleviated now that only Jean and her older brother remained at home. So, she decided to venture out on her own. Jean's mother didn't try to stop her, giving her a few dollars to help her out the door and sending her on her way without a tear in her eyes. Jean ended up in northern Virginia, where she rented a tiny room in a boardinghouse and got a job at a convenience store in Alexandria.

Bill Dexter had been stopping at that store each day for his morning coffee long before Jean started working there. His eyes lit up the first time he saw her standing behind the counter. Jean was an attractive young woman. She tried to make herself presentable, always doing her hair and putting on a little makeup. She was self-conscious wearing the shirt the store made her wear, but it didn't seem to bother Bill. He was always very polite, and he flirted with her in his own shy way. Eventually, he asked her out, and it didn't take long for their relationship to become intimate.

Bill had also experienced a sad upbringing. Although he didn't know it, his father had been killed in a drug-related incident before Bill was born. His mother was an addict who ended up in jail when Bill was only one year old, leaving him with an aunt who really didn't want to raise a child, but carried on as best she could. Four year later, when Bill's mother got out of jail and took him back, he had no idea who she was. His mother ended up back in jail several times, eventually for an extended stay due to an armed robbery charge. At the age of 14, Bill became a ward of the state and was placed at St. Andrew's Home for Wayward Children.

Bill spent most of his next three years at St. Andrew's. He was given one chance in a foster home, but he couldn't adjust and was shipped back to St. Andrew's. St. Andrew's housed a lot of tough, underprivileged children and could sometimes be a dangerous place. But Bill learned to take care of himself, and he actually liked the strict rules and rigid schedule which to him were a breath of fresh air compared to the chaos and uncertainty of his life before coming there. He was one of only a few residents of St. Andrew's who were completely sold on the values of integrity and hard work that were taught there. He made it a point to move forward, never looking back with regret or misgivings.

By age 17, Bill secured a full-time job on an asphalt crew at Alexandria Asphalt Company. Soon thereafter, he was able to afford an apartment and ventured out on his own. When he was 20, he met Jean Jones, and it didn't take long before he asked her to marry him. They lived in his apartment for five years. When they conceived Billy, they moved to a rental house in McLean, which was known for its strong public school system. It took them 10 more years of trying until their second son was born. Richie was now 10 days old.

It was a Monday morning. School had been back in session since the middle of the prior week. The summer was over, but life went on the same as always for Bill Dexter. He woke at 5 a.m., as was his custom. He quietly slipped out of bed so as not to wake his wife, went to the kitchen, made coffee and toast, and enjoyed the morning paper. At 6 a.m. sharp, he went to wake Jean before leaving for work, also his custom. But this morning, when Bill stepped up beside the bed and placed his hand on Jean's arm, squeezing gently, he noticed immediately that her arm was cold and stiff. His heart rate increased. He shook his wife a little more forcefully, but she didn't move.

"Jeannie," he said. "Jeannie, wake up!"

Bill turned his wife from her side to her back. He put his fingers on her throat to check for a heartbeat, feeling nothing. This and the unnatural stillness of her cold, pale skin informed him clearly that not only was Jean dead, but she had passed away quite some time ago. The medical examiner would later determine that Jean died in her sleep from an aneurysm, possibly related to the birth of her second child, but otherwise inexplicable. At the moment, however, Bill knew only one thing: She was gone.

Bill was a strong man, both physically and emotionally, and he knew he needed to be stalwart at that moment. He had a 10-year-old son and a 10-day-old baby who needed him. He sat down on the bed, and he thought. Bill had been taught at St. Andrew's to think things through before acting, no matter what the situation. Even with the heaviest of hearts, he knew he needed to think clearly now more than ever.

Bill decided that the first thing he should do was get Billy out of the house without him seeing his mother. Bill felt that if Billy saw his mother lying there dead in bed, that image would haunt the boy for the rest of his life. He figured he could manage the baby, but he needed help with Billy. Jean had friends from school, and from the pool, and from church, but Bill didn't know any of them. His life revolved around his job and his family. He worked six days a week, and he left the friend tending and Sunday churchgoing completely in Jean's hands. He worked around the house on Sundays, repairing things that were broken, changing the oil in the car, mowing the lawn and such.

Bill had worked at Alexandria Asphalt Company for 18 years. He'd been the foreman of the number one crew for the past 10 of those years. He was well-known and well-respected by everyone at the company, including the owner, Branford Stevens. All of Bill's crew members lived a long way from McLean, so none of them were an option to help. Bill needed someone close by to come pick up Billy. Bill had never called Mr. Stevens at his home, but he knew that his son Billy was very good friends with Mr. Stevens's son, Michael. He went to the kitchen and eventually found the School PTA Directory in the drawer where the family kept important papers. He leafed through it and found the phone number for the Stevens household. He called.

Branford picked up the phone. "Stevens Residence," came his deep voice.

"Hello, Mr. Stevens," Bill said nervously. "It's Bill Dexter."

"How can I help you, Bill?" asked Mr. Stevens, sounding somewhat perturbed.

"I'm sorry to bother you at home, sir, but I have a terrible situation over here at my house."

"What's going on, Bill?" asked Mr. Stevens, still somewhat impatient.

"My wife passed in the night. She's lying here in the bed, dead."

"My God, Bill. That's terrible."

"I need help," Bill said. "Jean has—had—lots of friends, but I don't know any of them. I need to get Billy out of this house without seeing his mom lying here dead. I just can't let him see her that way. Your family is the only one I know that's nearby. Can you help me, sir?"

There was a pause on the other end of the line, then Mr. Stevens spoke. "Yes, we can help. I'll get my wife up and ask her to come over and get Billy. She'll be there in around 30 minutes."

"Thank you, Mr. Stevens! I'll write a note so Billy can ride on Michael's bus."

"I'm happy we can help, Bill."

"Thank you, sir. You won't have to keep Billy long. I'll tell him to take the bus home to our house this afternoon. If I have time, I'll go to the school and pick him up after the arrangements are made for my wife."

"Okay, good."

"I'll have to take the day off work. I'll call the plant and let them know."

"Yes, of course. Take whatever time you need."

"Thank you, Mr. Stevens. I'll never forget this."

"I'm glad we can help, Bill. I'm sure you'd do the same for us if we needed your help."

"Of course, sir. Anything you need, just ask."

"I'm sorry for your loss, Bill. You take care." Branford hung up the phone and went to wake his wife, formulating a plan that he thought might convince her to help.

Bill hung up the phone and went to wake Billy.

"Hey, bud, how you doin'?" he asked his son, touching him on the shoulder.

"Okay," said Billy, stretching and rubbing his eyes. "What time is it?"

"It's early, son. Look, I need you to go over to Michael's house and take the bus to school with him, okay?"

"Why?" asked the boy.

"Uh, your mom's not feelin' too well. I gotta take her to the doctor."

"What's wrong with Mom?" asked Billy, concern in his voice.

"I don't know, son, but I need you to go over there, okay?" Bill said, struggling to keep the tension out of his voice.

"What's wrong, Dad?"

"I'm just tired, that's all. Now get dressed. Mrs. Stevens is gonna be here soon to pick you up."

"Mrs. Stevens? Uh, okay." Billy was very confused, but he could tell it was important that he do as he'd been told.

Bill left the room and went to call the plant. Billy brushed his teeth, changed into his school clothes, grabbed his backpack, and went into the living room. Bill was waiting for him at the front door.

"Can I say goodbye to Mom?" asked Billy.

Bill wiped sweat away from his forehead. "She's sleepin' right now, son," he said, choking up a bit but holding it together.

"Is everything okay, Dad?"

"Sure is, son. Now listen, give this note to Michael's bus driver that tells them I said it's okay for you to ride on that bus today." He grabbed his son's backpack and stuffed the note inside it. "The note's right inside here, okay? Now there's Mrs. Stevens pulling up, so let's go." Bill opened the front door and strode down the sidewalk.

"Should I ride Michael's bus this afternoon, too?" asked

Billy, following his dad toward Mrs. Stevens's car.

"No, take your regular bus home, unless I come and git you before that."

"Why would you come git me?"

"Please, son, no more questions. Just go with Mrs. Stevens and use your manners. I'll see you soon."

Christina Stevens drove a red two-seater Audi TT Roadster convertible. It drew the attention she craved. Her husband was much more conservative, preferring boring Mercedes sedans, but he never attempted to curtail her from her own, more extravagant tastes, even while he resolutely guided their son in a more traditional direction in all facets of his life. Christina cooperated in this endeavor, but only so far as her "Do what I say, not what I do" philosophy would let her.

The morning of the Dexter woman's death, Branford had woken her at 6:15 a.m., well before her normal rising time. He explained to her what had happened and implored her to go over, pick up Billy, and bring him to their home so he could take the bus to school with Michael. Christina was cranky and had resisted, but then Branford explained that perhaps this was the beginning of an opportunity to help encourage young Billy to pursue athletic endeavors more suited to his talents than swimming. This would need to be handled delicately over time, he explained, and subtle manipulations such as this were not his strong suit. Christina was intrigued. So, she had gotten out of bed, quickly brushed her teeth, thrown on some jeans, jumped in her car, and sped off to pick up Billy with the convertible top down.

When Christina arrived at the Dexter's neighborhood, which she'd driven past many times but never even glanced at, she was a bit shocked by the run-down condition of the homes she saw as she worked her way toward the Dexter home. She *did* notice that the Dexter's lawn was nicely mowed and trimmed, and the house was well painted, but it was *so* tiny! She couldn't imagine how a family of three—let alone four now that the baby had arrived—could live there.

As Christina wheeled her convertible to the curb, she saw Bill rushing Billy down the sidewalk. Bill was carrying the boy's backpack, and he placed it in the small space behind the passenger seat.

"Thank you for helping us, Mrs. Stevens," said Bill. He gave his son a hug, then opened the passenger door to the car.

"My pleasure," she said. "Hop in, Billy. We have to hurry to get back to my house so you can catch the bus with Michael."

Billy climbed in, and Christina sped off back toward the other side of town. She was hopeful she'd never have to return to this wretched neighborhood, ever again.

The red Audi convertible arrived back at the Stevens's estate around 7 a.m. Mrs. Stevens darted in through the massive gates at the front of the house, sped down the winding driveway lined with manicured trees and shrubbery, and stopped right at the front door to the home. She and Billy got out of the convertible, and she ushered Billy through the front door and toward the kitchen.

The few times Billy had been to the house to see Michael, his mom had driven him in from the back driveway where the big garage, pool, pool house, and tennis court were located. Billy and Michael played basketball back there because Billy didn't know how to play tennis. The boys always had their snacks in the pool house and had never gone into the main home.

"Have a seat," Mrs. Stevens said to Billy, gesturing toward the row of six stools lined up like soldiers at one of the three kitchen islands. "I need to check to make sure Michael is ready for school and let him know you're here."

Billy looked around the huge kitchen. In the center of the kitchen was a large island that seemed as big as a car. Billy put his backpack down on the floor and climbed onto one of the stools. He rested his arms on the island, immediately feeling the coldness of the black granite permeate into his forearms, so he raised his arms, then let them fall to his sides. This gave him a slightly slumped-over appearance. At this point, Billy didn't know what had happened to his mom, but his dad's abrupt manner had unsettled him quite a bit. He knew something was wrong.

Billy smelled the pleasant aroma of freshly brewed coffee, which made him feel a little more relaxed, but not much. He stared across the island at the long bank of gleaming stainless-steel appliances—a huge refrigerator and an eight-burner stove with a griddle in the center and two large ovens below—and a sink and cutting area, and lots of white cupboards above and beneath the black granite counters. He looked down at the wide-plank oak floor, which seemed warm compared to the granite island top. He had to resist the urge to get off the stool and curl up down there.

Mrs. Stevens came back into the kitchen. She was now wearing a tight, colorful outfit, which Billy assumed must be for working out, because Michael had once complained to Billy that his mom was always going to the gym before Michael went to school. In addition to the smell of freshly brewed coffee, Billy now smelled a pleasant, delicate perfume.

"Michael will be down momentarily, Billy," Mrs. Stevens said. "I'll be on my way to the club in a moment for my morning workout." She reached into a cupboard and pulled out a few boxes of cereal, put them and two bowls and spoons on the island, took a carton of milk out of the refrigerator, and placed it there as well.

"You boys should have some breakfast before school."

Mrs. Stevens went back to the cupboard and removed a coffee mug, poured herself a cup, moved back to the island, and poured some milk in her mug. She raised the mug to her lips with both hands and took a sip, emitting a soft moan as the coffee slid down her throat.

"Ah, that's good," she cooed, turning to look at Billy.

Billy had never seen Mrs. Stevens this close up, and he was somewhat stunned by her beauty. Her fair hair contrasted pleasantly with her tanned skin, curling forward attractively over her erect shoulders. Mrs. Stevens took another long sip of coffee.

"Billy, you are welcome at our home whenever you'd like to come. You've been a good friend to Michael, and we hope to see more of you in the future."

"Yes, ma'am," said Billy, somewhat intimidated and tongue-tied.

Michael entered the room.

"Hey, bud," said Michael.

"Hey," said Billy.

"You boys go ahead and eat and then run to the bus," said Mrs. Stevens. "I'm going over to the club now. See you later, alligators!"

"Bye, Mom," said Michael.

"Bye, Mrs. Stevens," said Billy. "Thank you."

Billy wasn't sure what he was thanking her for, but he was soon to find out. His dad came to pick him up at school just before lunch and shocked him with the news of his mother's death. This would be the first, but not the last, horrible tragedy in Billy's life.

CHAPTER 5

Fall 2007

Two years after the death of Billy's mom, the trauma of losing her had gone from a sharp pain to a dull, empty ache in his heart. He still missed her terribly and found that being busy with sports helped keep his mind occupied and held the empty feeling at bay. Fall football season had become the most important part of Billy's life. He'd given up summer swimming, primarily because of Mrs. Stevens's encouragement that he should pursue football more aggressively—not only because it was his favorite sport, but also because it would certainly provide his best chance of receiving a college scholarship. She'd also mentioned that he would be helping his family save money by leaving the swim club, which made him feel a lot better about quitting swimming. Billy still excelled at club wrestling in the winter, through a scholarship given to him by the club, but tackle football was what he loved. During the summers, Billy trained by running and riding his bike.

Michael was still swimming, but he often joined Billy for bike rides in the afternoons. While they still met up at The Fort from time to time, the allure of that secret oasis was fading as the boys grew older. By the time they reached high school, two years later, their visits to The Fort would become rare indeed, almost nonexistent.

Billy spent more time with Michael than ever, however, since being welcomed into the Stevens's home. Mrs. Stevens had become an important person in Billy's life, supporting him and strongly encouraging him to pursue his football dreams and the college scholarship that she assured him was out there waiting for him.

Billy *did*, however, enjoy running. He loved the way his mind relaxed after a mile or two, allowing him to hardly even feel the pain of the run, which sometimes went on for over an hour. But he had no desire to compete in running; it was simply a good way of training, and he found it relaxing. When fall football season arrived, 12-year-old Billy just wanted to play, and he wanted to win.

As this season began, Billy was concerned about his weight. He was solid as a rock, but he still didn't have the height he needed to be as heavy as many of the other seventh-grade boys he played football with. The prior season he'd played on Coach Kob's 85-pound team even though he'd weighed only 79 pounds. Nobody had ever mentioned his weight. He'd started on both offense and defense, and the team had gone undefeated, winning the league championship. Of course, the undefeated part was no big deal—Coach Kob's teams were always undefeated—but Billy had never played for a coach like Coach Kob in his six years playing organized tackle football. Coach had a way of making you think you could accomplish anything. The only other people in Billy's life who could make him feel that way were his dad—and Mrs. Stevens.

This year, however, Coach Kob was coaching the 95-pound team, and Billy weighed only 84 pounds. Somebody from the league office had sent a letter to all clubs in the region saying you had to weigh between 86 and 95 pounds to play for a 95-pound team. There had been an official weigh-in. Billy gorged himself on a pan of lasagna and guzzled a liter of root beer, but it still hadn't been enough to push his weight to the 86-pound minimum. The league had assigned him to an 85-pound team with a bunch of sixth graders on it and a coach rumored to not know anything about football. Billy had shown up at Coach Kob's practice instead. While Coach very much wanted Billy on his team, he had to follow the league rules. Billy had missed the first practice of the 85-pound team. When he arrived for the second practice, he learned that he was the second-string tailback, behind the coach's son, David. And that kid was pitiful.

One evening early in the season, the coach was scrimmaging the first-string offense against the second-string defense, followed by the second-string offense against the first-string defense. The first group would run plays until the offense either scored, turned the ball over, or went out on downs, then the second group would come onto the field and do the same. Billy had no idea why the coach would run such a ridiculous drill, except that it would give David the best possible chance to look good, while stacking the odds against Billy.

The funny thing was that no matter how many times the coach called a play for David to run the ball, he'd fall down the first time someone hit him. The good news for David was that the first-string offensive line usually wiped out the second-string defensive line, so no one even touched David until he'd gained five or six yards. But as soon as they did, he went down like he'd been hit by a freight train. Unfortunately, this sad state of affairs was so imbalanced that the first-string offense stayed on the field until they scored, every time! And the coach kept telling David what a good job he was doing. *Pitiful!*

And of course, when the second-string offense came on against the first-string defense, the imbalance shifted in the other direction. On about half of the plays, a defensive lineman or linebacker tackled the quarterback before he could even get the ball out of his hands. Passing was out of the question. The quarterback was sacked before he could take three steps back. But none of this really mattered to Billy. He knew that all he needed to do was get the ball in his hands, just one time.

But for some reason, the coach wasn't calling plays that involved Billy running the ball. He kept calling plays for the fullback, Tony DiAngelo. Tony was about four and a half feet tall, and he weighed 85 pounds only once that season—at the weigh-in. He'd crash dieted to make the 85-pound team, but within a few weeks he'd ballooned back up to nearly 100 pounds. The kid was so slow that on the rare occasion when the handoff actually took place, Tony was tackled before he even made it to the line of scrimmage, often fumbling the ball in the process.

But Tony was too much of a New Jersey macho man to complain. His parents had moved to Virginia from Jersey a few years ago. They lived a few houses down from Billy's family. Tony wasn't a bad guy, and his parents drove Billy to practice because his dad was always at work when practice started. But what bothered Billy was that the coach wouldn't let him run the ball. Not even once. He'd asked him several times, but the coach either ignored him or dismissed him with, "Do your job, son. Just do your job."

"But, Coach, in all due respect, I thought my job was to run the ball," pleaded Billy.

"Your job is to run your assignment for each play that's called. And if you bother me one more time, boy, you're gonna be running all right. Running laps! Now pipe down!"

Billy's face turned red, but he wasn't defeated. He knew what he'd have to do. He'd have to play fullback to get the ball. The next time his squad took the field, he grabbed Tony by the face mask while they were in the huddle waiting for the play to be sent in by the coach. He pulled the ear hole of Tony's helmet close to his mouth.

"Tony," he whispered. "I'm gonna play fullback on this play, ahright?"

"Ey!" exclaimed Tony, who began nearly every sentence with the word "hey," minus the "h." Tony opened up his arms as if preaching to a crowd. "You can play fullback da rest of da night! Only problem is, what position am I gonna play?"

"Tailback," said Billy.

"Ey! I ain't gonna play no tailback! I'm too slow to be a tailback."

"You're too slow to be a fullback, you turd," cajoled Billy. "Just one play, okay?"

"Ey! For you, my friend, okay. One play."

The wide receiver came in with the play call from the sidelines. Everyone in the huddle except him knew what was going to happen, but not one of them would cross Billy. And they were happy they might actually have a chance on this one play. Sure enough, the coach called a running play for the fullback. F22. Fullback up the middle, over the right guard. The boys broke the huddle, and Billy took the fullback position. Tony was directly behind him, trying to act like he knew what he was doing.

The quarterback barked the signal. "Down! Set!"

Billy got down in a three-point stance, jerking his head up. He looked across the line at the defense. The middle linebacker was looking right at him, a maniacal smile on his face, eyes wide and ferocious. Billy smiled back.

The snap was on two. "Hut. Hut." The snap came up, and the quarterback took the ball and pivoted right, raising the ball up to waist level. Billy shot toward the line and took a wobbly handoff just as the noseguard wiped out the quarterback. He hit the line without hesitation, still crouched and low to the ground, running literally as fast as he could. Not many running backs at any age level hit the line with that much utter abandon, at least that's what Coach Kob had said about Billy last year.

The right offensive guard held his block for about one second, but Billy's speed was enough to keep the defensive tackle from getting anything but an arm on him. Nobody could arm tackle Billy. He could run through players much bigger than he was without feeling it, and this guy wasn't that much bigger than him anyway.

The first real contact Billy made was with the middle linebacker with the maniacal smile. He saw Billy coming, but he'd never seen anybody shooting through the line that fast, or that low. He had his arms spread to make the tackle, but he was standing just a bit too high. Billy's helmet impacted the unsuspecting linebacker's gut, blasting him into the air and knocking the wind out of him. The linebacker hit the ground on his back, groaned, and curled into the fetal position. He was no longer smiling.

Billy lurched forward, head still up, and saw the safety coming in hard. The safety launched himself like a missile, flying at Billy while parallel to the ground. Billy jammed down hard with his left leg and cut right. The safety hit nothing but air on his way to the ground. Immediately, Billy cut back up field and saw the cornerback coming at him from the right with a good angle. There was no doubt the cornerback was going to hit him; it was only a question of whether he'd go high or low. If the cornerback tried to tackle him high, Billy would give him a stiff arm. A low tackle would call for either a limp leg, a spin, both, or neither. Sometimes things happened so quickly that Billy wasn't sure what he was going to do. He just did it.

The cornerback went low, very low. Without thinking, Billy hurdled into the air, still moving forward. The cornerback tried to adjust to Billy's move and got his arm up, managing to latch his hand around Billy's ankle. Still in the air, Billy spun 360 degrees and wrenched his ankle free from the cornerback's hand. Billy hit the ground hard on one foot and stumbled, but his powerful legs pushed him up and steadied him. And then he was gone, all the way to the end zone. Nobody was going to catch him. No one ever caught Billy Dexter.

When Billy returned to the sidelines, the cheers and high fives of his second-string teammates died out quickly as the coach grabbed him by the shoulder pads with both hands.

"What the heck were you doing in the fullback spot, Dexter?"

"Just trying to do my job, sir," said Billy, breathing hard, exhilarated by what he'd just done.

"Well, I gotta new job for you," said the coach. "Gimmie 10 laps!"

Billy's blood boiled. He wanted to say something disrespectful, but he wasn't raised that way. All he said was, "I'm sorry, sir, but I can't do that." Then he turned and walked off the field. Billy stared down at his feet, wondering if this was the last time he'd walk off a football field in full pads.

Billy didn't hear the coach yelling disparaging things at him as he walked away, but his dad *did*. Bill had arrived a few minutes before the last play, coming directly from work to pick up Billy from practice. He'd seen what had happened. He didn't approve of what Billy had done, but he wouldn't stand by while an adult verbally abused his son either.

Billy had almost reached the parking lot when he saw his dad striding purposefully toward the coach. Bill put his face up really close to the coach's face. The coach stopped yelling. Every child and parent at practice was watching. The field went silent. Bill was not a big man, but he was very strong, very tough, and very hard to ignore. When he looked you in the eye, it took a lot of willpower to look back into his hard, green eyes. Most people averted their eyes, but they always heard what Bill was saying.

Bill said what he had to convey to the coach quietly, then turned and walked off the field, catching up with his son near the car. They headed to the car side by side, neither saying a word. Billy tilted his head up and away from the ground, straightened his shoulders, and threw his chest out. He held his head high and jumped into the car.

Bill got into the ancient Ford Taurus, started it, and drove out of the parking lot onto Church Hill Road. When his dad had the car moving along smoothly, Billy asked the question he had to ask. "Do you think I did the right thing, Dad?"

Bill kept his eyes on the road, his mouth closed. Billy knew this was his father's way. He wouldn't speak until the right words came to him. Billy kept his eyes on his dad, waiting patiently. For the first time, he noticed dark circles under his father's eyes. Billy wondered if most 37-year-old men had dark circles like that. *Probably not*, thought Billy. He figured his dad looked a little older than other people his age because for the past two years he'd been working a full-time job and taking care of two children, all by himself.

Bill cleared his throat. He spoke with a slow, powerful, Southern-accented voice.

"The coach didn't tell you to play fullback, did he?" asked Bill.

"Nossir."

"Then why were you?"

"Uh, 'cause the fullback was getting all the running plays."

"So, you decided to make yourself the coach?"

"I guess so," said Billy, bowing his head, thinking he might be in trouble.

"Son, it's important for a player to respect the coach. Never forget that." Bill paused.

"Yessir."

"But it's also important for the coach to respect his players."

"Yessir," said Billy, a little too quickly, his head coming up a bit.

"And more than anything, it's the coach's responsibility to play the game to win. To do that, you have to play your best players."

"Yes, sir!" exclaimed Billy, with far too much enthusiasm.

"You see, son, the man on that field today who was running that practice was not truly a coach. He allowed his personal feelings for his son to get in the way of his duties as a coach. He was allowing the team to suffer so that his son might gain."

"Yessir."

"The sad thing is that his son will be the one to suffer, in the long run, by being handed a position he didn't earn. Anything in this world worth having, son, is worth working for."

Billy nodded his head, and his father continued. "So, when you quit, even though you weren't sure why you did it, you must have known deep inside that without a true coach this team doesn't have a chance to win. Now I'm not saying you should quit every time you think you have a bad coach or if you're playing on a bad team. I don't want you to ever do that! Before you ever do anything like this again, I want you to talk to me first. Do you understand?"

"Yessir."

"When you play football, or any sport for that matter, winning is everything, as long as it's done within the rules. When you step onto the battlefield, you must show no mercy to your opponents. Never maim or hurt a player on purpose. But when you run over someone, even if you think they're hurt, never look back. The world is a cruel place, son, and competition in sports can help prepare you to face it when you go out on your own. Just follow the three rules I've taught you, and you'll be fine."

Billy had been hearing the "Rules of the Game according to Bill Dexter" for as long as he could remember. He knew his dad had never had the opportunity to play organized sports because he'd been thrust into the working world at such a young age. But his dad had made a point of taking the lessons he'd learned in life and applying them to the world of sports for the benefit of his children. Bill had played by the rules of life, and he had earned a hard-fought victory that had resulted in gainful employment and the ability to provide for his family.

The loss of Bill's wife two years ago still hurt, but he hadn't let it deter him. He moved forward, refusing to get caught up in what might have been. He made the sacrifices he had to make for something that was important to him—the well-being of his sons.

Billy knew from many years of practice what he had to say now. It wasn't difficult for him, because he believed in his heart and soul that what he was saying was the gospel truth.

"Play Fair, Compete to Win, and Never Look Back," he recited reverently.

Unfortunately, Billy would live to regret these beliefs.

CHAPTER 6

2009–2012

Michael joined the cross-country team upon entering public high school in the fall of 2009. He hadn't been much of a runner prior to this, but it quickly became apparent that his tall, athletic frame and excellent conditioning were well-suited to the rigors of cross-country.

There was a period of adjustment when Michael switched from swimming in the summer to running in the fall. He'd joined a powerful long course swim team—which trained and competed in a 50-meter pool—and the training and competition were at a much higher level than what he'd experienced at Endless Woods. But he had a few weeks at the end of August to facilitate the transition to running before school started in late August.

Within a few months of Michael's freshman year season, he had established himself as the fastest runner on the varsity team. He went on to win the District Championship that year, followed by the Regional Championship his sophomore year, and then the State Championship his junior year.

In the winter season, Michael swam for his high school team, but he also trained with a private coach his parents had

hired. The high school team workouts were simply insuffi-
cient to keep Michael performing at the standards his parents demanded. Michael was okay with it because this higher
level of training ensured that he was on the hunt for the state
swimming championship from his freshman year forward.
He was second in the state in the 200-free and third in the
100-back his freshman year, then he went on to win both
events at the state level during both his sophomore and junior years.

In the spring, Michael ran for the high school track team.
His specialty was the 3200 meters, which was just about 2
miles. He performed equally well in the 1600 meters, but
he preferred the 3200. Longer distances felt more natural to
him, more compatible with his physical and psychological
traits. Michael was a top five finisher at states in both events
during his freshman year, a top three finisher his sophomore
year, and won both during his junior year.

In the summer between Michael's junior and senior years,
he began a new activity—work. He continued to work out
with his private swimming coach in the evenings and on
weekends, but his father had arranged for him to spend his
days working on the number two crew at Alexandria Asphalt
Company. Because the number two crew was short-handed
that summer, Branford also hired Billy to work on the crew.
He told the crew foreman, a man known as Rock, to push
them hard, but keep them safe. The work was dangerous, and
a few of the crew members could sometimes be dangerous
themselves in certain situations.

Both Michael and Billy performed the job of shovel man on
the crew. This was the entry-level position because it required

the least amount of skill and the most amount of effort. A shovel man carried a sturdy, wide-mouthed shovel that he used to spray a shovelful of asphalt over areas where the spreader—the machine that laid the asphalt down on the road—hadn't gotten even coverage. The roller—a large machine with huge, heavy round cylinders for wheels—would then roll over the newly spread asphalt to compress and flatten it.

To get the asphalt into the shovel, the shovel man had to walk quickly up to the front of the spreader jam the shovel into the bin that held the hot, fresh asphalt, remove the full shovel then race back to help repair the uneven areas at the back of the machine before the roller got there. It was back-breaking work.

Summer temperatures in the metro Washington, D.C., area were often 95 degrees or higher, with equally high humidity. The hot asphalt raised the road temperature to a sweltering 120 degrees. Two strong, determined young men who were used to intense exertion were perfect for the job of shovel man. A typical workday was 12 hours. If the foreman was under pressure to finish a job, he'd keep the crew out on the road until past seven in the evening.

One unexpected problem Michael encountered was the appearance of Billy's naturally competitive nature on the job. When they first started working on the crew, Billy would race back and forth, spreading asphalt as if it were a competition. He would literally run to the spreader to fill his shovel and then race back to the newly laid asphalt, making nearly twice as many trips as Michael did. Michael knew enough about asphalt work to understand that Billy's efforts were making very little difference in the final quality of the road. While he wasn't compelled to keep up with Billy, he felt a little uncomfortable because of Billy's intense efforts.

Rock, a stocky, middle-aged man with graying hair, had the perfect solution to Michael's problem, although Michael had never mentioned it to him. Rock took Billy and Michael aside and gave them a short talking-to.

"Now, boys, I know you're both young and strong, and you want to make a good impression on me and everybody else," Rock said. "But you see, come the end of summer, both you fellas are going back to school, and then one day you'll go to college, and after college us full-time people'll probably never see you again. But when you're gone, we'll still be here, still slinging that hot black rock. Most of us are too old to keep up the pace you boys been keeping. So, I'm telling you right now, SLOW THE FUCK DOWN!"

Michael realized that Rock's lecture had been more for Billy than for himself, but Rock was a wise man. He'd known Michael for many years, seeing him every year at the company picnic, talking to him about what he was up to, and watching him grow up into the handsome, talented young man he'd become. He knew Michael would take no offense at being included in this lecture. And the lecture worked. Billy slowed down.

Michael respected Rock more than almost anyone. Michael didn't know a lot about Rock's past, but it seemed to Michael that Rock was one of the most thoughtful and wise people he'd ever met. He had a perfect balance of kindness and firmness that motivated people to do their best. Unfortunately, sometimes balance could not be achieved on the unruly crew.

One day, a new guy—a young, strong man just out of the

Army—pulled a switchblade on Rock during a disagreement. Rock took that knife from the young man so quickly that no one even saw how he did it, and then he was behind the guy with the knife to his throat. The man raised his arms in surrender. Slowly, Rock pulled the knife away. Then he closed the blade and threw it back to the man.

"Go home," Rock commanded. "Don't come round here or the yard ever again."

The man walked away and was never seen again. The incident didn't seem to bother Billy at all, but Michael was shaken up by the whole thing. Later, Rock pulled him aside.

"I'm sorry you had to see that," said Rock.

"I am, too," said Michael. "But I'm glad you were here to take care of it."

"I've been around a long time. And unfortunately, I've had to learn the hard way how to take care of myself. Just keep your distance from guys like that, okay?"

"I certainly will," said Michael. "Thank you."

Michael also had the unenviable job of driving the truck that hauled the shovels, rakes, other small equipment, and several of the crew members to and from the job sites. A few of the men, including Rock, drove their personal vehicles to the sites so they could get home faster at the end of the day. But some of the men didn't have their own transportation, so they'd have to ride back to the yard on the truck and find a way home, usually on public transportation.

One day Michael was driving the truck back after a protracted, hot day on a job out in the country. It was a long drive back. Billy was sitting beside him in the wide cab, and another worker, a man everyone on the crew called Tommy-Lee, was sitting in the passenger's seat. Three other men from the crew sat back in the bed of the truck with the equipment. Tommy-Lee looked and talked like a real tough guy. He was really strong, and he could be the nicest guy in the world one moment, but he could also turn into the nastiest guy in the world, depending on the circumstances. On the drive back, Tommy-Lee asked Michael a question.

"Say, Mike," said Tommy-Lee. "You mind dropping me at home so I don't have to walk? My place is real close to the plant."

Michael had been warned in advance by Rock never to do this. Rock explained that if you did it once, you'd end up driving everyone on the crew home from that point forward, which was against company policy. More specifically, it was against *Rock's* policy, and that was a policy Michael did not want to violate.

"I'm sorry, Tommy-Lee, but that's against company policy," Michael said.

Tommy-Lee persisted. "Hey, man, I told you it was on the way. You just stop the truck, I get out, and that's it."

"I'm sorry. I can't do that," said Michael. At that point, "Nasty Tommy-Lee" made his appearance.

"You know I'll fuck you up if you don't do what I say, right?" screamed Tommy-Lee.

Then Billy got involved. "Stop the truck, bud," he said calmly.

Billy was no longer short. In fact, at six feet tall he was now only two inches shorter than Michael, and 25 pounds heavier. Billy was 195 pounds of sheer muscle, intimidating to almost anyone. Tommy-Lee was nearly as big as Billy, and he had the inherent advantage of being an experienced street fighter. But in addition to being strong and determined, Billy was also a state champion wrestler. Michael had seen Billy end fights and scuffles simply by taking his opponent down to the ground and putting him in a hold that prevented him from moving. But Billy had never fought a man as dangerous as Tommy-Lee. Michael's heart began to beat faster.

"What?" asked Michael.

"Just pull over to the side of the road," said Billy, a little more firmly. "This won't take long."

Michael pulled over and stopped the truck. Billy turned to Tommy-Lee.

"Get out of the truck," he said.

"Fuck you! *You* get out of the truck!"

"Okay. Let me out."

Tommy-Lee opened the door and got out, and Billy followed him. Tommy-Lee moved to get back in the truck, but Billy slammed the door shut and kept his hand on it.

"What the hell are you doing, man?" asked Tommy-Lee.

"Get in the back," said Billy.

"Go fuck yourself," said Tommy-Lee. "Let me back in that truck!"

"Get in the back or walk," said Billy. "Those are your choices."

Michael was concerned that Tommy-Lee had some kind of weapon on him. He wasn't sure what to do. Everyone knew that he was the owner's son and that Billy was foreman Bill Dexter's son, but it was impossible to predict what Tommy-Lee might do in this situation.

Tommy-Lee took a threatening step toward Billy, his hand moving to his back pocket. Billy grabbed Tommy-Lee's wrist and squeezed.

"Last chance, man," said Billy.

Tommy-Lee froze, obviously deciding what to do next. Suddenly, he relaxed and smiled. Billy let go, but he didn't take his eyes off Tommy-Lee. Billy's knees were slightly bent, ready to move, and his arms were loose at his sides, but tensed, like a gunslinger before he reached for his gun.

Tommy-Lee moved slowly to the back of the truck and jumped into the bed. He was still smiling, but his eyes were burning with anger. But Billy wasn't finished. He walked to the back of the truck.

"I'm sorry, Tommy-Lee," he said, staring directly into the man's furious gray eyes. "But that kid up there is a good person and don't know how to protect himself. That's my job. Please leave him alone, okay?"

Tommy-Lee didn't reply, but he never confronted Michael or Billy again.

CHAPTER 7

Way back when Billy was 12 years old and quit the 85-pound football team, he'd ended up playing for Coach Kob on the 95-pound team. Coach Kob had gotten wind of what happened and used his influence to allow Billy's weight to be rechecked. He explained to Billy that water weighed a lot more than food, telling him to drink as much water as he could and to eat plenty of salt during the 24 hours before the weigh-in. Immediately before the weigh-in, he had Billy chug a full quart of water, which by itself weighed more than two pounds. Billy weighed in at 88 pounds, well over the limit for the 85-pound weight class. He was officially placed on Coach Kob's 95-pound team.

Billy had a great season with Coach Kob's team. And soon after that season ended, Billy started to grow. By the time he was a 14-year-old freshman in high school, he stood 5 feet 6 inches tall and weighed 140 pounds. The coaches at McLean High School considered making Billy the first freshman ever to earn a spot on the varsity team, but they decided to give him one more year to grow.

Billy hit the weights in the spring, after wrestling season ended, and by the fall of his sophomore year, he was 5 feet 9 inches tall and weighed 165 pounds. He rushed for more than 1,000 yards that season and scored 17 touchdowns. He came into his junior year at 5 feet 11 inches and 180 pounds, rushing for nearly 2,000 yards and scoring 26 touchdowns. He received several unofficial offers from Division Two college teams and even a few second-tier Division One teams.

By the spring of Billy's junior year, he was well above 190 pounds and had reached 6 feet in height. The calls from top teams started coming in. By that point, very few D1 college football teams in the country didn't know about Billy Dexter.

The student body at McLean High truly adored Billy. He was a humble, unassuming person, like his dad, but because he was so popular, he learned to socialize. And with encouragement from Michael and Mrs. Stevens, he worked hard to improve his academic performance—with some success.

In stark contrast to Billy's genuine goodness was his nickname. Because Billy played with such reckless abandon on the football field, someone had said he played like a demon. The name caught on, and soon Billy was called "Demon" more than he was called Billy. Kids passing Billy in the hall would hold their hand up for a high five and say, "Yo, Demon!" When the offense took the field during a game, chants of "Dee-*mon*! Dee-*mon*! Dee-*mon*!" rose from the crowd.

Billy didn't really like the nickname, but it wasn't his style to make waves—unless something important was at stake. So he let it slide, hoping his unwanted nickname wouldn't follow him to college.

With Billy in the backfield, McLean was an offensive powerhouse. The school was riding a wave of football euphoria unlike anything it had ever experienced before. For the first time in a long time, kids who might not have tried out for the team were coming out in droves, from freshmen all the way to seniors who had never even touched a football before. Even the best athletes from other sports wanted in, and several of them became important contributors to the team.

Billy was the rock upon which the team's fortunes were built. All the top prognosticators were picking McLean to win the 2012 State Championship during his senior season. McLean had fallen just short the year before, losing by one point on the final play of the game.

This year, the opening game of the season was against Marshall, a perennial powerhouse that always fielded a fierce defense. Both teams had been thinking about and preparing for this game since the schedule had been released the prior spring. The game would be an early-season indicator of which team had the inside track to win the Northern Region championship and move on to play for the state championship.

In early September, the humidity was still very high. Even though the games were played on Friday evenings, it was still quite hot when the ball was kicked off. The game was one of the most physical contests anyone could remember. Several players from both teams were carried off the field injured during the first half. Two were taken to the hospital. The McLean offense could barely get a pass off due to the intensity of the Marshall rush, so they resorted to the one weapon that Marshall couldn't completely shut down—the Demon.

Billy carried the ball an unheard-of 27 times in the first

half, gaining a hard-fought 92 yards. His average of 3.4 yards per carry was far below his average of 6.5 yards per carry during the previous season, but it was enough to give his team a 10–7 lead at the half.

The McLean defense had performed admirably during the first half, but in the locker room at halftime it was obvious to the coaches that the defense couldn't hold out for the rest of the game. The players were lying on the benches in front of the lockers, panting for breath and begging for water, particularly the defensive linemen. The team's star fullback, Tony DiAngelo, now 5 feet 7 inches tall and 210 pounds of hard-earned muscle, ranted at the beleaguered defensive side.

"Ey!" shouted Tony. "What 'chou guys layin' around for? We been doin' all dah work! You see dat noseguard! Dat dude's 300 pounds! You boys ain't gettin' hit by no 300-pounders! What gives?"

"Pipe down, DiAngelo!" yelled the head coach. "We've got work to do here."

If the defensive line broke down, Marshall would march down the field and score every time they had the ball. The coaches desperately needed to keep the defense off the field, and to do that, they needed Billy to keep making first downs. To no one's surprise, the coaches told the team that Billy would run the ball nearly every play of the second half. But they went even further than that. Billy would run the *same* play—tailback to the left side, between the guard and tackle, with the center and the left guard double-teaming Marshall's 300-pound noseguard and with DiAngelo leading Billy into the hole and taking out the linebacker. The offense would run that play until the Marshall defense made an adjustment.

The assumption was that Marshall would shift their defensive line over or move an extra linebacker closer to the hole on the McLean left side. This would create opportunities on the right side that could be called up by the quarterback on an audible at the line of scrimmage.

On the first McLean possession of the second half, Billy ran the ball six straight times over the left side—gaining 33 yards and 3 first downs—before the Marshall coaches called timeout. After the timeout, when the McLean offense came to the line of scrimmage, the Marshall middle linebacker shifted to his right; there were now two linebackers near the hole where Billy had been running. Marshall's outside left linebacker pulled in toward the center to compensate for the adjustment of the middle linebacker. This took away the run up the middle on either side of the ball, but it left an opportunity wide on the right side. The quarterback barked the audible as loud as he could, fighting the rhythmic chant of his own fans: "Dee-*mon*! Dee-*mon*! Dee-*mon*!"

"Red Twenty-Nine! Red Twenty-Nine! Hut! Hut!" screamed the quarterback.

The ball came up into the quarterback's hands. He turned to his left, raising the ball as if he were going to hand off to Billy on the same play the offense had just run six times in a row. The fullback, DiAngelo, blasted toward the hole between the left guard and the left tackle that he'd led Billy into six straight times. Billy took one long step with his left leg in the direction DiAngelo was headed, then quickly pushed off with his left foot and sprinted to the right, parallel to the line of scrimmage. The quarterback spun counterclockwise and pitched him the ball. Up to the point when Billy and the quarterback had quickly changed directions, every player on the McLean offense had moved the same way they had on the previous six plays. The inertia of nearly the entire Marshall defense was moving in the direction of the McLean left side. But Billy was now running wide right, and he was running very fast. The crowd saw it too, and their rhythmic chant became a roar.

Billy easily skirted past the defensive end, who'd been moving down the line of scrimmage in the wrong direction. The linebacker on that side was also too far inside to get to him, so Billy turned upfield, hearing the rumbles of the crowd, digging his teeth into his mouthpiece, and breathing through his nose. He knew his team needed this score to have a chance to win this game, and winning was what Billy did best. He was in a full sprint now, his mouth falling open, sucking air over the saliva that had accumulated on his mouthpiece.

Billy looked left, and to his surprise he saw Marshall's All-State safety, Melvin Penrose, coming at him with a good angle. He'd spent some time with Melvin at the past year's All-State Awards Banquet. He knew that Melvin had run a 4.45-second 40-yard dash, which was equal to Billy's best time at that critical distance. Melvin was also a very smart player. He was the one player on the Marshall side who hadn't taken the bait. Instead of moving up toward the line of scrimmage, Melvin had backpedaled as the play progressed. He was still farther down the field than Billy was, and this gave him a good angle. He closed in easily on his target. But Billy was not going to be denied this score. He simply had to run through Melvin's hit. He didn't know how, but he was determined to find a way.

Billy kept sprinting, and Melvin kept sprinting. As Melvin

closed to less than two yards from Billy, he dove at Billy's legs. This was sooner than Billy had expected. Melvin was risking everything by doing this. Either he would hit Billy and make the tackle, or Billy would score a touchdown.

Billy saw Melvin dive, but the timing of his stride was such that his left leg was planting into the turf as Melvin's shoulder pads made contact just above his left knee. Billy attempted to spin out of the hit, a dangerous move at such high speed, but the force of Melvin's impact would not allow his left foot to come up out of the ground. Billy's spinning motion radically twisted his knee.

There was an audible snap as ligaments and cartilage ripped inside Billy's knee. The pain was so intense that Billy fainted before he hit the ground, looking like a lifeless corpse strewn out. Unmoving. Melvin heard the "pop" and bolted to his feet, jumping up and down, furiously waving for the trainers and coaches to come onto the field, horrified by what he'd done to Billy.

The team doctor rushed onto the field and knelt down. First he checked Billy's pulse and breathing and determined that even though unconscious, he was in no respiratory or pulmonary distress. Then he looked at Billy's knee. He carefully slit the fabric of Billy's football pants and pulled the knee pad up and away from the knee. It was obvious from a cursory inspection that Billy had suffered a serious, possibly career-threatening injury.

The doctor quickly imobilized the leg, saw Billy regaining consciousness, and injected him with a painkiller. Billy was taken off the field on a stretcher and rushed to the hospital in an ambulance. He would never play tackle football again.

CHAPTER 8

Late Fall 2012

Almost two months after Billy's knee injury, he took an extended walk on his crutches. He lived about a half mile from the Endless Woods Swim Club, now closed until summer, and it took him a while to get there. He had a chance to think while he walked, but he didn't think heavy thoughts. He was saving the soul-searching for when he got to his destination.

While Billy struggled along the sidewalk on his crutches, he was content to breathe in the fall air and look at the trees along Kirby Road. It was early November, and the trees were in the process of dropping their leaves, but a lot of the vibrant colors from the fall peak were still there.

Billy passed a few houses of people he knew, wondering what they were doing. It was nearly 6 p.m., and dusk was already approaching, so he figured a lot of people would be watching TV or doing homework, or they'd be just getting home from their winter sport practice—wrestling, basketball, swimming, or gymnastics. All but two football teams were done with their seasons, but there was still one game left to be played. Marshall would be playing for the state championship the following weekend. McLean hadn't even won districts. With Billy out for the season, the team had finished a disappointing 6–4.

When Billy finally arrived at the club, all boarded up for the winter, he worked his way around the fenced-in pool area to the woods in the back. He walked down the nicely manicured path to where the briar patch used to be, now cut down and turned into a children's playground. The stand of pines was still there, but the allure of the place had changed from a wild, mysterious hideout to a tame, domesticated leisure spot for parents and their little kids. There was a bench right in front of the pines. Billy leaned his crutches up against it, carefully lowered himself down to take a seat, leaned back, and tried to relax. His leg was still in a full cast, stretching out in front of him in a white line, with signatures and good wishes from just about everyone at McLean High scribbled all over it.

Before Billy could settle into his thoughts, he saw a lone runner jogging up the path in the forest. The jogger was tall and had good form, and Billy knew at once that it was Michael. Billy and Michael were still the best of friends, but with Michael's cross-country training and diligent approach to his studies, Billy didn't see much of him these days. He hadn't mentioned to Michael that he would be coming here, so he was surprised to see him.

"Hey, bud, what'cha doin'?" asked Billy.

"Hey," said Michael. "Just doing a little extra training, sort of."

"What do you mean 'sort of'?"

"Well, I stopped by your house, and your dad said I might

find you here. He said you wanted some time alone, so I hope I'm not interrupting."

"No," said Billy. "Not at all. I was just coming here to think. This place was always a good place for that. Not as good now as it used to be, but it can do the trick, I guess."

"What were you planning on thinking about?"

Billy paused, deciding if he should confide in his best friend. Then he spoke.

"I'm trying to figure out what to do with my life, I guess," he said, his voice cracking a little.

Michael knew that Billy's knee injury was not likely to be career-ending. Billy's medial collateral ligament (MCL) had been partially torn but had not required surgery. The meniscus cartilage, which cushions the femur and tibia where they attach to the knee, had also been torn and then lodged between the femur and the tibia. This was where most of the severe pain Billy had felt initially had come from. The doctors had been able to clean up the cartilage without any difficulty and had told Billy that with the right rehabilitation program, and a little luck, he should be able to play football again.

Unfortunately for Billy, luck was not part of the equation college recruiters used to select running backs. Michael knew the realities of big-time college sports recruiting himself because he was a candidate for track and field and swimming scholarships at dozens of schools. He knew an injury such as Billy's meant at best a temporary end to his hopes of playing college sports. His only likely option for a scholarship would be to play at the junior college level and hope he could get noticed again. If he didn't do that, he'd have to take his chances on getting into whatever college his grades and test scores would allow, and then waiting to see if he could qualify for financial aid. This option wasn't very appealing to Billy because in his mind, going to college had always meant playing college football. So unless an unexpected turn of events occurred, Billy might end up be working side by side with his dad at the asphalt company.

"Any ideas on what you might do next?" asked Michael.

"Nothing good. That's why I'm here. Trying to come up with something." Billy's Southern accent was still there, but his diction had steadily improved as he'd grown up. Michael's mom couldn't stand improper diction, so she always corrected Billy's diction mistakes when he was around her. While this embarrassed Michael quite a bit, Billy seemed to appreciate it. Billy always wanted to improve, in all aspects of his life, and Michael respected this.

"Well, that happens to be why I'm here, too," said Michael, rubbing the index finger of his right hand over the scar on his chin.

"What are you talking about, man? You know you're going to college on a full ride. What are you worried about?"

"I'm worried about *you*. But I have an idea. I came here to share it with you, if you're willing to listen."

"Oh *really*?" said Billy, intrigued. He had the highest level of respect for Michael's opinion on virtually any subject. Michael was a good, intelligent person, and he knew Billy better than anyone. "What are you thinking?"

Michael didn't hesitate. "I'm thinking you should run track next spring," said Michael.

"What? Why?" asked Billy.

"Because you're the Demon, that's why!"

Billy lowered his head. "Was," he said, his voice barely audible.

"The doctor said you could be jogging in as little as three or four months. You've been in that cast for nearly two months, and it's coming off next week. The spring track season doesn't even start until March. That's almost four months from now. It's true you won't be able to train much before the season begins, but you're so darn fast you could probably beat anyone on the team, at any distance, with no training. And that includes me!"

"You don't give yourself enough credit, man," said Billy, stalling a little, trying to think this through. "You're the best at the 3200. I could never touch you at that distance no matter how much training I do."

"Look," said Michael. "Track coaches don't worry about knee injuries as much as football coaches. You could go out for the track team and end up getting a scholarship after all, to a Division I school. I'm sure of it!"

"It's kind of hard to think about running right now, you know what I mean," said Billy.

"Sure, I do," said Michael. "But we're talking about your whole life here, bud. With all respect to your dad, you don't want to be pitching asphalt the rest of your life. Do you?"

Billy tilted his head and scratched his neck. "I don't know, man. Could be worse things."

"Just tell me you'll think about it, okay?"

Billy thought for a while, just like his dad would do. "Yeah, okay. I'll think about it."

Michael got up and started to move away. "I'll be back in 10 with my car. Meet me out front, okay?" Michael's house was only about a mile away. He could run home in five or six minutes and then bring his car down to get Billy and drive him home. It was almost dark.

"Okay," said Billy. "And thanks for thinking of me, bud. I appreciate it."

"That's what friends do."

Michael left the playground that used to be known by the boys as The Fort. Many of the cherished memories of their childhood came from this spot. Michael was hoping that on *this* day they could forge yet another good memory. As it turned out, this day *would* change the course of both boys' lives forever. Just not in the way that either of them had expected.

CHAPTER 9

2013

The 2013 Virginia Track and Field State Championships were held in late May. Michael qualified with the top times in both the 3200- and 1600-meter races. His time of 4 minutes, 3.54 seconds in the 1600 made him the favorite to win the state championship. Billy had logged the next fastest time—4 minutes, 4.93 seconds. Michael knew in his heart that Billy could run faster if he wanted to. A lot faster.

Billy decided to pursue the idea of joining the track team that Michael had presented to him in the early stages of his recovery from his knee injury. The idea gave Billy hope, which translated into a tremendous enthusiasm toward his rehabilitation. Just six weeks after Billy's cast came off, he was jogging slowly, and he was training with the track team when the season opened on March 1. Billy wore a knee brace as a precautionary measure, but when he ran, it was clear that the Demon was back—with a vengeance.

If Billy didn't have a recently injured knee, the track coaches would have entered him in the sprints, for which his build was better suited, most likely the 100-meter dash and the

200-meter dash. But the compressed stance of these sprints and the subsequent launch from the starting blocks were assumed to be too stressful on Billy's knee, at least for this season, so he was entered in longer distances, where the runners started in the standing position.

Billy ran the 800- and the 1600-meter races. This meant that Michael and Billy ran against each other in the 1600. Billy dominated the 800 from the start, but he struggled in the 1600. As time went by, however, Billy continued to train for the longer races, and he began to shed weight—literally molding his body into one that was more compatible with the longer distances. Fast-twitch muscles gave way to slow-twitch muscles. Billy's times in the 1600 got closer and closer to Michael's times.

By the end of the season, Michael was convinced that the only reason Billy didn't run faster in the 1600 was because he wanted Michael to win. Billy easily won his 800-meter races and had run times at that distance that were 5 seconds faster than any other times recorded in the state that season. Billy already held the state record in the 800 meters—1:47.24— and it made no sense that Billy would run the 1600 in well over 4 minutes. A runner who could break 1:50 in the 800 should be able to easily break 4 minutes in the 1600. Michael had never come close to breaking 4 minutes in the 1600. He knew Billy was holding back.

What neither Michael nor Billy knew was that Branford Stevens had approached Bill Dexter privately, early in the season, to ask Bill for a favor. Branford had sent word for Bill to come to his office at the Alexandria Asphalt Company one day after work. He closed the door and told Bill to have a seat.

The office was well-appointed, with a huge cherry desk and comfortable furniture, but the acidic smell of asphalt from the plant outside still hung in the room.

"Hello, Bill," said Branford. "How are things going with you and your crew?"

Bill had been with the company for 25 years at that point and had gotten somewhat comfortable being around Mr. Stevens. He'd seen Mr. and Mrs. Stevens often during the seven years since his wife had died. Mrs. Stevens had been very supportive of Billy, although she *had* seemed to withdraw somewhat since Billy had joined the track team.

"Things are going well, sir. It's great that the company has so much work lined up. Keeps us busy!"

"Well good, Bill. I'm glad to hear that. Now, Bill, do you remember the conversation you and I had over the phone on that terrible morning your wife passed?"

Bill thought back to that horrible day. He remembered asking Mr. Stevens if they could help with Billy while he sorted out what had to be done with his wife's body and made the funeral arrangements.

"Yes, sir. I remember. I wish I didn't because that was the kind of day you never want to have. But it happened."

"Yes, and my family has been very supportive of yours in the ensuing years, as I promised we would. And if you remember, you said you would do the same for us if the need ever arose. Isn't that right?"

"Yes, sir. And that still holds true."

"Very good. Because I believe the time has come for you to help my family."

"I see," said Bill, wondering where this was going and beginning to feel a little uncomfortable.

"Actually, Bill, this should be a fairly easy request for you to carry out. Simply stated, I'd like you to convince your son to choose an event other than the 1600 to compete in. That should be easy enough, right?"

Bill Dexter did not respond immediately. He sat and thought, which was his way.

"Bill?" asked Mr. Stevens. "Are you all right?"

"Yes, sir. I'm fine."

"So, we have an agreement then?"

"Well, sir, I'm not sure. I have some simple rules that I live by and that I've taught my sons to live by. And your request seems to go against my number one rule."

"And what rule is that?" asked Branford, his voice becoming edgy.

"Play fair," said Bill. "Your request just don't seem fair to me, sir. My Billy's already had a run of bad luck, and it don't seem fair to pile this on top of it."

"I see," said Mr. Stevens. "But you also know that my family has done nothing but help yours over the years, Bill. It just doesn't seem fair to me that you would pass up the opportunity to help my family, especially since you promised to do so many years ago. The reality is that it was Michael's idea for Billy to join the track team, and he has welcomed him with open arms. So why would you, or Billy for that matter, want to in any way tarnish the legacy that Michael has built in track and field?"

"I don't understand how Billy running the 1600 would tarnish anything, sir."

Branford's face began to redden. He was not patient in the face of resistance, especially when it was one of his employees resisting him. "Do I have to spell it out for you? Damn it!

I don't want *your* son to have the opportunity to defeat *my* son!"

"But, sir, Billy's trying to get a new start, and the coaches have told him he can't run the shorter races. The 1600 is one of the few races he can run right now."

Branford turned completely red in the face. "Then let him do the high jump, or the javelin. I don't care what! But not the 1600!"

Bill didn't respond, thinking again. After about 10 seconds, he made his final decision.

"Well, sir, you have a point. I suppose you could say I'm not a man of my word after this, but I can't hurt my son just to help you stack the odds in your son's favor, especially when Michael doesn't even need your help, or mine, or Billy's. My family truly needed your family's help back then, but this just don't seem the same."

Branford didn't hesitate. "I disagree, Bill. In my mind, it's you who's broken your number one rule. And since you seem to have no appreciation of all I've done for you, then you no longer need to accept a paycheck from me either."

This time Bill didn't hesitate. "I wouldn't have it any other way, sir. I can't work for a man who would stoop so low, for no good reason. You're not helping your son by trying to keep Billy out of the 1600. You're crippling him."

"My son will win the 1600 state championship, Bill, but with no thanks to you! Now get out!"

Billy was aware that his dad no longer worked for Alexandria Asphalt Company, but he didn't know why. All his dad said was that he was tired of it and wanted to make a new start. Unfortunately for Bill, the paving community in the area was very close. After a few phone calls from Branford to his competitors, Bill was blacklisted and could not land a job at one of the other paving companies. He was forced to take a job at Home Depot, which was a major pay cut for him. Finances got very tight at the Dexter household.

Bill had savings, and he hated to use them, but he had to pay the bills. Nevertheless, Bill felt good about his decision. What he didn't feel good about was that just like Michael, he knew his son was holding back in the 1600 meters.

Bill approached his son the day before the championship meet. He explained to Billy that there was no place for friendship during a competition. Billy pointed out that it was Michael's idea that he run track, and this had resulted in him receiving several scholarship offers from Division I college teams. Billy had Michael to thank for this and didn't want to hurt him in any way. Bill disagreed, vehemently.

"Son, if you don't make every effort to win that race, you'll be cheating yourself, your family, and even your best friend. Do you think he wants the race handed to him? And do you give him so little credit that you think he won't raise his game if challenged? Nobody but you has even come close to him in the 1600 this year. And the closer you've gotten, the lower his times have gone. Matter of fact, I'm not sure you could beat him even if you tried to."

That last comment got to Billy. His genetically and environmentally imposed will to win dominated his being. And now that his dad had said Michael would probably beat him even if Billy gave it his best shot, Billy was inclined to find out. But before making a final decision, Billy intended to discuss it with Michael.

On Friday night, two days before the 1600, Billy broached the subject with Michael. The championships were being held in the Hampton Roads area of southeastern Virginia, about a three-hour drive from McLean. Billy and Michael were roommates at the hotel. The boys were watching a college football game on TV when Billy decided to talk the issue through with his best friend.

"How you feelin'?" asked Billy.

"Okay," said Michael. The fact was that Michael didn't feel that well. He felt like he might be coming down with a cold. He wasn't sure he wanted Billy to know this, however, and that made him feel tense and confused. "How about you?"

"I feel good."

"You looked good in the 800 prelims today." Billy had coasted to an easy win in the 800 qualifying race, cruising in a few seconds slower than his state record. The 800 Finals would be the following day, Saturday, as would the 3200-meter Final. The 1600 Final would be on Sunday, the last day of the meet. There were no prelims in either the 1600 or the 3200.

"Thanks," said Billy. "Listen, about the 1600?"

"I'm listening," said Michael, bringing the index finger of his right hand to the scar on his chin and rubbing it slowly back and forth.

"I figure I'll win the 800 tomorrow, and I figure you'll win the 3200."

"We should be so lucky," said Michael.

"Yeah, a little luck always helps," said Billy, trying to lighten the moment. "But assuming we don't have any bad luck, we should win those races, right?"

"Okay, right."

"So, that leaves the 1600, right?"

"That would be correct," said Michael, stiffening. He was angry with himself for feeling this way. It had been his idea to bring Billy onto the track team, and he knew going in that Billy was the kind of athlete seen maybe once in a generation. He'd understood with clear eyes that Billy was going to excel in the sport. True, he hadn't expected to be competing against Billy, but circumstances that neither of them controlled had led to this. It wasn't Billy's fault, and it wasn't his fault either.

"So, what do you think we should do about the 1600?" asked Billy.

"What do you mean?" asked Michael, already knowing exactly what Billy meant.

"Well, I been feelin' pretty good lately. I'm really startin' to get the hang of these races. And I think I can go faster in the 1600."

"I'm sure you can," said Michael, sawing away at his chin with his index finger. "I think we've all known that for a while. So why don't you?"

"Uh, well. The 1600 is kind of your race, you know what I mean?"

Michael knew what Billy meant, and deep inside he felt that way too, but his pride wouldn't let him admit it to his best friend. "No, it isn't," he said. "No way. I won't be out there by myself on Sunday."

"Yeah, but you've owned the 1600 this year, man," said Billy.

"Thanks to you I have."

"What do you mean?"

"Look," said Michael. "We don't need to get into the details of this past season, okay? We've both had great seasons.

We're both going to college next year on scholarships. So, on Sunday, why don't we line up for the 1600 and let it all hang out? Who knows, maybe we can both go under 4 minutes. Wouldn't that be cool?"

Billy was stunned. He hadn't expected Michael to be so understanding about this. Maybe Billy's dad had been right after all. Maybe Michael wanted to be pushed. The conversation ended, and the boys got ready for bed.

On Saturday, Billy won the 800, and Michael won the 3200. Michael was still feeling a little under the weather, but he felt no worse than he had the day before. He took some acetaminophen and went to bed. Unfortunately, he didn't sleep well. Michael was scared. Just like old times, he was afraid of losing to Billy. Billy, on the other hand, slept like a log.

The day of the 1600 race arrived. The weather was overcast, with a breeze from the west. Michael woke up groggy, with a slight headache. He took more acetaminophen. The boys ate lightly, then took a shuttle over to the event venue together. Michael's thoughts drifted. He wondered if it was his destiny never to beat Billy when it mattered the most. He took two more acetaminophen and began his stretching regimen, frustrated that he wasn't at his best healthwise. He cursed his bad luck in his moment of need.

Race time arrived. Billy and Michael shook hands and moved onto the track. Michael looked up and saw his mother and father sitting together in the stands. They waved at him, and his father gave him the thumbs-up sign. Michael nodded his head, more nervous now than ever. He reached deep within himself for the confidence and willpower he would need to pull this off. An aura of determination took hold of him that he'd never felt before. Perhaps it was his anger at his own bad luck, but whatever it was, he'd never felt it before. He told himself that he wasn't going to let Billy take this from him. Not this time!

The starter called the contestants in the 1600 to the line. As the top two seeds, Michael and Billy took the spots closest to the inside of the track. The other competitors would have to battle with each other to get to the inside. A familiar chant rose from the McLean High School fans: "Dee-*mon*! Dee-*mon*! Dee-*mon*!" It wasn't as loud as the chants back in the fall because there were far fewer track and field fans at McLean High than there were football fans, but it hurt nonetheless.

Michael had been the captain of the track team for the past two seasons. He was a state champion in cross-country, track, and swimming, and while he was respected and well-liked by everyone, he simply wasn't the Demon. Billy's mythical status had only increased with his resurgence as a track star. He was a Phoenix risen from the ashes, and a double win at the track and field state championships would solidify his standing as perhaps the greatest high school athlete ever in the state of Virginia. Michael decided at that moment that *he* would be the one who kept Billy from achieving this destiny.

The starter called the runners to their mark, and the crowd fell silent. Michael's heart was beating too fast as he stepped to the line and leaned forward for the start, his left leg bent and out front, his left hand resting on his left knee. He wondered if it was the anxiety surrounding the race that was causing his heart to pump so fast or if it was something else. He told himself it didn't matter and forced his mind into a state of concentration.

The gun went off, and the race was on. Michael was astonished at how fast Billy went out, taking the lead from the start, moving quickly to take the inside from Michael. In all of the previous 1600s they'd run together, Billy had *never* been ahead of Michael. Now he was not only ahead, he was surging with a determination Michael had witnessed so many times in the past. *Too many times*, he thought.

Michael went after Billy, fighting off the bumping and grinding of the runners trying to get to the inside while Billy breezed out in the front, untouched. After about 100 meters of battling, Michael settled in just behind Billy.

Billy finished the first lap in 56 seconds. Michael was right behind him, but he felt he couldn't keep up this pace. The next closest runner was nearly 10 meters behind Michael. The crowd was beginning to rumble, sensing something thrilling was in the making.

At the halfway point, two laps, Billy was still in the lead, followed closely by Michael. Michael heard them call out the time—1:55—and was shocked. Michael's halfway split at the regional meet had been 2:01. He was breathing with difficulty and had some numbness in his arms. But his mind was strong. His mind was willing his body on with no regard for anything except the pumping arms and legs of the runner with the knee brace who was just ahead—the Demon.

As the two teens blazed by the stands at the end of lap three, the crowd was in a frenzy. Even students from the other schools had joined in the chant—"Dee-*mon*! Dee-*mon*! Dee-*mon*!!"

The 1600 had become a two-man race of historic proportions. The split after three laps was 2:54! The runners were on pace for an American high school record at the 1600-meter distance. Michael was now feeling pain in his chest. His heart pounded erratically. But his mind and soul said this was his chance, maybe his last, to prove he had a heart as big as Billy Dexter's.

The final lap was an epic struggle. Michael made his move on the back straightaway, knowing he needed to forge a lead on Billy before the final sprint. He passed Billy, succeeded in opening up a gap of around 1 meter, and tried to hold it. Coming around the final turn, Billy dug as deep as an athlete could and closed the distance. The crowd roared, telling Michael Billy was coming. Billy pulled even with Michael with 50 meters to go and began to edge ahead of him. Michael reached deeper still for a final push, but it was too much. In a wave of pain, his heart gave out. He crashed to the track surface in a flailing heap of legs and arms, coming to a rest on his side only 25 meters from the finish line. The crowd shrieked with fear and hysteria, knowing something terrible had happened. But Billy didn't know, and he wouldn't look back until he crossed the finish line, still bound by the third and final rule his father had taught him: Never look back.

Not until Billy finished, victorious, did he turn to see his best friend crumpled on the track. It was a horror scene Billy would *never* be able to erase from his memory.

The doctor and trainers rushed onto the track and examined Michael while the ambulance careened toward them. Billy ran up and knelt beside Michael, asking the doctor if he was going to be okay.

Michael's father ran up and screamed at Billy. "Get away from my son!"

"Let me work," admonished the doctor, frantically waving everyone away.

Billy backed away, tears streaming down his face. His dad rushed onto the track and grabbed him, squeezing tightly, a look of fear and confusion on his face.

The doctor pulled out a syringe and injected Michael with heparin, a drug designed to dilate the blood vessels and dissolve any blood clots. Michael was rushed to the hospital.

Billy was the state champion in the 1600 meters, setting an American high school record of 3:51:56 in the process. But he didn't care. Billy had come face-to-face with the ugly truth about winning at all costs. He had literally run his best friend's athletic career, and maybe even his life, into the ground. Billy's guilt was profound and would haunt him for many years.

PART TWO

CHAPTER 10

2015

Elizabeth Whitlock took her seat at the elegant rosewood chess table the school had purchased specifically for this event, noting the enthusiastic applause at her entrance. Bradenbrook College had spared no expense on the table. With an average student tuition exceeding $75,000 per year and a large endowment, the school could afford it.

The chess table had been placed on the stage in the school's performing arts theater. It was early April 2015, and all the colleges were back in session after their spring breaks. The theater was full this Saturday evening. Although Bradenbrook was a women's college—one of only four remaining in Virginia—a healthy percentage of young men were in attendance.

A tradition that remained strong at Bradenbrook was the presence on the weekends of students from nearby colleges and universities such as Hampden-Sydney, the University of Virginia, and Washington and Lee. Bradenbrook often hosted mixers for the young men and women to meet and socialize. Tonight's mixer would begin after the chess exhibition ended.

Elizabeth glanced up at the huge video screen that hung above the table, a few feet farther back on the stage. The screen would provide a close-up of the board so all in the room could see exactly what was transpiring in the game. Elizabeth's opponent was the president of the Virginia Chess Federation, a white-haired elderly gentleman named Winthrop O'Keefe.

In his prime, Winthrop had attained the United States Chess Federation's ranking of national master, which wasn't the highest ranking, but at any given time there were fewer than 1,000 active national masters in the United States, meaning it *was* a serious ranking. But Winthrop had long since retired from competitive chess, and it was well known in chess circles that his game had declined precipitously over the past several years.

Elizabeth had never officially competed on the chess circuit and had no desire to do so, but her natural abilities in the game were exceptional, and she sought out opportunities to play against accomplished players. She had recently defeated the Virginia state champion at a coffeehouse in town. Although the match was completely unofficial, it had drawn the attention of the state chess federation, which was always on the lookout for new talent to join their ranks. Winthrop had readily accepted the school's invitation to play against Elizabeth at this event, a fundraiser for a charity dedicated to providing educational opportunities to underprivileged children, a few of whom were current students at Bradenbrook.

Winthrop and Elizabeth had been introduced backstage prior to the match, and she had treated him with respect, bordering on adoration. Elizabeth was a confident young woman, but she also knew it would be a challenge for her to win against such an experienced opponent, even if the rumors about the decline of his game were true. She had dressed conservatively, wearing a dark blue pantsuit over a white cotton blouse. She assumed the demeanor of a nervous, underqualified, but nevertheless duty-bound participant in the match.

"You see, Mr. O'Keefe, I *do* hope you don't end the match too quickly," she said, demurely. "I know I'm not qualified to play you, but we *have* raised a lot of money tonight for the underprivileged, and if I can simply get out of here without being too embarrassed, I would be grateful."

The truth was that Elizabeth was not at all concerned about the underprivileged or being embarrassed. She was simply probing for a way to gain any small advantage she could in the upcoming contest.

"Now, now, Miss Whitlock," said Winthrop. "I'm led to believe you're highly talented, and we very much would like to see you join the federation."

"Why thank you, sir. I'd be honored to join if I can just not embarrass myself too much." Elizabeth had no intention of joining the federation, but she played along to continue her ruse.

"Please don't worry about that, my dear. I'm sure we'll have a very enjoyable match."

"I hope so," she said, turning her head down in apparent bashfulness.

"Why don't you take white, my dear. Would that help?"

Bingo, thought Elizabeth. In the game of chess, white always plays first. Data collected from more than 600,000 matches demonstrated that playing white achieved either a win or a draw 73 percent of the time, with white winning 37 percent of the time compared to only 27 percent for black. In a friendly exhibition, there are no firm rules on how to decide which player plays white. Sometimes, one player puts a black pawn in one hand and a white pawn in the other while his or her hands are below the table, then closes his hands over each piece and holds them up for his opponent to choose. The odds are the same as flipping a coin. However, there's nothing stopping one opponent from volunteering to allow the other to play white, as Winthrop had just done.

Elizabeth clasped her hands together, the helpless maiden being rescued by the heroic prince. "Oh, thank you, sir! Thank you!"

"Please, dear, call me Winthrop."

"Oh, yes, Winthrop. And please call me Liza, all right?"

"Certainly dear. Certainly."

The match began. In spite of Liza's apparent lack of confidence, Winthrop was still hopeful she would be a worthy opponent. He knew from experience that her first five or six moves would provide the answer. Unfortunately, as the game unfolded, he was sorely disappointed. Her opening was so poorly executed that he was uncertain how he could get this match to go much longer than 10 to 15 minutes. She had clumsily maneuvered one of her bishops to the side of the board, seemingly wasting several moves to get the piece out of the area where the battle was normally won or lost—the center of the board—and for no apparent reason. The bishop now sat directly in front of one of her rooks, wasting away and blocking any potential move forward by her rook.

Winthrop tried to keep his expression neutral, but every now and then he caught himself shaking his head, stupefied by her ineptitude. He tried to take his time, but it wouldn't take long before he would have no choice but to unleash his forces and end the match. It was quite obvious that he wouldn't even need to castle—a standard defensive move to help protect the king from assault—to emerge from this game as the master of his outrageously overmatched opponent. Reluctantly, he began his attack.

Winthrop reached for a bishop and shot it forward, plunging it into her knight, adroitly removing the captured knight from the board with the same hand that had moved the bishop, then placing the captured knight in the drawer on his side of the table. A subtle, dominating smile formed on his lips, and he reclined and folded his arms in front of himself, but when he realized how impolite he was being, he quickly sat up and regained a more neutral expression. Liza countered quickly, making an adjustment in her defense that he knew was the correct move, and this surprised him a bit. Nevertheless, he remained firmly convinced that she'd let things get too far out of hand.

He jumped one of his knights into the heat of the battle, brushing aside one of her pawns. Again, she made the proper move in response. *Too late, my dear. Too late.* He sliced his other bishop into the fray. She immediately used her long, slender fingers to castle to the queen's side, putting her king in a secure position and throwing off the rhythm and direction of his attack. Her side of the board was beginning to take on a more formidable shape. It was still highly defensive, but if he wasn't careful, it could become offensive as well.

Winthrop decided to prepare his side of the board for a queen-side castle. This would require him to bring his queen forward, but that was something he needed to do anyway, to enlist more firepower against her suddenly bolstered defense. He moved the queen up and sat back to wait for her next move, which was not forthcoming for some time.

Winthrop was unaware that Elizabeth Whitlock came from a long line of chess aficionados. She'd consulted with her father, the best player in her immediate family, who was an *active* national master and regularly competed in federation-sponsored tournaments. He'd done a quick study of Winthrop's matches from his days of active competition, which were archived online by the federation. This had led Liza's father to suggest a gambit that was rarely used in serious chess circles because of the high risk of failure. Nevertheless, he doubted if Winthrop had ever seen or studied this gambit, because his style was very conservative.

As Liza studied the gambit, she decided that she would use it only if she was comfortable prior to the match that her opponent was somewhat overconfident. She had concluded after their brief conversation prior to the match that Winthrop was either a very good actor or he was indeed convinced that he was involved in a mismatch. Otherwise, he would never have volunteered to allow her to play white. And of course, the opening of this gambit had thoroughly convinced him that she was playing out of her league, allowing her to take advantage at the appropriate time, which had now arrived.

The room began to feel oppressively hot to Winthrop. A bead of sweat trickled down the side of his puffy cheek.

Why did the school insist on using those blazing spotlights? he thought. *Are they purposely trying to put me at a disadvantage?*

He looked up and saw the girl staring at him, her piercing blue eyes wide and blazing, her perfect mouth open and loose. She wasn't smiling.

Is she gloating? he wondered. *What's going on here? Have I missed something?* He felt goose bumps rising on his skin.

Winthrop's opponent returned her attention to the board. She reached out with long fingers and delicately clasped the "wasted" bishop between the two curled fingers, her index and middle. This was the piece she'd maneuvered to the side of the board very early in the game. She dropped the two fingers all the way down, touching the surface of the board with her fingernails, then squeezed the piece between them. Slowly, she dragged the bishop diagonally down the board. The sound of her blood red nails lightly scraping against the board was audible to everyone in the silent room. Many in the audience didn't know the game of chess, but they could feel the tension of those who did. Something was coming. And it was coming soon.

The bishop came to rest on the square occupied by a pawn that was to have been one of her opponent's sentinels after he castled. But the pawn was gone now, and the queen-side castle was suddenly eliminated as a viable move for the old man. What was worse, he had no immediately available option for removing her bishop. It wasn't threatening his king, however, so he had to decide if he should position a piece to threaten the bishop or leave it alone for now. For the first time in the game, he didn't know what to do. He kept his eyes focused on the board, sweat beading up on his forehead. He knew the girl was staring at him again, but he didn't want to give her the satisfaction of looking back at her. He felt blood rushing to his cheeks, embarrassment beginning to cloud his judgment as it might for a novice player.

Settle down. Settle down. Think it through. Think it through. But when he thought it through, he realized that she was no more than three moves from checkmate, no matter what he did to disrupt her attack. Her king was protected, and his wasn't. He pressed his lips together, stood up, and extended his right hand.

"I resign," he said.

Liza stood and shook his hand, smiling, her eyes almost apologetic, as if she were saying, *I'm sorry I had to do that to you in front of all these people.*

The crowd burst into applause. The show lights were slowly faded down. Liza could now see out into the crowd. Up in the mezzanine, she saw a tall, handsome young man with blond hair. He was wearing a blue blazer and was staring directly at her as he clapped enthusiastically along with the rest of the audience. There was a look of awe on his face, which she was used to, but there was also something else. Some kind of unexplainable sadness. Liza smiled at him, hoping she'd have the chance to meet him later at the mixer. Michael Stevens was hoping exactly the same thing.

CHAPTER 11

In April 2015, Michael was finishing his second year at the University of Virginia. He'd originally planned on attending Virginia on a combined swimming/track scholarship, but that had been withdrawn after his heart attack. The school was happy to admit Michael on his academic merit alone if he could afford the tuition, which was no issue for his family, so he readily accepted.

Going to college on an athletic scholarship was never about the money for Michael. It was about finding a school where he could get a great education while continuing to excel in the sports he'd trained so hard for and come to love. He'd lost that opportunity when his heart gave out at the state championship meet, but Virginia still provided him a great opportunity to build a new life, even if that life didn't involve athletic competition. While Michael was heartbroken at the loss of his athletic career, he was grateful to have been given what seemed to be a good chance at finding a new path.

The cardiologist had determined that Michael had been suffering from myocarditis—inflammation of the myocardium, the heart muscle—which had probably been brought on by an infection, although it was impossible to know exactly how the disease had originated. The doctor said Michael had been lucky because the myocarditis was only in its early phases at the time it caused his heart to fail. The quick, accurate response of the doctor at the scene had been critical in minimizing damage to the heart muscle. The doctor was also happy to hear that Michael had been taking acetaminophen, which was known to work in a complementary way with drugs used in response to heart attacks. The best news of all was that there was a very good chance of a complete recovery if Michael was careful during the months immediately following his heart attack.

Michael spent the first few months slowly resuming the day-to-day activities of normal life, excluding athletics, of course. The doctor cautioned him not to allow his heart rate to get too high during the initial stages of his recovery. He'd even given him medicine to help prevent this, but the medicine made Michael sluggish, and he stopped taking it after only a few weeks, relying on his own diligence to keep his heart rate under control.

After four months, the doctor said Michael could resume light exercise and need not worry about his heart rate anymore, but that was easier said than done, considering the emotional damage that had accompanied the physical harm.

Perhaps an even greater tragedy than Michael's heart attack was the fate of Billy Dexter. Billy had gone to the University of Florida on a track scholarship, but he'd quickly lost the scholarship and had to return home. His discipline was gone, and he'd started drinking soon after the state meet. By the time he went to college in August, he was in poor shape, partying constantly, and barely made it to September before being dismissed by the team, losing his scholarship. Billy came back to the little house in McLean where he'd grown up, but he kept partying, telling everyone he would not compete until Michael competed again.

Many people thought this was a convenient excuse, but Michael believed Billy had made that decision at the moment he was told that Michael might never compete again. He'd spoken to Billy endlessly, urging him to get his life in order. He never blamed Billy for what had happened to him and wanted very badly to see his best friend get back on course and take full advantage of the opportunities that his extraordinary athletic abilities could open up for him, but to no avail.

Before long, as Billy's inexorable decline continued, Bill threw him out of the house. Billy's younger brother, Richie, was only eight years old at the time, and Bill didn't want the boy to grow up imitating his older brother's irresponsible behavior. Billy stayed with friend after friend, losing all of them, and he couldn't hold a job. Months at a time went by when nobody even knew where he was.

By mid-October 2014, early in Michael's sophomore year at Virginia, it had been nearly six months since he'd last seen Billy. Having just taken his last mid-term exam prior to fall break, Michael was driving home, proceeding north out of Charlottesville on Route 29. The weather was brisk, and a light rain was falling.

Up ahead Michael saw a man on the side of the road. A hitchhiker. You rarely saw hitchhikers anymore. There were just too many crazy people these days, both drivers and hitchhikers. Michael had no intention of picking the man up, but he slowed down to make sure he didn't soak the guy with a spray of water from his tires. As he approached, the man looked familiar. He slowed further and couldn't believe that he might be looking at Billy Dexter.

Michael brought the car to a stop well off the highway and got out. He approached the man, who was soaked from head to toe. Michael looked more closely. This person definitely looked like Billy!

"Billy?" he asked.

The man tensed, then turned and began to run.

"Billy, wait!" screamed Michael. "I won't tell anyone I saw you if that's what you want! I just want to talk!"

The man stopped, then slowly turned around. It was definitely Billy, although he was much thinner than he'd been the last time Michael had seen him. Michael continued to walk toward him, slowly, ignoring the rain and traffic whizzing by. He wanted to avoid spooking Billy, and he was still conscious of his own heart rate, continuing to try to keep it from going too high. This was in spite of the fact that the doctors had said his heart was completely healed and could easily withstand exercise.

"Billy, it's me, Michael. Can we talk?"

"Why?" slurred Billy. He appeared to be drunk, and his dilated pupils indicated maybe he was on something else, too.

"Because I've missed the heck out of you, that's why," said Michael. "Come on, let's get in my car."

Billy followed, tentatively at first, unsteady on his feet. Michael stepped in beside him and put his arm around him, leading him to the car. In the small confines of the car, Billy's alcohol-infused breath quickly dominated the air. Michael ignored this and started asking questions.

"Where in the heck have you been, bud? We've all been worried sick."

"Around," said Billy.

"What are you doing down here near Charlottesville?"

Billy hesitated, then confessed. "Partying," he said.

"Where?" asked Michael.

"Just somebody's place," slurred Billy.

"Where have you been living?"

"Around."

"What about money? How have you lived?"

"Why's it matter?"

"I don't know. I just want you to be okay."

"I been dealing powder, okay!" said Billy, angry.

Oh crap!, thought Michael. *I've got to get him back home.*

"Sorry, I just want to help," Michael said, his tone conciliatory. "Look, you know that what happened to me had nothing to do with you, right?"

"Not the way I see it," said Billy, folding his arms across his chest.

"But I'm fine anyway. Doing great. Joined a fraternity and loving school. I'm studying business. The only thing that's wrong with my life is that you haven't been around."

Billy seemed to be thinking, a good sign. "So, you're doing pretty good then?"

"Heck yes! Even better now that I've found you. Do I look like someone whose life has been ruined? Here I am, driving a hand-me-down Mercedes for goodness' sake, going to the college of my choice, and having the time of my life."

"But you can't do sports no more. Can you?"

"Well, that's not really true. I *choose* not to do sports. I've already told you this, but let me remind you because it's important. I had a heart condition due to an infection that had nothing to do with you, and that's why I didn't make it through the 1600 back at Hampton Roads. It had nothing to do with you, man! And the doctors say I can start working out again if I want to. I just haven't gotten to that yet. Too busy, I guess."

A small smile formed on Billy's face. "Well, then. That's good."

"Did you know I was still down in Charlottesville?" asked Michael.

"Yeah, I know. I come down this way every now and then, but never worked up the courage to come see you. I'm just so far gone I don't know what to do." Billy shook his head slowly from side to side.

Michael felt he was getting through to Billy. "Not true at all. There's always hope when you have friends and family to help you through a tough time."

"I should've been there for you, man." Billy hung his head.

"No, that's not what I mean, Billy! I mean I'm here for you, and I know your dad and Richie will be there for you, too, if you let them."

Billy was silent, obviously conflicted. He'd put his family through a lot. He'd certainly broken his father's first rule of being fair. He knew what he'd done hadn't been fair to anyone, especially to himself.

"You think they'll take me back?" he asked, his voice soft and timid.

"I know they will, bud. I know they will. I'm headed to northern Virginia anyway. Why don't you come with me?"

Again, Billy hesitated, thinking. "Okay," came his meek reply.

Michael was relieved—and excited. He pulled back out onto Route 29 and headed north, but he knew he had more work to do. As they drove toward northern Virginia, Michael counseled Billy that for his father to take him back in, Billy would need to make a commitment to getting off the booze and drugs and finding a job. Billy readily agreed to this. Michael then called ahead on his cell phone to tell Bill they were on the way. Bill insisted on speaking to Billy directly, and Michael handed him the phone.

"I want to come home, Dad," Billy wept into the phone. "I want to get right, but I need your help. Please!"

"Come home, son," Bill said. "We'll get started."

Michael drove Billy back to McLean and helped him reunite with his family. Bill and Richie, now nine years old, were overwhelmed with joy when Billy came in the door. There was no talk of fairness whatsoever. Billy was home. His family would help him get back on his feet.

Within a month, Billy was working at Home Depot for his dad, who was now the assistant store manager. Not long after that, he was jogging and lifting weights, looking a lot more like the old Billy. Michael returned from Charlottesville as often as he could, trying to rebuild the friendship that had meant more to him than almost anything else.

CHAPTER 12

The mixer at Bradenbrook in the spring of 2015, toward the end of Michael's sophomore year, started at 8 p.m. The chess match was over, with Liza Whitlock the winner. The school administration was ecstatic with the success of the fundraiser. Refreshments were served, none of them alcoholic. The boys who wanted to drink had flasks in their pockets that they discreetly poured into their soft drink glasses, offering the booze to girls who wanted a drink.

Michael wasn't a big drinker, never had been, even before he knew about his heart condition. The fraternity he'd joined was more of an academically minded group as opposed to the stereotypical heavy partiers that Virginia was known for. Michael's fraternity brothers knew how to party; they just didn't do it seven days a week!

Michael had heard a few of his fraternity brothers speaking about Liza on the drive over to Bradenbrook that afternoon. It seemed to him that they were more interested in the way she looked than the fact that she was good enough in chess to challenge a national master.

During the match, Michael noted that Liza was indeed

beautiful, but he was more impressed with her skill in the game of chess, a game he'd recently become enamored with himself. Michael wasn't intimidated by pretty girls, but he was most definitely intimidated by a pretty girl who was the best chess player he'd ever seen. But as he pondered his dilemma further, it became obvious to him that if he had the chance to meet her, he should ask her exactly what he wanted to ask, which was how she'd become such an accomplished chess player.

When Liza entered the room, many eyes turned her way. She'd changed into an off-white, springtime dress that hung loosely on her frame, ending about mid-calf. The dress made no attempt to show off any particular aspect of her body—actually, it seemed to somehow provide balance to her proportions. As Michael studied the dress from a distance, he noticed a discreet thin piping that traveled along the front and back of the dress in a closed loop. The piping was the same off-white color as the dress, so it was very subtle, delicately tracing around the natural curves of her body in a barely visible, understated way.

Liza was tall and slender, with the muscle tone of someone who worked out regularly. Her blonde hair came to just above her shoulders, curling forward elegantly at the ends. Her blue eyes had a greenish tint, like a tropical bay in the sunshine.

Okay, she's really pretty, Michael thought. *So what? I've been with pretty girls before.*

Nevertheless, he began to question his plan of how to approach her. Suddenly, she walked directly up to him, extending her right hand.

"Hello, I'm Liza Whitlock," she said, smiling and gazing directly into his eyes.

Michael smiled back and shook her hand, his face reddening from this unexpected turn of events.

"Hi, I'm Michael Stevens," he said, working hard to keep his voice steady. "That dress is, well, it's different," he said, struggling to explain what he meant.

"I hope that means you like it," she said. "I designed it myself for one of my classes. I'm studying fashion design."

Bradenbrook had one of the most renowned fashion design departments in the country.

"Well, I think you might have found the right field!" Michael said, too enthusiastically, but with truth in his voice.

"Thank you," Liza said. "I rather enjoy the world of design." She paused, appraising him up and down. "Michael, you're not a first-year student, are you?"

"Why no, I'm second year, at Virginia," said Michael, wondering why she would ask this.

"Ah, good. I'm a sophomore as well." She paused, thinking, looking deeply into his eyes. "Michael, would you like to get something to drink?"

"Sure," he said. "What would you like?"

"I'd like a scotch on the rocks," she said.

"Oh, uh, well."

"Not a problem," she said. "I have some scotch in my room."

"Oh, well, that's too much trouble, I'm sure. Maybe I can get some from one of my friends."

"I doubt they have anything I would like," said Liza. "Look, Michael, please don't get the wrong idea, but why don't you accompany me to my room, and we'll have a drink and then come back. I really can't stand these mixers, so the less time I have to spend here the better. What do you say?"

Stunned, Michael was at a loss for words.

"I'll take that as a yes," said Liza. She quickly took his hand and pulled him gently, yet resolutely, from the room. He floated along behind her, almost hypnotized by her brash, persuasive demeanor.

They arrived at Liza's room, and she quietly closed the door behind her.

"Please have a seat," she said, waving her outstretched arm at the two chairs and small table at the side of the room.

Michael took a seat. Liza went over to her desk, opened a drawer, and pulled out a bottle of scotch and two glasses. Michael noticed several black and white sketches pinned to a bulletin board on the wall behind the desk. Several of them were of dress designs, and a few were portraits, one of which was a nude of a woman. Michael considered asking about the drawings but decided that was too personal of a topic and could be saved for another time, *if* there was to be another time.

The scotch was a Macallan 12 Year, a favorite of his father's. Liza stepped over to the small refrigerator and got some ice, then poured the drinks. She returned to the sitting area and handed Michael his drink, taking a seat in the empty chair beside Michael's, casually crossing her legs, the dress riding up her calves and over her knee. Michael did not allow his eyes to stray and continued looking at her beautiful face.

"Thank you for the drink," he said, clinking his glass against hers.

"My pleasure," she said, taking a long sip of scotch.

"Where did you learn to play chess?" he asked.

"That's a boring story," she said, pulling the glass from her lips. Noticing she had stained the glass slightly with her red lipstick, she grabbed a tissue and wiped the lipstick off the glass, blushing slightly, as if embarrassed by this imperfection. She wiped the excess lipstick from her lips and dropped the tissue into a wastebasket.

"Tell me anyway," he persisted. "I've become fascinated with the game recently. Some of my fraternity brothers started an informal chess club."

Michael had found he was pretty good at chess. Not on the level of Liza, however—not anywhere close.

"My family has always played," she said. "My father, my mother, my brothers, my uncles and aunts. They all love it."

"And you? Do you love it?"

"I enjoy winning," she said. "So, I suppose from that perspective I *do* love it."

"Where are you from?" asked Michael.

"Manhattan. You?"

"McLean, Virginia, just outside of D.C."

"Ah," she said. "Did you go to private or public high school?"

"Public. You?"

"Private." She took a long sip of her drink. "What are your interests, Michael? Your hobbies."

Michael had very little to say on the subject of interests. He could no longer pursue the things he'd spent most of his young life doing. In a very real way, he was starting over, looking for new things to occupy his free time. He very much wanted to impress the stunning young woman in front of him, but he had no idea what he might say to do that.

"I'm sorry, Liza. That's a difficult question for me to answer," he said.

Liza sat back in her chair, perplexed. "Why?" she asked.

"Well," said Michael. "I was an all-state swimmer and runner in high school. Actually, I won a few state championships, but . . ." He paused, wondering if he should reveal his weakness to her.

"Oh, I love swimming and running! Please, go on," she said, sensing his hesitation.

"Well, during the last race of my high school career, the 1600-meter run at the state championship meet, I, uh . . ."

"Yes?" she implored.

"I had a heart attack," he blurted out.

She raised her hand to her mouth, sharply drawing in her breath. "No, that can't be true, Michael! Tell me you're joking."

"Sorry . . .," he said, lowering his head, ". . . but no, it's not a joke."

Liza reached out her hand and took one of Michael's hands, squeezing gently. "I'm the one who should be sorry," she said. "That had to be hard to reveal to someone you've just met. I apologize for putting you in that position."

"Thank you," he said, his eyes meeting hers. "I really don't share that with too many people. I guess it's obvious now why I don't have very many interests?"

"Oh yes," she said. "Presumably, to become so accomplished in swimming and running required a substantial level of dedication—and time. And now that you can no longer train and compete, there's a void in your life, which you've only had a short time to figure out how to fill."

"Couldn't have said it better myself," he said, feeling a profound sense of joy that Liza had so easily understood and sympathized with his situation. "But really, I'm working on it. I'm in a fraternity. I'm studying business, which I really enjoy, and I truly *do* enjoy playing chess."

"Oh, *really?*" she said, smiling. "So that's what you want from me. You want to use me to elevate your game!"

"Why, of course!" he played along. "If you want to be the best, you've got to compete against the best, right?"

She laughed. "Well, I'm hardly the best at chess. I'm not even the best player in my family!"

"Well, you're better than me, so let's start with that."

"Very well," she said. "Why don't we schedule a chess date? You can meet me next weekend at Bixby's, in town. It's the local pub. We can have our first lesson."

"Consider it a date," he said. "I'll be there."

CHAPTER 13

2015-2017

Michael and Liza dated for the next two years. He visited her in New York during the summer break and found that she lived in a luxury penthouse apartment near Central Park. The most stunning thing about the apartment was that she owned it herself. Technically, a trust owned it, but she was the sole beneficiary of the trust, so in essence it was hers. Her father, one of the most successful hedge fund managers in New York, had gifted it to her as a high school graduation present.

Michael learned that Liza kept in shape by running, swimming, and working out in the gym in her apartment. He asked her why she didn't compete in these sports, and she explained that she had in high school—winning a private school championship in track and placing in the top three in swimming. And while she'd been offered scholarships to compete in college, she wanted to pursue her interest in fashion design and had taken a break from athletic competition. But she continued working out and planned to compete in triathlons as soon as she became more competent on the bike.

"Why not just start now?" he inquired. "I've dabbled with the idea of one day taking a stab at triathlon. I'm not ready to take the plunge, but I've done a little research. There are plenty of events, some less competitive than others."

"I want to be good enough to win when I start competing," she said. "And I don't have enough time right now to train. When I graduate, I plan to work for a fashion design company for a year or two, then break out on my own and start my own label. I'll begin serious training as soon as I'm back in New York full-time, but I'll only compete in casual sprint distance races. Then when I'm working for myself, I'll make my own hours and begin training more rigorously, moving up in distance and level of competition."

"Do you think you can make it in fashion design on your own with so little experience?"

She looked at him incredulously. "Of course. Why wouldn't I?"

Michael hesitated before answering, a little taken aback by her extreme confidence, but then he remembered that some people were just born that way, even though he wasn't one of them.

"No reason I can think of," he said. "You seem to win at everything else, so I suspect you'll win at that, too. I hope you do because you're really good at it."

Liza smiled. "Thank you, Michael. You are just the sweetest."

Liza encouraged Michael to begin working out again. She arranged for him to meet with a renowned cardiologist her father knew in the city. The doctor told him his heart was fine and that he could work his way back to competing if he wanted to, but of course, that was Michael's decision. Michael began going for runs and swims with Liza and helped her with her technique in both disciplines. She bought a bike for him that she kept in her dorm at Bradenbrook, and he began riding with her, but had not yet resolved his misgivings about competing.

When they graduated from college, Michael got an entry-level job at a wealth management company in Manhattan and moved in full-time with Liza. Liza got a job with a well-known fashion house and began training more seriously for triathlons. She won her first triathlon, a sprint distance event that Michael had recommended, though he refused to participate himself.

Michael also kept up with Billy during his final two years in college and after he moved to New York. Billy worked full-time at Home Depot, and he'd enrolled in community college and was taking classes toward a degree. He'd also started to work out again, running and lifting, primarily. It was obvious to Michael that Billy could still get a college scholarship if he wanted it, and he had asked Billy why he didn't compete.

"I won't compete again unless you compete again," Billy decisively said.

The conversation ended at that point.

Four months after Michael moved to New York, he invited Billy to visit. Billy took a few vacation days and rode the Amtrak train up to the city on a beautiful sunny Wednesday in early October 2017. Michael went directly from work to meet Billy at Penn Station. Michael was wearing his standard work attire: a nicely tailored but boring gray suit and a red tie. They hugged, and Michael stepped back to look at his best friend.

"Wow, you look good, bud!" said Michael. Billy was dressed in khakis and a blue button-down shirt. "You could almost pass as a preppie!"

"Well, I've been trying to upgrade my wardrobe a little bit," said Billy. "Helps with the girls."

Billy and Michael had had little time for girls in high school due to their year-round training for their respective sports. Now that Billy wasn't competing, he had time on his hands and found that he was attractive to women. He had no serious girlfriend, but he dated regularly.

Michael hailed a cab for their ride to his apartment. After exchanging pleasantries with the doorman, they walked to the elevator. The elevator dropped them right at the apartment, which filled the entire top floor of the building, an exquisite 3,000-square-foot space with three bedrooms, a large living room with a view of Central Park, a well-equipped gym, and even a sauna. Billy seemed overwhelmed.

"You live here?" he asked.

"Yeah, I know," said Michael. "I felt the same way the first time I saw it."

"How much is the rent for a place like this?"

"I have no idea," said Michael. "Liza owns the apartment. I pay her $2,500 a month—even though she says I don't have to pay anything. But I can't do that. So, I pay her what my budget allows me to pay."

"Jeez," said Billy. "I had no idea you lived like this. I thought all the young people who came to the city lived like dogs over in Hell's Kitchen or some such place."

"That's probably where I'd be if I didn't know Liza."

A door from one of the bedrooms opened, and Liza

appeared. She was dressed in a tightly-fitting running outfit, headed for a run in the park. She walked right up to Billy and hugged him.

"Billy, I can't believe Michael and I have known each other for more than two years, and this is the first time I've met you." She released him and stepped back to take him in from head to toe. "Oh, my!" she said. "You have two different colored eyes! Michael, why didn't you tell me that? How amazing!"

Billy was flustered, of course. Michael remembered the first time he'd met Liza. He'd felt exactly the same way Billy was feeling now. She could be a very intimidating person.

"Nice to meet you, ma'am," said Billy.

Liza pounced. "Oh, no!" she said. "No 'ma'ams' around here. I'm Liza. You're Billy. Deal?"

"Of course, Liza," said Billy, relaxing a bit.

Michael also remembered how quickly Liza could put a person at ease, and her magic was working already on Billy.

"Anyone up for a run in the park?" she asked.

"Not me," said Michael.

"Maybe tomorrow, after Michael and I catch up a bit?" asked Billy.

"It's a date," said Liza. Michael remembered when Liza set up her first date with him. He wondered when the parallels between his first meeting with her and Billy's first meeting with her would end.

CHAPTER 14

Michael arrived at his midtown office the Monday after Billy's visit. It was around 8 a.m. Most people didn't show up until 8:30 or 9, but the newer people, especially those who wanted to advance in the firm, showed up a bit earlier. Michael stopped by the cubicle of his best friend at the office, Allie, and plopped down in the extra chair. Allie turned toward him, her dark, straight hair trailing behind her. "Hey. Good weekend?" she asked.

"Kind of," he said, slumping his shoulders.

Allison West was from Michigan. She'd graduated from the University of Michigan with a degree in business the previous spring, joining the firm at the same time as Michael. She was taller than average, with the broad shoulders of a swimmer, which she'd been doing almost her entire life. She had swum the distance events for the Michigan women's team, placing third in the 1650-yard freestyle at the Division I national championships in her senior year. When she moved to the city, she'd taken up open water swimming. Michael was intrigued by this and enjoyed hearing Allie's stories about the swims she'd done around the city and beyond. Sometimes they'd go for coffee or lunch, and Michael would listen with rapt attention as Allie described her swims. At the moment, however, Allie sensed that it was Michael who needed to talk.

"What happened?" she asked.

"Billy came to visit," said Michael. Allie had heard all the stories about Michael's best friend, and she was confused why a visit from Billy might not be a good thing for Michael.

"Great!" she said. "What'd you guys do?"

"More like what did Billy and Liza do," he said, frowning.

"Oh?" she asked, with concern in her voice.

"They went for runs in the park every evening. Worked out in the gym both Saturday and Sunday. Couldn't get enough of each other."

"Why didn't you join them?" Allie was familiar with Michael's trepidation about working out and could see how his old rival Billy being in town might aggravate his condition, but she was also frustrated that he'd been given a clean bill of health yet was still so reluctant to pursue athletics more enthusiastically. She knew his skills and abilities were through the roof, and it was maddening for her to see him waste the best years of his life on the sidelines.

"I was invited, of course," he said. "But I wasn't into it."

Allie was conflicted about what to say next. She and Michael had always been attracted to one another, but it was a given that because he had a serious live-in girlfriend, there would never be any intimacy between them. So, they'd settled for the next best thing and become fast friends. She was secretly angry, however, that Michael stayed with such a domineering, selfish person as Liza when he deserved so much better. She couldn't say that, however, because then *she* would be the one being selfish.

"I wish you would've at least run with them," she said. "It's not like it was a race, you know."

"Yeah. Just didn't feel right."

Allie decided to try a different approach. "I have an idea," she said, excitement in her voice.

"What?"

"I know a guy who lives down at the Jersey Shore. He's a coach for endurance athletes. He coaches me, actually, but he's also kind of a shrink. He really helped me in my training, but he also helped me get my head straight."

"Since when do you have head problems?" asked Michael.

"My issues aren't like yours," she said. "They're more in the area of being too competitive. But I think he can help somebody like you, too."

Michael was intrigued. "You know what? You're right. I admit it. My head is definitely not right. What's this guy's name?"

"Don't laugh," she warned. "His name is Ziggy."

CHAPTER 15

Michael pulled into Manasquan, New Jersey, in his hourly rental at around 2 p.m. on a Friday afternoon. He'd taken a half day off work and picked up a Zipcar, signing it out for six hours. The drive was less than an hour and a half, although he was sure the drive back would take more than two hours due to Friday rush hour. That left him more than enough time to meet with Ziggy, deal with any unforeseen delays, and get back to the city for a Friday evening run with Liza, then cocktails and dinner at one of her favorite restaurants.

Manasquan was the classic Jersey Shore town, full of well-worn, single-story crackerbox houses that vacationers rented by the week. There was also a good-sized population of col-lege-aged kids who rented for the whole summer and worked at the local bars and dining establishments, then partied into the wee hours nearly every night of the week.

Michael used the GPS app on his phone to weave his way to the main beachfront road, found a parking spot, and got out. It was late October, the off-season, so the town was virtually empty. It was a partly cloudy day, or partly sunny, depending on your point of view. For Michael, it was partly cloudy. He wasn't very optimistic about the prospects of a productive meeting with Ziggy, and he wondered if this was going to be a waste of time. But Allie had been persuasive, and he owed it to her, and to himself, to give it a go.

Michael switched his GPS app to walking mode and quickly found the spot where Ziggy's office was supposed to be. The building was a small, white, single-story structure in poor repair. A plywood sign hung on the door read "Two Cool Training." The font was a mix of green and black on a yellow background. Michael rubbed the scar on his chin with the index finger of his right hand and knocked on the door with his left fist.

"Yo!" came a yell from behind the door.

Michael assumed this meant "Come in," in whatever lingo this guy Ziggy used, so he opened the door and entered the space. Inside was an old metal desk, painted gray. The only other furniture in the room was a small end table, upon which sat a coffee maker and some empty mugs. On the desk were a MacBook Pro laptop, a pad of paper, a pencil, and a cup of steaming coffee. Behind the desk stood a man, presumably Ziggy. He looked to be about 40 years old, although it was hard to tell because he was bald. He had inquisitive brown eyes, a sturdy, flared nose, and a big smile. His bright white teeth were perfectly aligned and contrasted pleasantly with his dark brown skin. He looked to be about 5 feet 10 inches tall, was thin and wiry, and stood with his hands clasped behind his back. The room smelled of coffee. It smelled really good and helped Michael to feel a little bit more at ease.

"Dude!" said Ziggy, in a melodic voice. "Come on in!"

Ziggy's "lingo" reminded Michael of California surfer

slang, sounding like Chicken Joe from the animated 2007 movie *Surf's Up*. Surfer slang for sure. Michael walked into the room, took two steps forward, reached the desk, and extended his hand.

"Michael Stevens," he said.

Ziggy reached out and gave Michael a solid handshake.

"Ziggy Jalowski. Just call me Zig. If things work out, you might wanna call me Two Cool."

Ziggy's preferred nickname was a mystery to Michael. He was also intrigued by Ziggy's last name but didn't ask about the origin of the names at that point. He glanced around the room and noticed there were no chairs, not even behind the desk.

"No sitting allowed," said Ziggy, his voice still casual but with a hint of conviction.

"Why?"

"Standing is harder."

"So it is," said Michael, raising his eyebrows.

"Coffee, dude?"

"Sure."

Ziggy stepped out from behind the desk and over to the coffee maker. He poured the coffee into a medium-sized ceramic cup that looked to have been handmade and bore the face of a snarling wolf. Ziggy handed the cup to Michael.

"Thank you," said Michael. "Cool cup."

"Gotta be a wolf sometimes when you're out there, dude. Ride with the pack."

"I thought you were mainly a triathlon coach. Isn't drafting illegal in some triathlon bike legs?"

"It is," said Ziggy. "Sometimes you gotta be the lone wolf."

"I see," said Michael, beginning to think there might be more to this guy Ziggy than he'd thought when he arrived. "So, you mostly coach triathletes, right? If I were to compete again, that's the route I think I'd take. My girlfriend does them. By the way, do you have any milk?"

"No to the milk, dude. I like it pure. Try it?"

Michael sipped the coffee and found it to be the most delicious blend he'd ever tasted. It was deep and smooth, soothing and refreshing, all at the same time.

"What kind of coffee is this?"

"Sumatra Gold. Did a race there once and discovered it. Luckily, I was able to find a store out on Long Island that sells it. They ship me a batch every month."

"It's awesome."

"Indeed," said Ziggy. "Yes, to the tri question. That's my main focus. But I sometimes take on the odd swimmer, like Allie, a runner or two, even a pure cyclist every now and then. But I usually don't take on the purists unless I feel they have potential as a triathlete down the line. What are you?"

"I'm none of the above, I guess."

"Yeah, that's what Allie said. So, how can I help you, dude?"

"I don't know. But Allie said she thought you could."

"Tell me your story then," said Ziggy, taking a long slurp from his cup of Sumatra Gold, his brown eyes riveted on Michael's. Michael noticed that the face of a horned bull was on the side of Ziggy's coffee cup. He didn't ask what it meant, but Ziggy noticed him looking at it.

"Sometimes being a wolf's not what's needed, dude. Sometimes you just have to bull your way through 'til you get where you need to go."

A realization came over Michael that literally every aspect of Ziggy's office and behavior, down to the smallest detail, was about sending a message. The message seemed to be *You can do this. I'm going to show you how.* Michael was beginning to feel more hopeful, and more comfortable, with Ziggy. He took a sip of the wonderful coffee, gathering his thoughts, then got right to the point.

"I guess you could say I've been afraid for a long time," he said, surprising himself by his honesty, but feeling a burden being lifted in doing so. He went on to tell his long, sad story, leaving out the recent clouds on the horizon, which had been brought on by Billy's early-October visit to New York.

"What's the doc say now?" asked Ziggy.

"He says my heart is fine. No permanent damage."

"I'll want to see that report, if we end up working together."

"No problem. Say, why do they call you Two Cool?"

"No two people are alike, right?"

"Right."

"Even identical twins aren't alike. I trained some identical twins once, and they were more different than you could believe, up here." Ziggy raised his cup and pushed it against the side of his bald head. "So, no two people should *ever* have the same training program."

"Seems logical."

"No, it's cool, dude. Two Cool!"

"Indeed. And now that we're on the subject of names, do you mind if I ask if you're Polish?"

"Half Polish, half Jamaican," said Ziggy. "My dad was from a Polish family, and my mom came here from Jamaica. Both of them are gone from this world now, so my only family is the athletes I coach. It's important to me to have a strong relationship with my clients."

"That's really good to hear, Zig. That's important to me, too. I'll need to have a lot of trust in the person guiding me back into competition, if I decide to go that way."

"Dig," said Ziggy. "What do you say we go out on the beach and take a walk. You cool with that, dude?"

"Sure, I've got some time."

They stepped outside and made their way to the beach. The clouds were still in the sky, but the sun seemed to be staying out a little longer than it had been when Michael had first walked into Ziggy's office.

CHAPTER 16

Michael returned to Manasquan a few weeks later and learned that Ziggy had a master's degree in psychology from San Diego State University. He had stayed in San Diego after he got his degree and became involved in the triathlete scene out there, first as a competitor and then as a coach. Ziggy was now well known within StrongForce circles and had been bringing his athletes to StrongForce competitions around the globe for many years. He always had several athletes in his stable who qualified for the StrongForce World Championships, held every October in San Diego. He'd just returned from that year's championship when he and Michael met for the first time.

Ziggy had moved back to Jersey when his mother had gotten sick and needed help. She'd passed away, but he'd been back for a few years at that point, so he decided to stay. He continued to coach his West Coast athletes remotely and built up an East Coast clientele that he coached using a hybrid in-person/virtual approach.

"I'm not sure you'll ever do a StrongForce," said Ziggy,

during their second meeting. "You've got some other basic stuff we need to deal with first."

"I understand," said Michael.

"So, I'm thinking we need to take care of the fear thing first."

"Agreed."

"I want you to do that by getting involved in open water swimming."

"What?" said Michael. "That seems crazy! I've heard the stories from Allie. She's seen some wild stuff out there—dead animals and very much alive sharks—in the ocean swims! Plus, the water can be filthy, full of infection."

"Wrong," said Ziggy. "The East River and the Hudson are cleaner than they've ever been. Ninety percent of the time, they're fine. The only time they get a little dicey is after a heavy rain when a little sewer water from the city might get washed into them. When that happens, the races get postponed or canceled. And you won't need to train in the rivers anyway. Most NYC-based open water and triathlon swimmers train out at Brighton Beach when they go outdoors."

"I don't know, Zig. This seems kind of radical to me."

"Radical is what you need, dude. And you've got an in with somebody who does these races all the time. She can give you the ins and outs and all that stuff. Anyway, give it some thought. We can start you slow, maybe the Verrazano to Sandy Hook race. That's not even 5 miles."

"Five miles in the open water on my first race!" screamed Michael. "That's ridiculous!"

"Look, dude, Allie's already done the 20 Bridges swim, and she's only been in the city for five or six months. That's 28.5 miles. You're worried about 5 friggin' miles! What gives?"

"I'm scared! That's what gives!"

"Yeah, I know. I know. Look, even the veterans like Allie get scared when they go in for a long swim. But not 'cause they think they're gonna drown! You get your own spotter boat and all that. It's safe. You can't drown out there, dude, I'm telling you. Look, we'll take it slow. You'll do some training with Allie, and eventually we'll do a dry run, all that stuff. I'm not gonna throw you overboard. You gotta trust me, okay?"

"Zig, I haven't competed in swimming in more than five years. I'm not ready to have my first race be a 5-mile ocean swim."

Ziggy was quiet for a minute. Then he spoke. "Okay, listen. Whether you know it or not, what you're dealing with here is PTSD. You know what that is, right?"

"Yeah, I know what it is. Post-Traumatic Stress Disorder."

"Right. And there are a few different ways you can deal with that, okay?"

"Okay," Michael said, still upset about what Ziggy was trying to make him do.

"We can send you to a program that deals with PTSD. Those things last about a month and cost a boatload of dough, so I'm guessing that's not an option, right?"

"Right. Not an option."

"The other option is to put you in a situation where you confront your fear head-on. A situation you're very uncomfortable with. That's the 5-mile ocean swim. I wouldn't put you in that race to win, dude. You'd do it simply to survive it. And I'd have Allie swim right beside you the whole way. That's the fastest way to get you on the right path. The goal after that would be a run, maybe a 10K, something not at all similar to the 1600 meters, but a running race, nevertheless. Then we'd do a bike race, and by then you'd have it all under control, and you'd be able to begin training for triathlons."

"I just don't see why it's necessary to slam me into a 5-mile ocean swim to get the process moving. Isn't there a more gradual way to do it?"

"Dude, I may seem mellow, but I'm not into gradual. I know from your medical report that you're ready to rock 'n roll right now. But hey, I'm no dictator. That's not the way it works with me. I hear what you're sayin', and yes, there *is* another way."

"What is it?"

"The Coney Island swim. One mile along the Coney Island Beach. Half mile out, half mile back. Lifeguards on kayaks, and EMTs all over the place. The course runs parallel to the beach so you can bail anytime."

"Now *that* I can handle," said Michael.

"Fine. It's a new race, so I don't know how many people will participate, but I'd expect a lot 'cause it's so tame it won't scare anybody off. There'll be lots of lame swimmers in the event, but I figure a few of the local hotshots might show up, too."

"Sounds good," said Michael.

"Cool. But one more thing."

"Yes?"

"I'll want you to win that race," said Ziggy.

Michael wasn't happy to hear this, but he was so relieved that Ziggy had backed off of the 5-mile ocean swim that he didn't fight it.

"When's the race?" he asked.

"June of next year. That gives us more than six months to

get you ready. We'll train inside until the end of April, then we'll start going outside with wetsuits, and from late May on, we'll ditch the wetsuits if at all possible. We'll want you to swim the Coney Island race with no wetsuit even though most of the swimmers will be wearing them."

"Okay," said Michael. "So, what about my training plan? I assume you have some ideas."

"Oh yeah. You'll be ready for Coney Island, dude. I promise you that."

CHAPTER 17

Summer 2018

The Coney Island race was held on June 27, 2018. Michael had trained indoors at the same pool Allie trained at until the end of April. He was completely back in swimming shape by the time they started going outdoors. The bulk of their training continued to be indoors, but once or twice a week they'd go outside. Allie and some of her open water pals trained outside in the Brighton Beach area near Coney Island.

Michael quickly found out that open water swimming was very different from pool swimming. He learned the proper breathing technique easily—hard exhale under water, exaggerated turn of the head to make sure your mouth was well above the water line, opening the mouth as narrowly as possible to avoid taking on excess spray from splashing or breakers.

Sighting was more difficult. To keep swimming in a straight line, you have to have an object to sight, which in races was usually the buoys that marked the course. In the Brighton Beach practices, it was an object in the distance, sometimes a buoy, other times a stationary boat, and still other times there was nothing available so you just tried to stay parallel with the shore. The hard part was that to see, you have to raise your head straight up every five or six strokes. This takes a lot of energy and slows you down.

Michael developed a pattern of breathing to the left after three strokes, then taking three more strokes, then raising his head to the front to see and breathe, then taking three more strokes and breathing to the right side, then taking three more strokes and raising his head to see and breathe, then repeating the pattern. It took some time for him to get comfortable in the open water, but soon he began to feel just fine, as long as he was swimming with Allie and her pals.

During the six months of training for the Coney Island swim, Michael had spent far more time with Allie than he had with Liza. Ziggy had gone over Michael's training plan with both of them. In a private conversation with Allie, Ziggy had explained to her that Michael's PTSD was directly traceable back to his heart attack during the 1600 meters, and that while the 1-mile race at Coney Island the following June might not seem like much to her, it was a huge leap for him. If Michael could get through the race and do well, Ziggy believed he would be on his way to taking firm control of the disorder. He explained that you never could fully eliminate PTSD, but training and competing were excellent ways to firmly tamp it down.

Ziggy had always known that Allie would be the key to helping Michael through this, and while he was acutely aware that she might end up getting hurt emotionally before it was all over, he had a strong feeling that things would work out the way they were supposed to, for her and for Michael. Allie had thrown herself into "Project Michael" with pure dedication, the way she did everything in her life, guiding him through the principles of open water swimming and encouraging him to overcome the obstacles that came up along the way.

On race day, Allie was wearing a red, white, and blue competition suit, because July 4th was only a week away and also because she wanted Michael to be able to easily spot her during the race.

Michael's feelings for Allie had grown from friendship to affection during the past six months, to the point where he was somewhat concerned about his emotional dependency on her with regard to training and competing. But he didn't feel guilty about his time spent away from Liza. She was training more and more, following her plan to increase her primary triathlon distance from Sprint to Olympic distance. It was all part of her plan to become a top StrongForce competitor.

Liza was also poised to launch her own fashion label during the coming year, and she had secured funding and a few initial clients. Her idea was simple. She would design one-of-a-kind dresses for the women of privilege with whom her family had been associated her entire life. As with all things fashion, even this limited approach came with intense competition, but Liza was talented, and she'd earned the respect of her current employer. They had already let her attach her name to a few of the dresses she'd designed for them. These accomplishments, and her relationships with the people she was selling to, helped her gain promises from a few open-minded friends of the family. She felt no shame in using her family connections. Liza consistently used every advantage she had to win—both in sports and in life.

Billy came up to visit at least once a month and worked out constantly with Liza when he was in town—swimming, biking, running, lifting, or cross-training. They'd become good friends. Michael had been surprised that Liza in no way seemed to hold Billy's vastly different upbringing against him, and this led Michael to respect her in a whole new way. But it was also clear to him that Billy was falling in love with Liza. While Michael sometimes experienced moments of jealousy, he realized intellectually that he was contributing to the deterioration of his relationship with Liza as much as she or Billy was, perhaps even more.

Michael knew Billy would never sever their unshakable bond of friendship by initiating an affair with Liza, even if she pressed him toward that end. But there were times when he wished it might happen so he could make a clean break and start a new life. He was fairly confident that Allie would be waiting for him if he made that choice, but he remained hesitant to do so. He tried to convince himself that he still loved Liza and fantasized that events would transpire that would bring them back together, especially if he could begin competing again and ultimately take over Billy's role as her training partner.

Billy continued his boycott of all forms of formal competition, waiting for Michael to begin competing again first. On June 27, Billy was at the Coney Island race. Liza was in Connecticut doing a triathlon on her own, so she wasn't there. Michael was a little surprised Billy had chosen to be at *his* race rather than Liza's, but he was glad to have him there. Ziggy was there as well, and when Michael and Allie were in the water warming up, he hammed it up with Billy like he was an old pal, breaking whatever ice needed to be broken, staying loose until about a half hour before race time. Then he took Michael and Allie aside.

"Okay, you two, here's what I know," said Ziggy, all of a sudden getting more professional than Michael was used to. "There are more than 500 people entered in the race. It's a rolling start, meaning they'll ask the athletes to self-seed based on your anticipated finish time. They've spaced the signs based on how many people they estimate will be in each group. You two will both be in group 1. Look for the sign that says 'Under 20 Minutes,' and that'll be you."

"How many people do you expect to be in that group?" asked Allie.

"Maybe 10, maybe less," said Ziggy. "You might be the only woman in the group."

"Who's the favorite to win the race?" asked Michael.

"You see the guy over there wearing the bright orange suit?" asked Ziggy.

Michael and Allie looked over at the guy. He was over 6 feet tall, built like an Olympic-caliber breaststroker, meaning he was stockier and more muscular than Michael. In fact, he looked a lot like Billy except for his fair hair and two blue eyes.

"Yeah. I see him," answered Michael.

"He's the guy I've picked to come in third."

"And I suppose I'm the guy you've picked to come in first?" asked Michael, somewhat perturbed.

"No, I think you'll be second," said Ziggy. "Allie's gonna win this race." Ziggy had a big smile on his face, but Michael was confused.

"Then I'll draft on her," he said. He really wasn't sure if he could beat Allie or not, nor was he sure if Ziggy was kidding or not. Allie trained for and competed in much longer races than 1 mile, so he probably *could* beat her at this distance, but he really wasn't sure. Ziggy quickly cleared things up.

"Draft on him, dude. Allie'll draft on you. This race is not her distance. She's doing this for you, man, and both she and I want you to win, okay?"

"Okay," said Michael, feeling the pressure that Ziggy obviously wanted him to feel. "So, who *is* the guy in the orange suit?" asked Michael.

"He's the world champion at 10 miles. Name is Danny van Devers. From the Netherlands. That orange suit he wears is the Dutch national color. They say he trains in the canals over there or some such thing. This race is just playtime for him. He's probably got a real race somewhere nearby next week. He's not that good at the short distances. You can take him. I mean it, Michael. You can take that dude at this distance."

Allie leaned up against Michael and whispered in his ear. He felt her warm, muscular body, and it felt good, giving him a feeling of calmness that he rarely experienced.

"He's telling you the truth," she whispered. "He knows for sure you can swim a mile faster than this guy. He wouldn't say it otherwise."

Allie pulled away from him, and he resisted the urge to pull her back. The sensation he'd experienced when she was touching him was almost hypnotic, and he wanted more of it. But now was not the time for that, and he had the fleeting thought that there might never be a time for that in his future with Allie. This produced a feeling of sadness that he quickly forced out of his mind with an abrupt shake of his head.

The announcer called the swimmers to their start positions. As Michael and Allie moved up to look for the "Under 20 Minutes" sign, Billy came up to them.

"Go get 'em, folks!" he said, enthusiastically. Then he looked Michael straight in the eye. "I believe in you, brother. This is your time."

Billy shook Michael's hand and moved away. Allie grabbed Michael's hand, and together they pushed their way to the front. They found their sign and moved up right behind Danny van Devers. Including them, there were only six people in the Under 20 Minutes area, and Allie was indeed the only woman. After about five minutes of nervous waiting, the announcer came back on over the sound system.

"One minute to start," came the blaring voice from the speakers.

Michael had butterflies in his stomach that he hadn't felt in a long time. He was sawing away at the scar on his chin like there was no tomorrow. Allie could tell he was extremely nervous. She took his hand and pulled it away from his chin, squeezing tightly.

"I'll stay with you as long as I can," she said quietly. "But if you have to go after that guy, go, okay?"

"Okay," he said, breathing deeply and rapidly. "Okay."

Allie pressed up against Michael and kissed him on the cheek. Once again, the contact between them helped him feel calmer. The contact didn't last long, however. Allie gave his hand one more squeeze, then pulled away and did a final check on her goggles.

"This is it," she said, jumping up and down lightly and shaking her arms. "Get ready to rock 'n roll!"

The horn went off, and the swimmers ran toward the beach. Most of the over-20 minute crowd had wetsuits on, but none of the six under-20 minute swimmers did. Michael assumed this meant they were all very serious swimmers using this race for training. Still on his feet, Michael hung with the lead pack and nestled in beside van Devers as they entered the water.

They all kept running until they arrived at the first breaking wave, then they all dove into the wave, pulling under it, surfacing on the other side, and swimming hard to get far enough out to avoid the next breaker.

The water felt cold at first. Ziggy had said the water temperature was around 70 degrees, but the adrenaline burning through Michael's bloodstream quickly wiped away that feeling. The first buoy was only 150 or so yards from the shore. The lead swimmers reached it quickly, then turned left and began to separate. Michael kept pulling but raised his head up out of the water to take a look at who was where. He saw the orange suit of van Devers just ahead to his right. Looking back to his left, he saw the red, white, and blue of Allie's suit just behind him. She was drafting off his wake, just as Ziggy had told her to.

Michael felt good, better than he'd felt in a long time. It was as if each stroke he took helped him shed the dead skin of another life, a life of fear and complacency. He settled in just to the left of van Devers and drafted off him nearly the entire half mile up to the turnaround. Because it was a given that van Devers was good at swimming in a straight line, Michael didn't need to waste energy raising his head every six strokes to get a sight line. He simply followed van Devers, which he found to be surprisingly easy to do during the first half of the race.

The weather gods had blessed Michael in his first open water race. The sun was shining, and the wind was still, so he didn't have to cope with unsettled waters. The swimmers were far enough out that they barely noticed the wide, gentle swells on their way to becoming breakers a hundred yards or so closer to the shore.

Apparently, Allie also found it easy to stay with van Devers because she held her position on Michael's left-side wake all the way to the turnaround. The three of them had opened up a large lead on the other swimmers. Unless something changed dramatically, one of the three was going to win the race.

However, when they rounded the turn for home, things *did* change dramatically. Danny van Devers shifted into another gear. In no time, he was 10 yards ahead of Michael. Allie saw it happening before Michael did and raised her head up.

"Go!" she screamed. "Go, damn it, go!" She put her head down and increased her pace, giving it all she had to pull back to van Devers. Michael did the same.

Now Michael started to feel the pain. Not the pain in his heart. His heart was fine. The pain was in his muscles as they filled with lactic acid. He remembered this pain, and thankfully, he remembered it fondly. You could never win a difficult race without this pain, so he figured he was on the right track. Unfortunately, when Michael looked up, he saw that he'd hardly narrowed the gap between himself and van Devers. Michael had pulled well ahead of Allie, but he was still nearly 10 yards behind van Devers. There was only about a third of a mile to go in the race.

Michael took one look ahead, sighting the line of buoys, and put his head in the water. He made the decision not to spend time and energy looking up until he felt he was going off-line. The risk was that if he drifted much farther toward the shore, he could possibly hit the rock jetties that ran out perpendicularly from the beach. Michael was assuming one of the lifeguards in a kayak would stop him before he did that, at least he hoped they would. He needed to gain on van Devers, and he decided to keep his head down and increase his stroke count to do it. He proceeded aggressively with his plan.

After around 3 minutes, Michael took a quick look and saw that he was gaining on van Devers, who was now only about 5 yards ahead. Michael was slightly off course, however, having drifted about 10 yards toward shore during the 3-minute span. He saw the end of a rock jetty only 25 yards to his right. He made a slight adjustment to his direction and gradually moved out from the shore. There were now only about 400 yards to go.

Michael increased his stroke count further and resumed his pattern of raising his head out of the water every six strokes. He could see van Dever's head come up every now and then, so he didn't feel at a disadvantage. What Michael needed right now was something to give him an advantage, and he needed it fast.

Michael thought back to the time when he was 10 years old when Billy had beaten him in the 100 IM. He remembered his parents telling him he should have tried harder, and it made him angry. The anger pumped adrenaline into his system. Michael traveled back to that time nearly 15 years ago, and he saw Billy up ahead of him.

Michael's long arms tore at the water, refusing to let Billy defeat him yet again. His stroke count approached that of a swimmer in a 50-meter sprint even though he would have to cover nearly five times that distance to get to the finish of this race. It didn't matter to Michael. He wasn't going to lose this race. He realized that this same reckless abandon was what had led to his heart attack back in high school, but he also knew that he was no longer suffering from myocarditis. That affliction was long gone, at least according to his doctor. He had to believe that if he was going to win this race.

Michael pulled up beside van Devers at the final turn to shore. With only 150 yards to go, the swells were getting bigger. Michael knew he'd have to literally body surf when he got into the breaking waves, and he'd been practicing this with Ziggy and Allie for the past month. He approached the wave that would become the breaker he'd ride, still right beside van Devers, swam hard to catch the wave, did so, and slid into a glide with his hands clasped in a knot in front of him. He rode the wave until he could feel the sand below him, pushed himself up, and began running in the shallow water. The finish line was a 100-yard run up the beach.

Van Devers was right there with him, but Michael believed he had him. Van Devers wasn't a runner, and Michael was, at least he had been in a prior life, and he knew at that moment that he would be so again. But van Devers stayed with him.

Sand flew up from both men's feet as they surged toward the finish line, still neck and neck. Michael edged ahead and blasted across the finish line as the crowd roared. He was the winner of the Coney Island swim, in a time of 18:53! He shook hands with van Devers, then turned to look for Allie. She was already out of the water and running up to the finish line. She passed through in third place overall, the winner of the women's bracket with a time of 19:21. She ran straight into his arms, and they embraced, both of them with tears in their eyes and smiling at the same time. At that moment, Michael understood with great clarity that his life was going to change, in more ways than one.

CHAPTER 18

Michael and Allie made their way out of the finish area and joined up with Ziggy and Billy, all sharing hugs and tears. The race, as well as the result, had given each of them their own unique reason for profound joy.

"Told you, dude," bragged Ziggy.

"I don't think I believed you," said Michael. "Until Allie told me you were telling the truth."

"I'll let that go this one time since it's our first race together, dude, but from now on, if I say something, you'll know I believe what I'm saying to be true, right?"

"You got it, boss," said Michael.

Billy handed both Michael and Allie a bottle of Gatorade and a banana. They thanked him and started the hydration and replenishment process. Billy stepped up to Michael and whispered to him.

"Hey, bud, can we get some time alone a little bit later, before I head back to Virginia?" he asked.

"Sure," said Michael. He suspected he knew what Billy wanted to discuss, but he also had some important thoughts he wanted to share. It would be a crucial conversation.

The race had started at 8 a.m., and it was a Sunday, so Michael invited Ziggy, Allie, and Billy to join him for breakfast in the city. Ziggy bailed, saying he wanted to beat the traffic back to the Jersey Shore. Allie said yes, so she, Michael, and Billy Ubered back to midtown and went to a coffee shop near Liza and Michael's apartment. They enjoyed a massive breakfast and lots of coffee, talking more about the race and enjoying each other's company.

"I didn't know you cussed," Michael said to Allie, smiling, remembering when she'd screamed at him to go after van Devers after the turn at the halfway point.

"Not my normal approach to motivation," she said. "But considering that you were about to lose any chance of winning, combined with the fact that I was trying to get the words out before coming to a complete stop or taking on water, I said it, and I'm glad I did."

"Well, it worked," said Michael, still smiling.

"You two are a great team," said Billy. "I walked with you all the way down the beach and was a little worried when that Dutch guy opened up a lead after the turn, but then you tracked him down and got him on the run up to the finish. Man, was that exciting!"

After they finished breakfast, Allie said she needed to get home and take care of some things. Michael walked Allie outside so that he could speak to her privately while Billy held their table. He looked directly into her eyes, tears welling up in his own.

"Thank you," he sputtered, barely able to get the words out. "Thank you." Tears rolled down his cheeks.

She embraced him, not saying a word, then broke free and

walked away. He could see that she was also crying, and he wondered if it was from the emotion of the race or something more than that. He wanted to go after her, but he held back, watching her disappear into the distance, then went inside to rejoin Billy.

Michael sat down, still not fully recovered from his emotional parting with Allie, but knowing more than ever that he needed something to change. He suspected he knew what Billy wanted to discuss, and it was important, but there were other things to discuss that were important to Michael as well. Michael looked over at Billy, who seemed anxious.

"I guess you know I've been waiting for you to do this for over five years now," said Billy.

"I know you have," said Michael. "But you didn't have to. For the millionth time, I don't blame you for what happened to me at Hampton Roads. It had nothing to do with you, bud. It was just a freak episode of bad luck for me. That's all."

"I know I had your blessing to compete again before this. But I needed it to be this way. We don't have to talk about it anymore. Please just accept that I needed to know you were all the way back to being the Michael I knew before Hampton Roads. And, man, you didn't let me down! You're more than you were then. And that is just the icing on the cake."

"Thank you, bud. I wish you hadn't waited, but I understand why you did. Now that we got this done, can I have your word that you'll start competing again?"

"You got it. As long as I have your word that you'll keep competing, too."

"What? Are you saying that if I decide to stop competing, then you'll stop again?" asked Michael. "That's ridiculous!"

"No, no, no, that's not what I mean. I mean you're too dang talented to sit on the sidelines anymore. You've got a great, cool coach, and you've got an awesome training partner. Man, is she great."

"Tell me you're not going to fall in love with her, too!" Michael blurted out, unintentionally opening up the next topic of conversation.

Billy's face reddened. He was speechless for a moment. Finally, he spoke. "Is it that obvious?"

"I've known you almost 20 years, bud. It's obvious to me, and it's probably obvious to her, too, although we haven't spoken about it."

"I'll never allow anything to happen with Liza. You know that, right?"

"I *do* know that," said Michael. "It's not an issue. But it might be an opportunity, for both of us."

"What do you mean?" asked Billy. Just then his phone beeped with an incoming text.

"Anything interesting?" asked Michael.

"It's from Liza," said Billy. "She won the Ditka Olympic distance race. Set a race record." Billy texted back to Liza, congratulating her and letting her know that Michael had won his race.

Michael pulled his phone from his pocket and looked at the text message icon. No incoming texts. He held the phone up and showed it to Billy. "That, my friend, is the evidence we need. She texted you, but she didn't text me."

Billy had a look of astonishment on his face. "Are you saying you don't want to be with Liza?"

"I guess that *is* what I'm saying. Look, I love her. I'll always love her. But not in the way I love Allie. And not in the way you love her. You guys are much more in sync than she and I. You're apples and apples, and she and I are apples and oranges. But Allie and I are oranges and oranges." Michael wondered if he was making any sense at all to Billy, trying to fight off a growing feeling of excitement.

"But I'm not from the same kind of wealthy family that she's from," said Billy.

"Look, dude, I'm not saying she'll marry you, but she *might*. I don't know for sure how she feels about your family, but it seems to me it doesn't matter to her at all, and it shouldn't. And I know she sent that text to you and not me, and that's a good indicator of where things stand."

"So, how are we going to do this?" asked Billy.

"I've made my decision. I'm moving out. I'll speak with her as soon as she gets back. I think it'll be okay, maybe even a relief for her. Let's head up to the apartment so I can get started packing. And I'm going to need to look for a place."

Michael called the waitress over and paid the bill, got up, and made his way quickly to the exit. He was excited. Billy followed him.

"Are you going to leave tonight?" asked Billy.

"I think so," said Michael. He pulled his phone from his pocket and sent a text to Allie.

"Where will you go?" asked Billy.

"I'll let you know in a minute," said Michael. It didn't take a minute. His phone beeped. He checked the text. "I think I'm going to stay with Allie tonight, but let's see how things go with Liza first."

"I've got a train at seven tonight," said Billy. "I have to be on it."

"That's probably for the better. Liza will be home in a couple of hours. You'll need to give us some privacy, and then we'll see if she wants to speak with you after she and I talk."

When Liza returned, Billy wasn't there. He'd gone back to the coffee shop, thinking he'd probably be awake all night from all the caffeine *and* from the excitement revolving around a possible future with Liza.

At the apartment, Michael hugged Liza and congratulated her on her win at Ditka. She congratulated him on his win at Coney Island.

"There's something else I need to talk to you about," said Michael.

"Oh?" said Liza. "What's that?"

"It's about Allie," he said.

"Well, that's interesting because I need to speak with you about Billy."

"Sure," he said. "But can I go first?"

"Of course," she said, reaching out and taking his hand in hers.

Michael appreciated Liza taking his hand, just as she'd done back when they met for the first time and he revealed his dark secret about his heart attack. But the physical contact awoke him to the fact that this was a very serious, delicate moment. Still, it needed to happen, and he proceeded, telling the truth about his feelings.

"For the longest time, I thought my feelings for Allie were just appreciation for her helping me find a coach and with the training for the Coney Island Swim. But after the race today, it was clear to me that what I feel is more than profound gratitude."

"So, you're in love with her?" asked Liza.

"I think so," said Michael. "And what about your feelings for Billy?"

"Kind of the same as yours for Allie, I think," said Liza.

Michael was relieved, and he sensed in the energy from Liza that she was, too.

"Maybe it's time for us to make a change?" he asked.

"I think so."

"So, you're okay with this?"

"Yes, I'm fine."

"And what about Billy?" asked Michael.

"Is he still in New York?" she asked, trying not to sound too eager.

"He is. He's down in the coffee shop, but he has a seven o'clock train tonight."

"Well, we should speak to him then," she said.

"And you're sure you want to be with him?"

"Yes, I want to be with him," she said firmly. "But, Michael, you know I'll always love you, don't you?"

"And I'll always love you, Liza. Meeting you gave me hope for the first time after my accident. I'll always cherish what we had together."

The two sat down for a moment, still holding hands. The emotion was high, but the relief was even higher, for both of them. They realized that this big change had been coming for many months, and they appreciated that it was happening without the drama that usually accompanies such breakups.

They'd shared a lot during their three years together. Michael remembered the first time he saw Liza, when she was onstage winning the chess match. He remembered think-ing she was the most amazing woman he'd ever seen. She'd helped him begin the process of getting back the things he'd lost, and he would never forget that. But even though it hurt, it was definitely time to move on. Liza broke the silence.

"I'll have to set some ground rules with Billy. He's not going to just walk in here and start sleeping with me. He can take one of the extra bedrooms. And he's going to have to agree to some private etiquette lessons. He'll need to be able to carry himself in the circles that you and I find so natural."

"I think he'll be okay with all of that," said Michael. "He's always been open-minded about learning things he's not fa-miliar with."

"Well then, what is your plan for tonight?" she asked.

"I was thinking I'd grab some things and head out. If it's okay with you, I can come back for the big stuff later."

"Sure, that's fine. Why don't I text Billy and ask him to come up? We can bring him up to date on things, and he and I can talk later, privately."

"Yeah, that's good," said Michael.

Liza texted Billy. He came back up to the apartment. Liza made sure that a potentially awkward situation went smooth-ly. She explained to Billy that she and Michael were breaking up, but that they still cared for each other, and they wanted things to be okay between all four of the involved parties. She told Billy she'd like to speak with him on the phone about her ideas for the future and that he should run and catch his train. They all hugged, Billy departed, and Michael and Liza went to finish up his packing. They managed to get most of his clothes into two large suitcases. They embraced and kissed one last time.

Michael caught an Uber to Allie's apartment down in the financial district. It was a tiny studio. Michael hoped they could pool their funds and get a one-bedroom apartment, down the line, if that was something Allie would consider.

When Michael arrived, Allie opened the door and rushed into his arms. She kissed him fully on the lips for the first time, with passion that had been building up for a long time. Michael kissed back, and he knew in his heart that *this* was where he wanted to be.

CHAPTER 19

Summer 2019

The horn went off, and Michael and Allie rushed into the water, bumping and pushing against the mob of swimmers at the 2019 Battle of Titans triathlon at the Jersey Shore. They were entered in the Olympic distance—a 1.5K swim, 40K bike, and 10K run (.93-mile swim, 24.9-mile bike, 6.2-mile run). This was their last race at this distance before moving up to the StrongForce 100 distance—a 2.4K swim, 76.5K bike, and 21.1K run (1.5-mile swim, 47.5-mile bike, 13.1-mile run), and when the race was over, with both of them winning, it was clear that they were more than ready to begin competing at the StrongForce 100 distance.

Michael and Allie had spent most of the past year getting up to speed in the bike and run. Allie had been a championship runner in high school, but she needed some work to get her swimmer's legs readjusted to it. Both of them needed a lot of work on the bike.

Ziggy had asked one of his pure cyclist athletes, a guy named Russ Baxter, to ride with them a few times to decrease their times. Ziggy told them not to spend a lot of money on their first triathlon bike and recommended a Cannondale with an aluminum frame that cost only $1,500, which they both acquired.

Ziggy was an expert on bike fitting, and he fit them both onto their bikes really well, maximizing the power they could generate on the bike while making sure they were comfortable. He said that as they progressed, they'd need to convert over to more expensive carbon fiber or titanium bikes, but those could cost up to $15,000. No need to go there until they were much further along in their training and competing at a higher level.

A year had passed since Michael and Liza's mutually agreed-to breakup. He and Allie were still living together. Just as he had hoped, they'd pooled their funds and moved into a really nice one-bedroom apartment in the up-and-coming Hudson Yards area of Manhattan. The apartment cost about $4,000 a month in rent, but between the two of them, they could afford it. The building had a doorman, a gym, and an underground garage. They'd bought a used Audi because they were traveling out of the city so much for training and competitions. Both Allie and Michael had been promoted at work and were doing quite well for two people who were only 24 years old.

Michael and Ziggy had to push Allie to give up her exclusive focus on open water swimming. Part of the deal was that Michael would continue training with Allie in the open water, and they would do at least two open water races each year. Michael had refused to do more than 5 miles in any open water race, and Ziggy concurred. Even in StrongForce full-distance competitions, the swim was only 3 miles, so training for a longer swim distance than 5 miles would be unproductive.

Michael and Allie had both done well at the Sprint and Olympic distances, each of them winning several races and always placing in the top three in their respective brackets, but both of them were anxious to begin racing in Strong-Force competitions because these longer races seemed more appropriate for both of their skill sets.

While it went unsaid, Michael and Allie were frustrated at their progress compared to that of Billy and Liza. Those two had already been competing in StrongForce 200 races—a 4.8K swim, 153K bike, and 42.2K run (3-mile swim, 95-mile bike, 26.2-mile run)—and both had won their age group in most of these races. They were still amateurs, but there was talk of them going pro in the near future, depending on how they fared as age group athletes at their first StrongForce World Championship race this coming October in San Diego, for which they'd already qualified.

Michael, Allie, Billy, and Liza got together socially every now and then. They had all remained friends, but a tension had been building between the two couples, not at all related to the former relationship between Michael and Liza. Michael and Allie were simply tired of hearing about all the success Billy and Liza were having in their competitions. Billy was his same humble self, but Liza frequently went on and on about it.

Liza's personalized fashion concept, which she'd named "une seulement," French for "only one," had done well. She was now limiting the number of clients she'd take on, which gave her the time she needed for training, and it boosted the price of her services to an astronomical level. Billy had left his job at Home Depot and moved to New York City a few months after Michael and Liza's breakup. As promised, Liza had made him sleep in one of the other bedrooms for several months before they became intimate.

Billy had gladly accepted her offer to receive etiquette lessons from a well-known private instructor—table manners, cocktail party etiquette, formal dancing lessons, and basic socializing. His logic for submitting to this potentially humiliating requirement was simple: If he was going to win Liza over and live in her world, he had to know how to behave in that world. After six months of working at it, one would have thought he'd lived in the upper strata of society his entire life. And it took only an hour or two of his time a few days a week. The rest of it he devoted to full-time training, which Liza had facilitated by setting up a joint bank account for the two of them that provided Billy with ample funds for his day-to-day expenses. To Billy's credit, he kept detailed records of his spending and treated all of his withdrawals from the account as a loan. His intent was to pay the loan back as soon as he started earning money as a pro triathlete, which was about to become a reality.

Even though there was really no comparison between Michael and Allie's early triathlon accomplishments compared to Billy and Liza's, the tension was still there. It was different for Michael than it was for Allie. Michael had no desire to ever compete against Billy again. In fact, he was traumatized by the mere thought of it. Allie, on the other hand, was offended to her core by Liza's arrogance. She hadn't liked the way Liza had dominated Michael's life, just as she was now dominating Billy's life. Allie dreamed of competing against Liza and defeating her, while any such dream by Michael of a competition against Billy was a nightmare he very much wanted to avoid. Somewhere deep inside, however, it bothered him at how natural it was for both Billy and Liza to simply win, regardless of the level of competition. And while this emotion was buried deeply in his subconscious, as time went by, it climbed closer and closer to the surface of his mind.

CHAPTER 20

"Okay, class. Let's talk StrongForce."

The "class" Ziggy was referring to was composed of two people—Michael and Allie—who were now preparing for StrongForce 100 Ocean City, their first try at a StrongForce race. The Ocean City race was being held in September this year, so they had a few months to train after their last Olympic-distance event.

"The first thing you need to know, dudes, is that StrongForce is not a race. It's a religion. Yeah, there are always people like your pals Billy and Liza who race in StrongForce just to win. But most people, and I mean even most of the pros, do it because it means more to them than just trying to win a race. Much more."

"You mean that people are just trying to be the best they can be, something like that?" asked Allie.

"Sure," said Ziggy. "For many people it's like that. But it's been proven that endurance races like StrongForce can help people heal, both physically and mentally. Plenty of people with a lot worse PTSD than Mikey has have found that training for and competing in StrongForce events keeps that stuff under control. Some of them literally can't stop doing StrongForce because when they do, the PTSD comes back."

"So, you're saying it's an addiction for some?" asked Michael.

"I suppose you could say that," said Ziggy. "But that's an unnecessary negative spin on it, dude. Why not just say it's a 'way of life' for some people. How 'bout that?"

"I like that better," said Michael.

"Cool. Now let's lay out our plan. First thing is that so far you two have been inseparable in your training and in your competing. You're literally side by side every friggin' second, until Michael makes his move in the run. Now look, that's been just what the doctor ordered, until now. At this point in your training, we're going to have to separate you two every now and then, okay?"

"I don't like it," snapped Michael. "The main reason I do this at all is to be with Allie. I don't want to be separated from her."

"Now, dude, listen to me. You guys work all day in the same office, you live all night in the same apartment, you work out in the gym and on the road together, you share a car that you drive together to training and to competitions. I mean, this might be getting a little unhealthy! And it certainly isn't maximizing either of your performances going forward."

"Who cares?" said Michael.

"I care," said Allie.

Silence filled the room. Michael was a little shaken by what Allie had said. What was she talking about? He thought she loved their lifestyle as much as he did. Was she becoming just like Liza and Billy now?

"What do you mean by that, Al?" asked Ziggy, ever the shrink. "What are your feelings about my idea?"

"Well, first of all," said Allie, "I want to hear more of what your specific plans for both of us are. And while I love the life Michael and I have built with all my heart, if we can both improve without compromising the essence of what we have together, I could do that."

"Mikey, what do you think of that?" asked Ziggy. No one Michael knew ever called him Mikey except Ziggy, and he kind of liked it.

"Well, the way Allie put it, I can go along with that. I'm at least willing to hear what you have in mind, but if it crosses a certain line, I'm out."

"Now just wait a minute!" said Ziggy, raising his voice as much as Michael had ever heard. "Let's not get dramatic here, dude. I said we'd separate you 'every now and then' and you know the Zigmeister don't lie. But if you're going to let Two Cool work his magic, you gotta let me develop two plans for two people. One plan for you and one plan for Allie. I've been putting up with this one-plan stuff long enough. We gotta elevate now, you dig?"

"Dig," said Allie, before Michael could respond. "What do you say we hear him out, honey?"

"Fine," said Michael, sitting back and crossing his arms. He was afraid he might be losing what had been the most wonderful year of his life. He began running his index finger along the scar on his chin. Allie reached up and grabbed his hand, pulling it gently away from his face.

"This is no time for that, Michael. It's going to be fine. *We're* going to be fine." She looked him straight in the eye with her piercing green eyes, squeezing his hand tightly. His heart rate slowed, and he felt calm.

"Dig," was all he said.

Ziggy's plan was simple, hardly compromising their time together at all, so they both readily agreed to it. Each Saturday or Sunday, Michael and Allie would have separate workouts. Ziggy would choose people from his stable of athletes to compete against each of them. One workout, for example, he'd schedule a top-flight female cyclist to go head-to-head against Allie in a 60-mile ride. That same day, Michael would compete against a top swimmer in a 2-mile swim.

They trained that way for six weeks, culminating in a five-woman/five-man practice triathlon in a rural area without a lot of traffic. The participants were all athletes being trained by Ziggy. In official races, the triathlon organizers would work with local officials to limit traffic during the race, but this was completely unofficial, so the athletes had to be especially careful. Ziggy's number one rule for the practice races was to stay alert and not take any chances just to gain an advantage. Yes, he wanted people to give it their all, but in the end, this was just training, not a real competition. He'd hired three lifeguards on kayaks to patrol the swim course, and he set up hydration and feeding stations at T1 and T2, the transition areas.

The distances in the practice race for the swim, bike, and run were as close as Ziggy could make them to the actual StrongForce 100 race, also known as a "half" StrongForce. The StrongForce 100 distance was a 2.4K swim, 76.5K bike, and 21.1K run (1.5-mile swim, 47.5-mile bike, 13.1-mile run), with the three legs totaling exactly 100 kilometers

(62.15 miles). In a StrongForce 200, the distance of each leg was doubled, yielding a total distance of 200 kilometers (124.3 miles) for a "full" StrongForce race.

By the end of the StrongForce 100 training race, it was obvious that Michael and Allie were Ziggy's two best athletes, by far. Even though he started the women 10 minutes behind the men, Allie ended up catching all the men except Michael, coming in second overall. Michael finished in 3:55, and Allie finished in 4:14. Ziggy was stunned. These would be top three finishes at many StrongForce 100 events and would have won the Ocean City event some years. Both Michael and Allie knew this.

After the athletes left for home, Ziggy went back out on the course and measured to make sure he hadn't made a mistake when he set it up. The course was 101K long (62.8 miles), with the extra distance being mostly in the bike leg, although the swim and run were both slightly longer than the official distances as well. Ziggy shook his head, wondering how he'd stumbled onto two athletes like Michael and Allie.

With four weeks to go until StrongForce 100 Ocean City, they would soon begin their taper. Theoretically, this would mean their times would drop even further in the actual race. That would prove to be true for one of them, but for the other, a roadblock would resurface that changed everything.

CHAPTER 21

Michael stunned both Ziggy and Allie when they met to plan their three-week taper prior to the 2019 StrongForce 100 Ocean City. They were meeting virtually on a Monday evening. Ziggy was back at his training shack in Manasquan, standing as always, while Michael and Allie were gathered in front of a laptop in their Manhattan apartment. Ziggy began laying out their daily regimen, slowly reducing the amount of work they'd be doing each day. Suddenly, Michael interrupted.

"Two Cool, I need to say something," said Michael.

"What, dude?" asked Ziggy.

"I'm not going to race at Ocean City."

Silence ensued. Ziggy's face was blank. Allie's mouth opened in confusion, turning down into a frown. She was the first to speak.

"You're not going back there, are you?"

Michael knew exactly what Allie meant by "back there," and Ziggy probably did, too.

"Yes, I'm going back there," said Michael. "Billy's my best friend, and he'll always be my best friend. My time in the practice race was good news and bad news for me. The good news was it meant I was good enough to compete at the highest level. The bad news was it meant I was good enough to compete at the highest level."

"So, you're doing this for him?" asked Allie, anger in her voice.

"I'm doing it for me," said Michael.

"How so?" asked Ziggy.

"I don't want to compete against Billy," he said. "I know he's not in this race, but I also know where this is all headed if I stay on this course."

"And how do you think he feels about competing against you?" asked Ziggy.

"I know that he won't," said Michael.

"You do not know that!" screamed Allie.

"It doesn't matter," said Michael. "I know that *I* won't."

"Dang," said Ziggy. "Bummer."

"I want Allie to continue on with her StrongForce training," said Michael. "I'll continue to train with her, but I won't race."

"That's ridiculous!" screamed Allie. "It's a fucking waste of extraordinary talent!"

Allie was as angry as Michael had ever seen her, but his mind was made up.

"Look," he said. "Do me this favor. Go for it in Ocean City. Then we'll all regroup."

"Hell, yes, I'll go for it," said Allie. "I've worked too hard for this, and so have you."

She was settling down, but tears were still streaming down her face. Ziggy stepped in.

"Okay, dudes, let's table the meeting for now. Get a good night's sleep and let's talk again tomorrow."

"Okay," said Michael. "Sorry, you guys, I just can't do it."

"No need to be sorry, dude. We'll figure something out."

The next night, Ziggy had it all figured out. He could tell that Michael wasn't going to change his mind, so he'd come up with an alternative plan. Ziggy had heard about the up-and-coming Iconic Triathlon Series, only in seven cities in Europe at the time. He knew it was a possibility for Michael, *and* for Allie. In Ziggy's mind, the Iconic would never have the purity and originality of StrongForce, but it was a way of continuing to compete at a high level if StrongForce wasn't an option, which seemed to be the case for Michael.

Ziggy did a small presentation on the Iconic for them, and they were both intrigued. Allie loved the fact that it had really long swims, and Michael appreciated that Billy wasn't involved. It was agreed that Allie would compete at the 2019 Ocean City StrongForce 100, after which they'd take a hard look at the Iconic.

Allie was the first woman to cross the finish line in the Ocean City race, qualifying for the StrongForce 100 World Championship, but that event was coming up soon. It was too soon, in Ziggy's opinion, for Allie to be fully recovered and adequately trained, so she opted out of it. Michael's future path in the Iconic series was charted, but it would take many discussions between the three of them, and between Allie and Michael alone, before Allie's future in triathlon was determined.

One of the initial hurdles in getting Allie to convert to the Iconic series was her intense desire to compete against Liza in StrongForce, something that had been building and festering for some time. Billy and Liza were advancing quickly; both would win their age groups in San Diego that October.

But even before that, it was obvious they would be forces to be reckoned with in StrongForce competitions during the coming years. They were already faster than most of the pros.

Now that Allie had won in Ocean City, beating several pros herself, her future in the sport looked bright as well. Ziggy helped Allie to sort out her personal distaste for Liza from her desire to compete against her, and there was some discussion of the jealousy she had felt when Michael was with Liza. In the end, Allie was able to make the change, primarily because she wanted the joy of training and competing together that she and Michael shared to continue just as much as he did. Her desire to compete against Liza never wavered, but that would have to be put on hold for the foreseeable future. The Iconic Triathlon awaited them.

PART THREE

CHAPTER 22

September 2025

On the morning of his 30th birthday, Michael woke at 4 a.m. He and Allie were scheduled to race in a few hours in the 2025 Iconic Triathlon World Championship in the city of Nijmegen (pronounced *Nigh-meg-en*) in the Netherlands. Six years had passed since Michael and Allie had made the decision to begin competing on the fledgling Iconic Triathlon circuit. At that time, the Iconic Triathlon had been in existence for only a few years, but it was now expanding rapidly.

The Iconic Triathlon was founded by a group of European triathletes with a slightly different perspective than the founders of StrongForce had back in 1995 in Australia. From the beginning, StrongForce offered two distances—100K and 200K—each designed to offer a serious challenge in each of the three disciplines. And that was the essence of it—three tough legs—based on the knowledge and experience of the StrongForce founders. And it caught on. Within three years, an American company purchased the worldwide rights to StrongForce competitions and began a rapid expansion. More StrongForce events were now held in the United States than in any other country and San Diego had become the home to both the StrongForce 100 and StrongForce 200 World Championships. By the time Michael and Allie had become involved in triathlon, StrongForce was the largest endurance triathlon in the world, by far, drawing more than 400,000 participants annually, with millions of fans, and it was still growing. As Ziggy had said, StrongForce had become more than a race. For many, completing a StrongForce was the most defining moment of their lives.

The Iconic founders knew from the outset that their event would never rival StrongForce for a variety of reasons, not the least of which was the founding principle of the Iconic: The athletes were to spend approximately the same amount of time in each of the three legs of the race. To that end, they increased the distance of the swim to 10 kilometers (6.2 miles) and reduced the distance of the bike to 100 kilometers (62.1 miles), but they kept the run at the marathon distance of 42.2 kilometers (26.2 miles). Top swimmers would complete the swim in around 2 hours. Top cyclists would complete the bike in around 2.5 hours. The top runners were expected to run the marathon in as little as 2 hours and 40 minutes (2:40). This expectation was fueled by the fact that the bike leg was 35 percent shorter than the StrongForce bike, meaning fresher legs going into the run.

The goal was for the fastest racers to complete an Iconic distance race in just over 7 hours. This was only a half hour less than the total time it took for the top competitors to complete a StrongForce 200 event, even though the full StrongForce distance was 48K (30 miles) longer than the total Iconic distance. This was due to the fact that the Iconic swim was more than double the distance of the StrongForce swim.

The biggest impediment to participation in an Iconic event was, of course, the swim. Ten kilometers was a very long swim for most triathletes, and most already considered the swim a "necessary inconvenience," with a main goal of surviving the swim to get into the bike and run. It was well known that you couldn't win a StrongForce with a great swim alone, but you could lose it if you took on too much water or failed to train properly for the swim leg. To help make the Iconic swim less intimidating, the founders eliminated one unpredictable aspect of many StrongForce events—rough seas. Whereas numerous StrongForce events, including San Diego, were held in saltwater bays or the ocean—which added uncertainty to an already daunting challenge—Iconic events were held in calm water venues in every race location. This was easily accomplished in countries where canals were an integral part of the local infrastructure, such as the Netherlands. But calm water can be found in many other countries, too. Medium-sized lakes surrounded by wind-blocking hills were a great choice, and this allowed for more challenging bike and run courses. The Netherlands was very flat, so the bike and run legs were not as challenging there as in many of the other venues that had been established in other countries during the young life of the Iconic Triathlon series.

Both StrongForce and Iconic permitted drafting on the bike, allowing riders to get in behind other riders to reduce wind resistance and save energy. The reason for this was that it was difficult to monitor such large numbers of racers to fairly impose penalties for drafting. The downside was that triathlon teams could take advantage of these rules and help each other during the bike leg. This was more of a problem in StrongForce events than in Iconic events, because the long Iconic swim caused a natural separation of athletes who might want to work together in the bike, but even in Strong-Force, most riders *wanted* to work together in the bike, regardless of team affiliation. StrongForce participants were a brotherhood and sisterhood, and most preferred to help each other to make it through the daunting challenge rather than take advantage by drafting only with team members.

As of 2025, there were 18 Iconic venues—12 in Europe, 2 in Asia, 2 in Australia, and 2 in North America (in Vancouver and Montreal, Canada). The pool of competitors was approaching 20,000 annually worldwide, the vast majority of whom were highly trained, competitive athletes.

A significant number of the Iconic participants were StrongForce athletes who excelled in the swim and were intrigued by a triathlon where a great swim could actually win the race for you. Another large block came from the open water swim community, distance swimmers who had not yet tried triathlons because they didn't feel the swim in traditional triathlons was emphasized enough. The result was that the Iconic was helping to expand the universe of people participating in triathlons worldwide.

Even though there were far fewer entrants in any Iconic event than StrongForce events, there was a high level of competition in each race. Competitiveness was further enhanced by a strict rule that all competitors must complete the Iconic race in less than 12 hours. In a full StrongForce event, participants had up to 16 hours to finish.

Iconic races could handle up to 1,000 total entrants, although not all Iconic events sold out. StrongForce competitions, on the other hand, sometimes sold out in less than 24 hours and handled more than double the number of entrants of an Iconic event.

The Iconic World Championship was limited to 500 participants. There were 10 Iconic divisions—five for men and five for women—and the 50 top-ranked athletes in each division qualified for the championship event, earning points toward their rankings in races throughout the year. If athletes who ranked in the top 50 of their division opted out of the championship, the Iconic organizers worked their way down the rankings until each division was full.

For the 2025 championships, there were 100 pros—50 men and 50 women—and 400 age group competitors from the eight other divisions. Michael and Allie were pros, not because they were trying to make a living doing triathlons—although both had been earning good money from sponsorships and prize money over the past several years—but because they were two of the top swimmers in the Iconic series and wanted to go out in the first two waves of swimmers. The pro men went first, followed five minutes later by the pro women.

Michael and Allie had done very well in the Iconic format, both having excellent open water swim experience and abilities. Additionally, both had never trained for or competed at the 153K (95-mile) full StrongForce distance in the bike, so the shorter bike leg wasn't so intimidating to them. And both were great runners. The Iconic distance was made for them, and they loved it, steadily moving up in the world rankings.

Originally, Michael and Allie didn't like having to travel

to Europe to compete, but they were eventually able to turn those trips into mini vacations, so it actually became something they looked forward to three or four times a year. As the number of race venues expanded, with two in North America currently, albeit in Canada, their hope was that Iconic events would eventually be established in the USA.

The big challenge for most endurance triathletes around the world is time management. Only a limited number of people in the world can train full-time without needing to supplement their income. Only around 200 professional triathletes train full-time. The rest fit their training schedules around their work schedules.

Just a handful of Iconic triathletes trained full-time, and Michael and Allie were not part of that group. They put in 45 to 50 hours a week at their jobs, and then another 20 to 30 hours a week in training, not including travel time. Thirty hours a week of training for people with a full-time job was an extremely challenging goal, and was often unachievable due to the vagaries of travel for work, unexpected illnesses, and family matters. But it was a rare week when either Michael or Allie put in less than 20 hours a week in training, and they averaged around 25 hours per week. If they'd been pros racing at the StrongForce 200 distance, they would have had to dedicate 30 to 35 hours a week to training to compete for a championship, which would be impossible for them unless they left their jobs. But because the bike leg for the Iconic did not require as much training time as it did for the full StrongForce, the amount of time they trained each week was more than enough to prepare them for optimal performance in the Iconic races.

Allie and Michael enjoyed one advantage versus most other triathletes: They were *both* elite athletes and could do most of their training together. Unlike couples where only one person was an endurance triathlete, the challenge of spending time with your partner and family was not an issue for Allie and Michael. They were literally always together, except when Ziggy made arrangements for each of them to go head-to-head with another athlete on a weekend run, bike, or swim session.

Ziggy had helped them put together a comprehensive training plan that involved several key elements—big training volume; balance between the swim, bike, and run; balance between hard and easy sessions; recovery; and nutrition. Their seven-day-a-week plan evolved throughout the season.

Because Michael and Allie were based in New York City, they were lucky to have a USA Triathlon Certified Training Center nearby—Chelsea Piers. With an indoor pool, CompuTrainers (sophisticated bike trainers that allowed the riders to use their own bike while racing on a pre-programmed course of their choice), an indoor track, and state-of-the-art strength training facilities, Chelsea Piers was the place to go for many triathletes in the city. Michael and Allie did the vast majority of their training there throughout the year, although they went outside of the city on weekends for roadwork on the bike and to run, weather permitting.

Some core elements remained somewhat consistent for them. Tuesday was their recovery day when they did no workouts. Instead, they'd put in 12-hour days at the office on Tuesdays to help make up for the fact that they were working only 8 to 9 hours per day the other four days of the week. The six days a week when they trained included four swims, three bikes, and four runs. On Monday, Wednesday, Thursday, and Friday, they swam before work at Chelsea Piers. The Monday and Friday swims were only one hour and were preceded by a one-hour strength session in the gym. The Wednesday and Thursday swims were two hours long and very intense sessions, often involving interval training. When the weather got warmer, they swam outside at least one day a week, even if it meant adding a swim into their weekend work, which was primarily dedicated to the bike and run.

Monday and Thursday evenings were bike training sessions, while Wednesday and Friday evenings were dedicated to run training. The Monday bike was a hard two-hour private endurance session on the CompuTrainers that for Allie and Michael always included a lot of hills. They enjoyed the CompuTrainer feature that allowed them to race virtually against each another on the chosen course. The Thursday bike session was a one-hour private session on the Compu-Trainers that was mostly steady base training, but sometimes involved time trials and interval work.

The Wednesday run session on the indoor track at Chelsea Piers was one hour in total, with 45 minutes of base training at-less-than race pace, transitioning into 15 minutes of fartlek training—30- to 60-second spurts at 5K pace followed by equal periods of less-than-race pace for recovery. The Friday runs were hard—up to two hours of race pace running, depending on how far away their next competition was.

On Saturdays, they combined the bike and run into a brick workout—a long bike going right into the bike-to-run transition, then into a relatively short run. The Saturday bike was never shorter than 100 kilometers (62.1 miles) and was sometimes longer, but the Saturday run was rarely more than 5 kilometers (3.1 miles), although as they got closer to the competition, the distance of the brick run was gradually increased. The Saturday workout was primarily meant to be a challenging bike day, a time to practice the T2 transition and to get used to shaking the "bricks" out of the legs during the first few kilometers of the run.

The Sunday session was dedicated to long, intense run training, which included intervals, hills, and time trials. They would run one full marathon during a Sunday session between each competition, but only at around 80 percent of race pace. The marathon was simply too grueling of a race to run at full speed more than four or five times a year, according to Ziggy.

Weekend training was done about an hour's drive from the city, in the foothills of western New Jersey, weather permitting, but there was no problem duplicating hill work on the CompuTrainers and treadmills at Chelsea Piers when they couldn't go outside. Sunday evenings, they received a two-hour massage to work out any kinks they might have developed during the week. Overall, Michael and Allie did 11 workouts each week, with only one hard session on each of their six workout days—two hard swims, two hard bike sessions, and two hard runs per week. The other workout sessions were less intense, base level, and strength training. They did two-a-days on every training day except Sunday, which was a hard run day followed by the Sunday evening massage.

Nutrition was also important. Michael and Allie always ate a big breakfast after their morning workouts before they went to work, and they snacked regularly throughout the day. There was an emphasis on real food, including eggs, hummus, lots of fruits and vegetables, and also lean meat, especially fish. They drank chocolate milk. They ate a light dinner at least an hour before their evening workouts, and they always replenished after the evening sessions as well. Overall, they consumed a massive number of calories, but the food was healthy and helped them rebuild the muscles they were depleting in workouts to make them stronger than they were before.

Equally important to nutrition was rest—getting at least seven and a half hours of sleep per night on weekdays and nine hours on weekends. This meant they were normally in bed by 10 p.m., up by 5:30 a.m. on weekdays, and up by 7 a.m. on weekends. Neither one of them were big drinkers, although they both enjoyed red wine, but they stopped drinking altogether eight weeks before a competition.

Because the Iconic was a European-founded event, the metric system was the basis for measuring distances. Race organizers made no provision to accommodate the imperial system of measurement that was used in many athletic events in the United States. All Iconic race literature, web postings, and course markings were based exclusively on the metric system. While it was possible for Ziggy, Allie, and Michael to continue to train and race based on imperial system measurements, Ziggy felt it was important for each of them to become fluent in metric measurements. He developed their training programs based on the metric system and insisted that their communications during the race should be based on metric speeds and distances. Over time, they all became very comfortable in all aspects of the metric system. However, they never mastered the conversion of temperature from Celsius to Fahrenheit. While Ziggy sometimes gave them temperatures in Celsius, he always made sure to communicate the air and water temperature readings in Fahrenheit as well, no matter where they were competing.

Michael and Allie were now veterans of the Iconic triathlon circuit, but neither one had ever won an Iconic World Championship. In the year 2025, however, each of them had a legitimate chance of winning the race, and both of them were as well prepared as any athlete in the competition. For six years, they had sacrificed and climbed the ladder, and now they were both hopeful this would be their year to ascend to the top of the Iconic Triathlon world.

CHAPTER 23

The Netherlands had been a cornerstone of the Iconic Triathlon from the beginning. Three Iconic events were held annually in Holland, of which Nijmegen was one. Canals were not approved for recreational use in most areas of the Netherlands because they were important cogs in the country's infrastructure for moving goods from point A to point B, but due to efforts by the national and local governments to improve the quality of canal water, many athletic events were now sanctioned and permitted. Nijmegen had been very progressive in using its canals for athletic events for the past four or five years.

The Netherlands had the additional advantage of being the most cyclist-friendly country in the world, with strict right-of-way laws favoring cyclists and dedicated cycling paths and lanes throughout the country. Many people rode bicycles to work daily, and Nijmegen had a Fast Cycle route—for bikes and pedestrians only—that would be used for today's race.

Michael and Allie enjoyed competing in Holland. The Dutch were a very hospitable people, and literally all of them spoke English. For the world championship event, they were staying at the Van der Valk Nijmegen-Lent. Van der Valk was the largest hotel chain in the Netherlands. It was known for its clean, functional rooms and good food, and it was a great value compared with the big, international chains. The Nijmegen hotel was relatively new. It was 15 stories tall, and Michael and Allie were staying on the 10th floor, in a corner room with views through the floor-to-ceiling windows of much of the racecourse. Ziggy's nearby room also had a good view, and he studied the course from his window nearly every free moment, using his binoculars.

The evening before the race, Michael and Allie had prepared their pre-race meal, gone to bed at 8 p.m.—after a carb-heavy dinner with some easily digestible protein in the hotel restaurant—and slept soundly. When Michael arose at 4 a.m., he turned on the coffee maker, and the liquid started streaming out. Because the hotel provided only instant coffee for the rooms, Ziggy had gone to a nearby MediaMarkt electronics and appliance store and bought two small coffee makers. Then he'd figured out a way to get his Sumatra Gold into the machines, and that's what the coffee maker was brewing. The rich smell filled the room.

"Coffee?" Michael asked Allie, who was still in bed.

"Not yet," she said, sluggishly. "I'll get a cup when you go into the shower. Happy birthday, by the way."

"Thank you," said Michael, grabbing the cup and heading for the shower. Neither he nor Allie would drink much coffee before the race because it was a diuretic, meaning it would rob them of water they wanted to remain in their systems. But they loved Sumatra Gold, and all it took was a few sips to help them get going in the morning.

"We'll celebrate your birthday tonight, right?"

"Darn right! Can't wait."

When Michael came out of the shower, he went to the small fridge in the room and pulled out the energy shakes they'd made, then opened two of the peanut butter–and-banana sandwiches. Every endurance athlete had their own pre-race ritual. The idea was to get some easy-to-digest, high-energy food into your system a few hours before race time. The race start for pros was at 8 a.m., so it was time to begin eating. Allie didn't like to shower before races because she knew she'd be filthy within a few hours, but it was part of Michael's routine. They ate their sandwiches and sipped their shakes. At two hours before the race, the eating would be dramatically reduced, but the hydrating would continue. Ziggy mixed a special drink for them that he said was a secret formula, claiming it was better than Gatorade or any other sports drinks, but he wouldn't tell them what was in it.

Because the top 10 finishers at Iconic races were drug tested after the race, Michael and Allie had confirmed that the drink didn't contain any illegal substances, but they didn't know much more than that except that it tasted pretty bad. Ziggy made two versions of his special brew, a thin version and a thick version. They drank the thin version before the races. They also drank it during the bike portion of the event, placing the bottle of the thin version brew on the left-hand bottle holder behind their saddles. The thick version, which included a gel, was part of their eating regimen during the race and was placed in the right-side bottle holder behind the saddle.

At 5:15 a.m. sharp, there was a knock at the door.

Allie meandered over and opened it.

"Mornin', dudes!" said Ziggy. "Everybody ready to rock 'n roll?"

"Almost," said Allie.

"I'm ready," said Michael.

Allie and Michael gathered their things and headed to the elevators with Ziggy. Both triathletes had come a long way since they first raced together back at Coney Island six years previously. Allie was now the number one ranked Iconic woman in the world. Michael was the number three ranked man, but he had won his most recent race and seemed to be peaking at the right time. Ironically, the number one ranked Iconic male was Danny van Devers, the former open water swimmer Michael had edged out in the 1-mile race back at Coney Island. Danny had become a good friend to both of them, and they often spent time with him after races, touring around Europe. He was especially helpful taking them around Amsterdam, knowing all the special places where tourists were scarce.

The most endearing thing about Danny for Michael was that he'd picked up Ziggy's habit of calling him Mikey. In fact, while Ziggy seemed to call Michael "dude" more than he called him Mikey, Danny called him Mikey exclusively, and Michael liked it. It made him feel more like a regular person, something he'd been struggling to feel his entire life.

It wasn't raining that morning, but it was overcast, typical for Holland. Their first stop was T1, the area where they would transition from the swim to the bike. As was the case in many Iconic events, T1 was nowhere near the area where the race would start. This was quite inconvenient for the athletes because they had to visit the T1 area to check their bikes, then get back in the car and drive to the start area. The advantage was that it gave the organizers a lot of flexibility in their layout of the extremely long swim, often resulting in a swim with no turns, as would be the case today.

The T1 area was well lit because it was still dark. Michael and Allie found their bikes and went through their pre-race checklist. Both of them were now riding top-of-the-line Cervélo carbon bikes with integrated, aerodynamic storage units to carry the tools and food they would need during the bike. While no bikes could be taken out of T1, there was still important work to be done. They double-checked the tire pressure on their bikes, placed fresh hydration bottles into the holders, balanced their helmets on the seats, and verified that their shoes were locked securely into the pedals. Both of them used the flying mount technique to get on the bike, which they'd practiced endlessly with Ziggy. They would run the bike out of transition in their bare feet, swing onto the bike and put their feet on top of the shoes, and while pedaling slowly to keep their speed up, they'd work their feet into the shoes one at a time, pulling and securing the Velcro straps to tighten the shoes. Both of them raced with no socks, not wanting to waste time putting them on in the transition area.

After each of them did a final inspection of the other's bike, they joined Ziggy, sipping from the Ziggy-made drinks they always kept with them before race time. They scrunched up their lips in exaggerated ways when Ziggy was looking to show him how much they disliked his custom formula. All he did was smile.

They jumped back into the car. Ziggy dropped them off at

the swim start and went to find a temporary parking space. After their warmup, he would drive the 10 kilometers back to T1. He'd be ready for them when they came in from the swim with updates on their competitors.

Michael and Allie ran into Danny when they arrived at the race start area, high-fiving and making small talk. Danny was a lot trimmer than when they'd competed against him six years ago at the Coney Island swim. Whereas back then Danny had carried about 190 pounds on his 6-foot, 2-inch frame, he now weighed about 180. Michael was 6 feet 3 inches tall and weighed 175 pounds. Allie was 5 feet 9 inches tall and weighed 130 pounds. She'd weighed nearly 140 pounds when she'd switched from open water swimmer to endurance triathlete, but it was inevitable that all of them would lose weight after years of intense training for endurance distance triathlons. Another inevitability was that they'd all be even lighter when the race was over, 2 to 5 percent lighter, no matter how much fluid they took in during the race.

Ziggy returned from where he'd parked the car nearby, in a spot where no parking was allowed. He figured he wouldn't get towed or ticketed this early in the morning on a Sunday, a safe bet in the Netherlands, where everybody, including the police, enjoyed their Sundays. The Dutch knew how to enjoy life, and this philosophy was something that Michael and Allie hoped to one day incorporate into their own busy lives, but that time had not yet arrived for them.

Ziggy was very flexible regarding warming up. He told Michael and Allie to do what they wanted to warm up. It didn't surprise him that they spent every second of their warmup together. They'd never shaken their intense desire to be with each other, and Ziggy found this quite charming, although sometimes frustrating. But because Allie was faster than 95 percent of the men who competed in triathlon, it didn't really hold Michael back to do most of his training with her. To start their warmup, they jogged a mile or so together, laughing the entire time, relaxing each other in a way that even the greatest practitioner of meditation techniques would envy. Then they made their way to the swim area, where they were joined by Ziggy.

"Okay, dudes," said Ziggy. "Forty-five minutes till the race starts. Water temp is only 22 Celsius, 71.6 Fahrenheit, so it looks like you'll be wearing wetsuits, as expected."

Iconic rules stated that wetsuits were *required* at temperatures below 24 Celsius (75.2 Fahrenheit). Due to the long distance of the swim, the race founders felt making wetsuits optional in colder temperatures was too risky. No matter how hearty an athlete was, the risk of hypothermia was always present when the body was immersed in water that was substantially lower than the body temperature, especially for two-plus hours. Most triathletes preferred wearing wetsuits because they increased buoyancy and speed significantly, but they made sure to equip themselves with suits that were thinner in the shoulder and elbow areas than in other areas of the suit. This allowed for more flexibility and greater arm speed.

Iconic limited the thickness of wetsuits to 5 millimeters, as did most triathlon organizations, although they were often as thin as 1 to 2 millimeters in shoulder and elbow areas, and some athletes opted to use wetsuits with short sleeves, which was permitted. Wetsuits were optional in Iconic events at temperatures between 24 Celsius (75.2 Fahrenheit) and 27

Celsius (80.6 Fahrenheit). Above 27 Celsius (80.6 Fahrenheit) wetsuits were prohibited.

Ziggy continued his pre-race briefing. "Air temp is 60 Fahrenheit right now but going up to 72 by race end. Heck, the sun might even come out later. The best news is that the wind isn't expected to be a factor today, so the bike should be a lot less challenging than it would be on a windy day in Holland. Bacteria in the water should be no problem either. *E. coli* reading for the course ranges from 20 to 28 colony-forming units, so like I said, no problem. But take on as little canal water as you can, goes without saying. You dudes ready for the swim warmup?"

Michael and Allie responded by nodding and wading into the water, holding hands, of course. Ziggy watched them go, feeling both happiness and envy. *I wish I could love somebody like that,* he thought.

Michael and Allie had been married three years ago in a small ceremony in Rochester, Michigan, Allie's hometown. Allie's parents had met more than 35 years ago at the Ford plant where they both worked. They had good-paying union jobs with great health and retirement benefits, and they were lucky enough to have survived the seemingly endless layoffs in the auto industry and worked their entire careers for Ford. They were now retired, and while they'd never been to any of Allie's Iconic competitions, primarily because they were uncomfortable flying, they were very happy that at least one of their three children had finally gotten married.

Allie was now officially Allison West-Stevens, but she continued to use her maiden name at work and in events. This in no way reflected her love and absolute adoration for her husband; it was just more practical.

Allie and Michael spent 15 minutes warming up in the water. Ziggy handed them towels and they dried off. It was 7:45 a.m.

"Okay, let's win this thing, dig?"

"Dig," came their voices in unison.

"See you at T1," said Ziggy, who would watch the start and then drive back to T1. Michael and Allie handed their drink bottles to Ziggy and found their way to rolling start areas one and two. Michael stayed with Allie in area two until there were 5 minutes left to the race start. When it was time for him to move up to join the pro men, they embraced and kissed. As always, the contact with Allie put Michael into a state of calm that was just what he needed at the start of the race.

"Have a nice birthday race, dear," said Allie, squeezing tightly.

"Thank you, my love," he whispered into her ear. "You, too."

Michael finally pulled away and made his way to area one, found his friend Danny van Devers, and lined up for the run into the water. He was very happy to be in that spot, at that time. Life couldn't be better.

CHAPTER 24

At 8 a.m. sharp, the horn went off, and the pro men began the short run to the Maas-Waal Canal. This canal got its name because it connected the Maas and the Waal rivers. It was 13.5 kilometers long (8.4 miles), so the swim could go straight from the start near the town of Malden all the way to the finish in Nijmegen—a straight shot with no turnarounds. The swimmers had to run down a set of temporary stairs that had been installed to get them from land to water. There was a little bumping along the way, but because all groups in the world championship race were limited to 50 people, the normal chaos of the start was reduced significantly. The cheering spectators at the start would get to see them again because both the bike and run routes passed through Malden as well. They would miss the finish, however, which was in Nijmegen, unless they chose to make their way there via many of the routes available to them.

Michael dove in from the platform at the bottom of the stairs and swam north. When he hit the water, he felt the shock of the cold on his face, hands, and feet as well as the disorientation of going from an air to a water environment.

He was bumped a few times and kicked on his shoulder once by another swimmer, but he avoided a blow to the face that often occurred during the swim start. He began looking for Danny, found him, and as was his custom, he fell in just to the left and slightly behind him, something he'd done more times than he could remember since that first 1-mile race at Coney Island. Danny didn't mind. He was the stronger swimmer at this distance and would pull away from Michael when he chose to, usually around 2 kilometers from the finish.

The water felt good and didn't have the dirty taste that was sometimes present in canal swims. It was a Sunday, and there was never much commercial boat traffic on Sundays, but to ensure a safe swim, all boat traffic had been blocked beginning at 6 a.m. and would stay blocked until noon. Any swimmer who didn't make it out of the water in 4 hours would be removed from the race and disqualified. Iconic races, particularly the swims, were designed to be tamer than Strong-Force races. However, Iconic races were focused exclusively on determining which athletes were the fastest, and therefore, Iconic cutoff times were much more strict than Strong-Force cutoff times. All racers participating in Iconic events were in the race to win, or at the very least, to come in as far up the leaderboard as they could.

Danny and Michael made it to the midway hydration and feeding station, which was floating in the center of the canal, after about 55 minutes, a full minute before any other swimmers. Stations like this weren't needed in StrongForce races because the swim was so much shorter, and the fastest swimmers in the Iconic races didn't stop to use them, but the slower swimmers did. Four hours was too long to go without hydration during an endurance event like this, and many of the slower swimmers would accept food—usually a packet of energy gel—at the station as well. Danny and Michael swam past the station without stopping.

Michael knew that Danny would begin picking up his pace in the second half of the race, and that is what happened. Michael increased his stroke count to keep up, staying in his favorite spot in Danny's bow wake, and powered on. He was able to hang with Danny for another 2 kilometers, but with 3K (1.9 miles) to go, Danny pulled away from him. This was sooner for Danny than normal, but after all, it *was* the world championship race, so Danny was obviously doing everything in his power to win. Michael would have to swim the final 3K (1.9 miles) without the energy savings provided by Danny's wake. This was okay for him. It was the way he and Allie trained anyway. They didn't draft off of each other in practice, unless of course, they were practicing drafting.

After another 30 minutes of hard swimming, the buoys marking the course started to curl left, and Michael knew he was approaching the end of the swim. He increased his stroke count with about 500 meters to go, looking once to try to spot Danny. He was at least 250 meters ahead of him, about double the distance he'd normally be ahead. When Michael emerged from the canal on the western side, Ziggy was there, on the edge of the racers-only zone.

"He's got a 2½-minute lead on you, dude," said Ziggy. "Do what you can on the bike, dig?"

"Dig," said Michael, running hard into T1, the first transition area, unzipping his wetsuit and pulling his arms free as he ran. He approached the "strippers," quickly laid down on his back, and two strippers adroitly ripped his wetsuit from his body. The strippers were local volunteers who had to put up with crazed athletes wanting to cut as much time off their transitions as possible. The pros were generally calmer than the age group athletes, but even some of the pros yelled at the strippers to hurry up. Michael never did that, however, knowing intellectually that the strippers were doing the best they could to help each athlete move through the transition as quickly as possible. After his wetsuit was off, Michael got up, grabbed the wetsuit, and ran to his bike, ripped off his goggles, dried his feet with a towel, put on his helmet, grabbed his bike, and ran it out of the corral area. He executed the flying mount and raced out onto the course to try to catch Danny. Michael was ahead of the third-place competitor by more than 2 minutes, but he was behind Danny by more than that.

Michael reached back with his left hand for the hydration bottle containing Ziggy's thin homemade brew and drank deeply. It always tasted better during a race. He jammed the bottle back in the holder and weaved his way from street to street, crossing back over the canal on the bridge on the S102, then turned south to work his way to the start of the main circuit for the bike. The MaasWaalpad was a Fast Cycle route along the F73 that ran all the way from Nijmegen to the town of Cuijk. It was 12 kilometers (7.5 miles) long and restricted to cyclists and walkers. There was even a bridge, known as the Maasover, which allowed cyclists and walkers to cross the Maas River without worrying at all about cars and trucks. Today the MaasWaalpad had been cleared of all non-competitors until 6 p.m. Any cyclist who hadn't finished the bike leg by the 8-hour mark since the race start would be removed from the course.

It was 3K (1.9 miles) from T1 to the MaasWaalpad. A full circuit of the MaasWaalpad was 24K (14.9 miles). After the initial ride from T1 to the MaasWaalpad and four roundtrip loops of the MaasWaalpad, the riders would have covered 99K (61.5 miles). The final kilometer (.62 miles) was the ride from MaasWaalpad to T2, located at the Radboud Sports Centre. Michael joined up with the MaasWaalpad, switched to a higher gear, and increased his speed. As soon as he got a good rhythm going, he reached into the integrated storage box and pulled out an energy bar, already unwrapped, and stuffed it into his mouth.

After he finished chewing, he reached down for the Aero Bottle on the diagonal front tube of the frame and washed the remains of the energy bar down with the water from the bottle. He returned the bottle, got into the tri bars, and bore down hard on the pedals. The tri bars projected forward horizontally, rather than curling downward and back, and allowed the racers to put their bodies in the most aerodynamic position on the bike. Tri bars, also known as aerobars, got their name because they were allowed in triathlon races only and were prohibited in most traditional cycling races, with the exception of time trials. The theory was that because triathletes expend energy in two other disciplines in addition to the bike, reducing the air resistance they experienced during the bike would help them save energy for the final segment of the race—the run.

Michael knew it was going to be tough to make up time on Danny during the bike leg, but he had to try. Danny and

Michael would both be traveling at a speed of about 45 km/ hour (28 mph) at any given moment during the MaasWaalpad bike loop, so at that speed, Danny's 2½-minute lead would be equal to a gap of nearly 2 kilometers. The 24K loop on the MaasWaalpad was 12K out and 12K back along the same road, so Michael would see Danny when they passed by each other as Danny headed back toward Nijmegen. Unless he passed Danny at some point, which was unlikely, he'd see him four times during the bike leg of the race. Michael settled into the aerobars and carried on, making sure to hydrate and eat as much as his stomach could tolerate. When he was about a kilometer from the turnaround in Cuijk, he saw Danny coming at him on his way back to Nijmegen.

"Hey, Mikey," shouted Danny, a smile on his face.

"Hey, Danny," Michael yelled back, not smiling, because Danny still had a 2-kilometer lead on him.

Each time Michael and Danny passed by each other, it was clear that Danny was slowly increasing his lead over Michael. Michael's strategy going into the race was to average 85 percent of his FTP (functional threshold power), and the power meter on his bike display confirmed that he was doing that. He considered increasing his wattage, but then decided not to since Danny's lead wasn't widening that much during the bike leg. By holding his power output to 85 percent of FTP, Michael would have plenty of strength left in his legs for the marathon. Danny, on the other hand, was obviously pushing a higher percentage during the bike, and this might come back to haunt him during the run. At least that's what Michael hoped would happen.

The singular most redeeming feature of the out-and-back

loop along the MaasWaalpad for Michael was that he got to
see Allie four times. Each time, she was the first woman he
saw, meaning she was leading the women's field. They waved
and yelled "Love you" as they passed each other, but the further the race progressed, Michael thought he saw a look of
concern on Allie's face—concern for him no doubt, because
she would have been able to see that Danny's lead over Michael was increasing, just as he could see it.

Danny's lead would stretch to 3 kilometers before the end
of the bike leg, a full 4-minute gap. Michael would also be
passed by Vlad Popescu toward the end of the bike. Vlad was
from Romania and was the number two ranked male on the
Iconic circuit.

As Michael pulled into T2 at Radboud Sports Centre on
the southern side of Nijmegen, he slipped his feet out of his
shoes while still riding and executed a flawless flying dis-
mount, throwing his right leg over the saddle, putting all of
his weight on top of his left shoe while his right leg dangled
behind him, and then hitting the ground running with his
bare feet. He grabbed the back of his saddle with his right
hand and ran the bike into T2, racked his bike, ditched his
helmet, changed into his running shoes, and headed out onto
the run course. He passed Ziggy on the way out of T2.

"You're 4 minutes down!" yelled Ziggy, jogging along to
minimize the distance between him and Michael. Michael
was a slightly better runner than Danny, but the 4-minute
deficit loomed large.

"How much is Allie's lead?" Michael yelled back. It was
hard to talk while competing, and Ziggy always encouraged
Michael and Allie to minimize their words and leave the

brief seconds they had for communication to him. But he also knew the couple well enough to know the one question they were guaranteed to ask if they were going to talk, and that was about how the other one was doing.

"Four minutes!" screamed Ziggy. "Looking strong!"

And then Michael was gone, out of earshot.

Michael was aware that Allie was ahead because he'd seen her on the bike loop, but he was excited to hear that she had a 4-minute lead and was almost done with the bike, which was her weakest leg of the race. He knew she could win the race even if she was behind after the bike leg, so unless something disastrous happened, she was going to win! This thought gave him a shot of adrenaline, and he increased his own speed, hoping he still had a shot at this thing himself.

The marathon course at Nijmegen was laid out as a half marathon that you ran twice. The first 5K (3.1 miles) was from T2 at Radboud to the town of Malden. The fans from the swim start would see the runners passing by once again. The next 5K (3.1 miles) was Malden to Mook, where they turned back north and took an 11K (6.8 miles) route back to Radboud in southern Nijmegen. The roads were all blocked to prohibit traffic, and the pavement was smooth. The Dutch prided themselves on the conditions of their roads. Michael and Allie had never seen a pothole on any Dutch road, regardless of whether it was a narrow cobblestone street or a superhighway. This helped reduce the possibility of a twisted ankle or a nasty fall on either the bike or the run.

Michael shook out his legs and arms as he ran to help clear the lactic acid that had built up during the bike leg. But this didn't take long because the bike leg was much shorter than the StrongForce distance, and his legs weren't that tired or strained. He saw Vlad about 100 meters ahead of him. Vlad was just under six feet tall and rail thin, with more of a distance runner's frame than a triathlete's build. Triathletes were typically thin, but they had more muscle mass, particularly in their upper bodies, than pure distance runners. If the contest were simply a marathon, Vlad would have an advantage, but because Vlad lacked the muscle mass of competitors like Michael and Danny, he couldn't rely on his muscles to give him extra energy when he needed it.

In endurance triathlons, the body inevitably turned to the muscles for food and energy, literally eating them from the inside to get to the stored glycogen and lipids found there. Vlad had long since used up most of what his muscles had to give in that regard, so he would theoretically be weaker by now than many competitors. Regardless, he would need a bigger lead than 100 meters to hold Michael off.

After less than a kilometer, Michael felt completely ready to run and established a good rhythm. He slurped down some water from one of the hydration stations. He turned left onto the N844, the long, straight road that would take him the final 3 kilometers to Malden. After about another kilometer, he caught Vlad, wishing him good luck as he passed by him. His next priority was to find out what kind of a time lead Danny had, so he began looking on the side of the course for Ziggy. Ziggy had said he'd find a spot just past the McDonald's on the left side of the N844, about a kilometer in from the turn. He said there was a grassy area just past the parking area, and he didn't expect many fans to be there. Ziggy knew all the tricks of getting from point A in a race to point B. In this case, he'd made his way to the McDonald's using back roads, by bicycle, beating both Danny and Michael there. By referencing an app on his phone that reported each racer's progress and speed, he could tell Michael how far behind he was when he passed by. In this case, he'd also be able to check his calculations by pressing a stopwatch when Danny passed by and stopping it when Michael passed by.

Michael moved to the left side of the road as he approached the McDonald's, easily spotting the shiny bald head of his coach just past the group of fans who were watching the race from the McDonald's parking lot.

"He's 4½ minutes ahead!" yelled Ziggy, running along beside Michael as best he could. "Keep your current pace! He'll slow down!"

Then Ziggy was gone from sight and earshot as Michael surged forward.

Michael looked at his watch. He was averaging 3 minutes, 50 seconds per kilometer (6:10/mile). If he could keep up this pace, he'd finish the marathon in around 2 hours and 42 minutes, which wasn't *impossible* on this flat course, but not at all likely. Michael would be ecstatic to go under 2:45, which he'd never done before. And even though Danny had extended his lead in the first 3K of the run, Michael was confident that Ziggy was right in saying that Danny's pace would fall off. It was just a question of when.

Michael kept his rhythm and made his way into the town of Malden. He passed through town, waving to the fans on the side of the road who urged him on. Many of the fans were decked out in the orange color that was such an important symbol of Dutch national pride. The Dutch believe strongly in fair play and are a polite people, so even though most of them undoubtedly wanted Danny, their countryman, to win the race, they also respected the fact that Michael was here, giving it his all. They rewarded him for that with polite cheers and applause.

A few kilometers out from Malden, the N844 merged left onto the N271, a larger, busier road that had been shut down for the race. Mook was a few kilometers south. Michael wished he would see Ziggy there, but he knew the timing was too tight for Ziggy to make it that far. Ziggy would move east from the McDonald's and position himself on the route back to Nijmegen.

Upon reaching Mook, Michael turned left off of the N271 onto Groesbeekesweg, then made a quick left onto Bovensteweg, now heading north back to Nijmegen. Bovensteweg was a quiet road, traveling through quaint Dutch neighborhoods with their sturdy homes made from brick, several with orange tile roofs. Bovensteweg became Lindenlaan, then Lindenlaan merged with Lierdwarsweg, and Michael found himself in a rural area with forests on both sides of the road. He took Gatorade from an aid station as he continued north, slurped it down, then looked at his watch. He was still holding the 3:50/K (6:10/mile) pace. He looked ahead up the road, and way out in the distance he thought he could see the orange suit of Danny, about a kilometer ahead of him. About 3K (1.9 miles) from Radboud Sports Centre, he spotted Ziggy on the side of the road. The area was still quite rural, and no spectators had gathered there. Ziggy was alone, and he started running as Michael approached.

"He's 3½ minutes ahead. Just hold your pace. I'll see you at the McDonald's again."

"Okay, thanks," said Michael, struggling to get the words out between his deep, rapid breaths. He was nervous that he was about to finish a half marathon and had only regained a minute on Danny. But he trusted Ziggy. He held his pace and carried on into Nijmegen toward the halfway point of the marathon.

Michael reached the Radboud Sports Centre and turned left onto Willem Nuyenslaan to rerun the half marathon he'd just completed. After 3 kilometers, he approached the McDonald's on the N844 and saw Ziggy.

"He's crackin', dude!" yelled Ziggy. "You're 2 minutes down! See you at the finish line!"

Ziggy disappeared as Michael sped past. He looked ahead and saw that Danny's orange suit was much closer than it had been just 6 kilometers earlier in the race. He was excited because he felt good, and he tried to follow Ziggy's advice to stay steady at 3:50/K (6:10/mile), but it was becoming more difficult. Michael looked at his watch and saw that his pace had slowed to 4:00/K (6:26/mile). However, by the time Michael reached Mook, Danny was only 100 meters ahead and was obviously struggling. They turned left onto Groesbeekseweg, then made the quick left onto Bovensteweg, heading north. There were only 10K (6.2 miles) left in the race.

Michael pulled alongside Danny in the first neighborhood along Bovensteweg. Danny was gracious.

"Looks like you've got this, Mikey," he said, panting. "I'm hurting."

"Keep moving," said Michael. "Vlad's back there somewhere."

"Okay. See you in Nijmegen, brother!"

Michael sped by, running loose, feeling good. He didn't even remember the last 10 kilometers of the race, finding that nirvanic place that so many distance runners speak about. He crossed the line to cheers from the crowd, his name coming over the loudspeaker as "The 2025 Iconic Triathlon World Champion, Michael Stevens!"

Ziggy ran into the finish area and hugged him tightly.

"You did it, dude! You did it!" Ziggy was happier than Michael had ever seen him.

"What about Allie?" asked Michael, breathing hard.

"She's got a 5-minute lead! She's gonna win, too!"

Danny came in about 3 minutes behind Michael, and they hugged. Vlad came in 2 minutes later, and they all shook hands. Thirty minutes later Allie came across the line, a World Champion herself. They all hugged, cried, and smiled. A lot of work and sacrifice had gone into this. Both of them had broken the Iconic Triathlon world record times. Michael's marathon time of 2:45:15 was a personal best for him in that leg of the race. It didn't get any better than this. But they were completely blindsided by what happened next.

CHAPTER 25

A month later, in San Diego, Billy won his third StrongForce 200 World Championship in a row. It was his sixth appearance at San Diego and fifth as a pro. Billy had won his age group in 2019, but in 2020, San Diego and most other events were canceled due to COVID-19. In Billy's pro debut at San Diego in 2021, he placed third, then second in 2022. He won in 2023 and repeated his winning performance in 2024 and again in 2025.

Liza had also competed six times at San Diego, winning her age group in 2019, placing third as a pro in 2021, fourth in 2022, second in 2023, second in 2024, and third in the 2025 race. For most people, a second- or third-place finish at StrongForce would be a cherished accomplishment. For Liza, it was a stain on her reputation. Liza's weakness was the swim, and she had yet to find a way to overcome this handicap at the pro level. She couldn't handle it. As far as Liza was concerned, her repeated failures had nothing to do with any shortcomings she might have as an athlete, but they must in some fundamental way reflect her training. She decided to walk away from StrongForce, but it wasn't the end of her

triathlon journey. In fact, she had every intention of returning to StrongForce competitions once she got her head, and
her swim, straight. To do that, she needed to concentrate
more on the swim without losing touch with the bike and
the run.

Michael and Allie learned about Liza's new direction one
evening in mid-October in Manhattan. They were dining at
one of Liza's favorite spots, a small, discreetly located French
restaurant that could have been found in the heart of Paris.
The restaurant seated only 16 people and provided privacy
for each of the tables. The staff spoke exclusively in French.

Michael and Allie were doing fine financially, although
their careers in the business world had plateaued somewhat
due to their time commitment to training and competing.
Many of their peers at the wealth management firm where
they worked had been spending their time outside of work
studying for the CFA (Chartered Financial Analyst) exams,
a comprehensive three-level certification process that took
years to complete and many, many hours of preparation. The
CFA was needed to continue to advance at their firm, and
neither one of them had the time to prepare for it.

On the other hand, both were earning more than $100,000
a year from their triathlon sponsors and prize money, so this
helped compensate for their slowed progression in the business world. Nevertheless, they would never have dined at a
restaurant like this without Liza's invitation, because they
wouldn't want to spend that kind of money on a mere dinner and also because they wouldn't have been able to get a
reservation anyway. It went without saying that an invitation

directly from Liza meant that she was paying, and while they were somewhat uncomfortable with this, they also understood that Liza wouldn't have done it unless there was something important she wanted to accomplish. Michael and Allie wondered if there was an engagement announcement in the offing.

The four friends still got together every now and then. Billy had been the best man in Michael and Allie's wedding. Michael and Billy still loved each other like brothers. Allie and Liza, on the other hand, had a chilly relationship, mainly because Allie just didn't care for Liza. Liza wasn't uptight at all about getting together with Michael and Allie, but she could feel Allie's negative energy toward her and tried to be sensitive about it. Considering what she was about to tell her friends, she would need to choose her words carefully.

A waiter came over to their table and poured the wine, asking in French if they'd decided what they would like to order. *"Avez-vous pris une decision?"*

"Veuillez nous donner une minute," said Liza, fluent in French and never shy about using it. The waiter bowed and left the table. Liza raised her wine glass in the air.

"Congratulations on your double win last month, you two!" she said, with enthusiasm.

"Thank you," said Allie.

"Thanks," said Michael.

They all clinked glasses and sipped their wine.

"Did you two spend a little extra time over there after the event?"

"As always," said Michael. "Our friend Danny enjoys showing

us around Holland when we race there."

"Oh, yes," said Liza. "Danny van Devers, the swimmer, right?"

"Used to be," said Michael. "Now he's a triathlete and a good friend."

"Yes, of course," said Liza. "But I'm sure his swimming talent comes in handy in those Iconic races."

"Indeed," said Michael.

"A toast," said Billy. "To Michael and Allie. Iconic World Champions!"

They all raised their wineglasses and clinked them lightly together again, then drank.

Allie raised her glass, "To Billy and Liza. Two of the best StrongForce athletes on Earth!"

They all toasted and sipped more wine.

"Well, I think Billy deserves all the credit, really," said Liza. "He's the World Champion. I'm simply an "also-ran" at this point."

"Hardly," said Allie, and she meant it. Liza was a force to be reckoned with in all aspects of her life, including Strong-Force.

"Would you trade your Iconic World Championship for my third-place San Diego finish?" asked Liza.

Allie didn't hesitate. "I wouldn't trade that for anything," she said.

"Of course not," said Liza. "It was hard-earned."

"Your finish was also hard-earned," said Michael, peering at Liza and wondering what she was up to. He began rubbing his index finger over the scar on his chin.

"I suppose," said Liza. "But I think I need a change of pace."

Michael glanced at Billy, noticing a sheepish look on his face, then returned his gaze to Liza. "What kind of change of pace?" he asked, warily.

"I'd like to take a go at the Iconic distance," said Liza, a humble smile on her lips.

There was a moment of quiet after the blow was delivered. Allie was the first to respond.

"We love the Iconic format," she said. "It would be great to have you and Billy join us over there."

"I won't be racing the Iconic," Billy blurted out. "And Liza fully intends to return to StrongForce. She's looking at the Iconic as a kind of cross-training. Her bike and run are strong, but she needs work in the swim. The Iconic can give her that."

"Indeed, it can," said Allie. "And we'll be happy to help in any way we can, right, Michael?"

Michael could see the anger in Allie's eyes, but there was also a hint of excitement. It seemed she was going to get what she had wished for after all.

"Of course," he said, perhaps not as enthusiastically as he should have.

"So, are we going to get some dinner tonight, folks?" asked Billy, trying to change the subject. "What looks good?"

CHAPTER 26

One Tuesday morning a few weeks later, Michael was at his office when his cell phone rang. It was Ziggy.

"I'm comin' to the city today," Ziggy said. "Wanna join me for lunch?"

Michael was a little confused but certainly not opposed to seeing his coach and friend.

"Sure, Two Cool, but you know Allie's out of town right now," said Michael.

Allie was currently on a two-day business trip, visiting key clients in Chicago.

"Yeah, I know," said Ziggy. "That's kind of why I think we should meet."

Michael's confusion grew.

"Not sure what you mean," he said.

"Dude, I'll explain when we get together. I'll just come to your building, and we can grab a bite right there. Cool?"

"Okay," said Michael, absentmindedly rubbing his index finger over his scar.

"See you at noon, Mikey," said Ziggy, clicking off before Michael could even say goodbye.

At noon, Ziggy and Michael met up at the café in the lobby of Michael's building. They grabbed some food from the self-serve area, paid for it, and found a seat. Ziggy was eating a veggie burger and an apple. Michael was having a salmon cake and sweet potato fries.

"So, what's up, Two Cool?" he asked.

"A lot," said Ziggy.

"Such as?"

"Such as your old friend Liza jumping off the StrongForce battleship and landing on the Iconic life raft, that's what. What do you think of that?"

"I think Liza is free to do whatever she chooses to do," said Michael, stiffening.

"Of course, dude. Sure. But how does that make you feel?"

Here we go with the psychology session, thought Michael.

"I don't know, Zig. Do we have to talk about this?"

"That's why I'm here, dude. No other reason for me to be in the city today."

"Then why didn't you come in when Allie could join us?" asked Michael, a bit too aggressively.

"That's also the reason I'm here. I knew she was out of town, and I took the opportunity to talk to you alone."

"We could have spoken on the phone."

"This is important, dude. I need to talk to you face-to-face about this."

"About what, specifically?"

"About the impact this Liza thing's going to have on Allie, and on you, Mikey."

As Michael thought this through, he realized that Ziggy had been spot-on in his decision to come and see him. He'd tried several times to broach the subject with Allie, but she didn't want to talk about it. He literally had no one he could talk to about this, except Ziggy.

"Okay," he said. "What do you think the Liza thing means for us?"

"Look, dude, isn't it obvious what you two are going to lose from this, what you've already lost?"

"I admit I'm confused about it right now, but I'd really like to figure it out, Zig, 'cause I've been stressing a little bit."

"And that's the answer, right there, dude. No joy, man. No more joy for Allie, no more joy for you."

Michael thought about this. Allie *had* been different since the dinner when Liza informed them of her plan to compete on the Iconic circuit. She'd been a little less patient. A little more intense. As he thought about it, so had he.

"It's not like I don't think Allie can beat Liza, although for sure it'll be a challenge," Michael said. "It's more like what you said. It's like the wonderful bubble Allie and I had built for ourselves by pursuing the Iconic has got a small leak in it."

"Dude, the bubble's burst!" said Ziggy. "Forget about a small leak. The joy is gone, man. I'm here to work on a plan with you to get it back."

"What? You want us to quit Iconic, something like that?"

"Heck no, dude. More like I want you to double down on Iconic."

"What do you mean, 'double down'?"

"I mean I want you to get Billy into the Iconic scene as well, dude."

"And that's supposed to bring the joy back for us?" Michael asked, feeling anger boiling up inside him.

"Settle down, Mikey. Hear me out, okay?"

Michael sat back in his chair and folded his arms. He'd barely touched his salmon cake.

"First," said Ziggy, "we gotta think of Allie. She's a tough cookie, and she's ready for the challenge. And we'll all work hard to up her game even further. But hey, dude, in a very real sense, she's alone. She has to face this challenge by herself. Like I said, I know she's up for it. But right now, it's *her* problem."

"Why do we have to look at it as a problem?" asked Michael. "Why can't we look at it as an opportunity?"

"Funny you should say that," said Ziggy. "It *is* an opportunity, but it's not the opportunity you may think it is."

"Go on," said Michael.

"Clearly this thing is going to put an imbalance into your relationship with Allie. It already has. Am I right?"

Michael thought about the silly bickering that had been going on between him and Allie since the dinner with Liza and Billy over completely unrelated things, like who did the dishes and who took out the trash, things that had never even come up in their lives before. Their life together had been harmonious, with each of them gladly doing everything they could to help the other, in every aspect of their lives, no matter if it was mundane or critically important. He wondered if this bickering was going to escalate further into downright fighting, and he shivered at the prospect. He sawed away at his chin, but Ziggy's logic was starting to make sense to him.

"So, you think me having the challenge of competing against Billy will create a balance with the challenge Allie has from Liza?"

"I do. But it'll do a heck of a lot more than that, for you."

Michael knew what Ziggy meant. The terror of competing against Billy was the most enduring fear of his life.

"You get it, right?" asked Ziggy.

"Yeah, I get it. Doesn't mean I have to be happy about it."

With Liza all in against Allie, Michael would essentially be standing on the sidelines, no matter how much he trained with Allie and rooted her on. Allie had left StrongForce and come over to Iconic to help Michael run away from one of the central issues of his life. And now the life they'd built together around Iconic had been severely damaged by the selfish whim of a woman obsessed with winning. By bringing Billy into the Iconic, balance would be restored in the lives of Allie and Michael. Allie would have her challenge, and Michael would have his challenge. They would help each other in facing their individual challenges, just as they always had. The only problem was that Michael was terrified. Ziggy sensed this and tried to help.

"It's inevitable anyway," said Ziggy. "Liza dominates Billy, and if she wants him in the Iconic, she'll eventually get him into the Iconic."

"I'm not completely sure about that," said Michael. He paused, and Ziggy let the silence continue. He knew Michael was processing something important.

"Doesn't matter," said Michael. "I don't know if I can beat Billy, but does it make me a loser if I don't?"

"Better to try and fail than to never try at all, dude."

"Old wisdom that still rings true. But I'm scared, Zig."

"That's why I'm here. We gotta deal with that fear, Mikey."

"I hear you. But the first step is for me to talk to Billy."

"Do it before Allie comes back," said Ziggy. "Otherwise, she might talk you out of it."

CHAPTER 27

Michael and Billy met the next morning at the same coffee shop near Liza and Billy's apartment where the "Big Change," as they called it, had been planned. Michael arrived first and had a good look at Billy when he entered the café and approached the table. His dark hair was still wet from his shower after an early morning workout with Liza. Billy was a lot thinner than he used to be, carrying about 180 pounds on his 6-foot, 1-inch frame. His relentless training for StrongForce competitions was responsible for that, of course.

Liza had a client meeting early that morning, so she wasn't there. Her dress design business continued to prosper on her terms. She worked with only one client at a time. Michael had asked Billy to come alone, and it was convenient that Liza had something else on her schedule. Nevertheless, Billy expected something important was to be discussed.

Throughout their lives, the two always discussed the important things one-on-one before involving others. This meeting was no exception, although Michael was more nervous than he ever had been for any such meeting with Billy. He scraped his finger back and forth along the scar on his chin, wondering if he was about to do to himself exactly what he'd done back when he and Billy were seniors in high school. Billy sat down, reached over, and gave a fist bump to Michael.

"What brings you uptown?" Billy asked.

"I need to ask a big favor of you, bud," said Michael. "A huge favor as a matter of fact."

"If it's in my power to do, I'll do it," said Billy.

"It's a big one, Billy. A serious one."

"Okay, let's have it."

"I'd like you to take the next year off of StrongForce and race in the Iconic series."

Billy was stunned. "Holy moly. Where did that come from?"

"Bottom line, I need this for me," said Michael. "I need to get over my fear of competing against you."

"Is that why you went the Iconic route instead of Strong-Force?"

"Yes, it was. At the time I needed to *not* worry about you. My primary focus was to make sure I could race with no physical issues. And I've done that."

"You sure have," said Billy. "Look, I've got my baggage, too, you know. I still blame myself for what happened to you."

"Which you know is not the case. I had an infection that led to my heart attack. It had nothing to do with you."

"I pushed you to the limit, man." Billy was shaking his head from left to right. "I don't want to go there again. Never again. It almost ruined my life, too."

Billy looked like he was starting to panic as he relived the terrible pain of their respective tragedies, but Michael had more cards to play.

"And who got you started on your way back?" he asked.

"You, of course," said Billy.

"So, now I need you to help me. Look, I'm not worried anymore about having a heart attack. I'm just tired of being afraid of losing to you. And it really isn't about me wanting to beat you so badly, although I'm sure that would feel good. What I really have to get over is how terrible I feel emotionally when I lose to you. You're the one person in this world who I could never beat, but does that mean I should change my life to avoid competing against you? I don't think so. Not anymore. And from what I'm hearing, it could help you as well. Like you said, you've got your own baggage. You need to unpack that stuff, Billy."

"It's more complicated than that, a lot more complicated," said Billy.

"What do you mean?"

"Well, let's start with our dads."

"What in the heck do they have to do with it?"

Billy scrunched up his nose, making an expression that said he didn't understand Michael's reaction.

"You remember my dad, right?" asked Billy.

"Of course! He's okay, isn't he?"

"Yeah, he's fine. Still working at Home Depot. Became a store manager quite a few years ago, and he's doing great. He's in his mid-fifties now and still going strong. Anyway, he came out to San Diego for the last World Championships. Did you know that?"

"No, but that's awesome. He must be so proud of you."

"He is. But he also told me something after the race I had a lot of trouble believing. He told me that back in our senior year, early on during track season, your dad called him into his office. He demanded that my dad tell me not to run the 1600 that season. And when my dad said that wasn't fair, your dad got angry and fired him from his job."

"That's crazy!" said Michael, stunned. "I had no idea that happened."

"Really?" asked Billy. "Because I've been angry at you ever since I heard that. I figured you had to know about it, maybe even asked your dad to do it."

Now it was Michael's turn to get angry.

"I thought you knew me better than that," he said, shaking his head in disgust and turning down his lips into a frown, looking down at the table. "I can't believe my dad did that."

"Well, he did," said Billy. "I'm sorry I had to be the one to tell you. Your old man was a jerk to do that. A real lowlife. But what makes it worse is that I wish my dad *had* talked me out of the 1600. Then none of the bad things that happened to us would have ever happened."

Michael realized he was losing a grip on his main objective for the meeting, but he was also very upset at the news about his father and needed to work it through with Billy.

"Look, dude, we've been over this a hundred times. My problem was my problem, and you didn't make it happen! But that stuff with my dad. That's not right, and I'm going to confront him about it."

Michael still saw his parents on holidays, and once they'd even come to an Iconic event while they were vacationing in Europe. His heart attack back in high school had changed them profoundly. In one awful moment, they realized how trivial their desire to see their son win at all things truly was. They'd also sought therapy to help them with their anger at the Dexters. Eventually, they had thoroughly convinced themselves that what the doctors said was true—that Michael would have very likely suffered the heart attack whether or not Billy had been in the race. Their relationship with Michael became more normal, except for the fact that they shied away from his competitions. It seemed to him that they might be more scarred from what had happened than he was. But now this new revelation brought back all the anger Michael used to feel toward his parents. He was absolutely livid.

"No, please," said Billy. "My dad told me not to say anything to you. He just wanted to get it off his chest after all these years. There are no hard feelings. It worked out really well for him to get off that asphalt crew."

"I'll have to think about that," said Michael. "My dad really stepped over the line, and he should know how wrong I feel that was."

"Well, just try to let it go if you can," said Billy. "Your old man was wrong, of course, but he was trying to do what he felt was best for you."

"That may be true, but it doesn't make it right. And I had absolutely no knowledge of that, and I want you to know I'm glad the way things worked out. Both of us are doing as well as we could have ever hoped to do."

"What does Allie think about this idea of yours?" asked Billy, turning the conversation back to Michael's original proposition.

"She doesn't know," said Michael.

"Why?"

"Because this is between you and me. It has nothing to do with her. Well, that's not true. It has a lot to do with her, but it's complicated."

"Try me."

"I don't think it's fair that Liza's jumping in to go against Allie while I run away from competing against you. My relationship with Allie has been very balanced. We've faced all of our challenges equally, helping each other through things. But with the prospect of Liza coming into the Iconic, with no equal challenge for me, it's thrown things off between Allie and me. Do you understand what I'm saying?"

"Kind of. But that's not really the kind of relationship Liza and I have. I mean, we help each other and all, but it's really more about mutual success than it is about our undying love for each other."

"Wait a minute," said Michael. "I know you adore Liza. Are things okay between you two?"

"They've gotten a little dicey since I won again at San Diego and she didn't, again."

"Sorry to hear that. You think it's going to work out?"

"I do. Especially if she hears that I might commit to Iconic. I'm not saying I will, but it would be music to her ears."

"That's hardly a basis for repairing a relationship, is it?"

"Oh, it isn't?" asked Billy. "I thought that's what you just told me you're trying to do by getting me into the Iconic?"

Michael paused, chuckling to himself. Billy might not have finished college, but he sure could understand the heart of a matter in quick order.

"Good point," said Michael. "Maybe we can justify this crazy idea by saying that life and sport have merged as far as our relationships go."

They had a good laugh at that, but the truth of what Michael had just said was not lost on either of them.

"What would I do about my sponsors?" asked Billy. "You

know I've been paying rent to Liza same as you did—$2,500 a month. And I've paid back all the money she loaned me while I was working to get started in my pro career. It's a matter of pride for me just as it was for you."

"I suspect your sponsors will be fine with it. You have an agent, right?"

"Yeah, some guy Liza's family knows."

"Let him handle it."

"Okay. I'll think about it."

"Thank you," said Michael. "I hope we can both get some closure on this."

In spite of what Michael had just said, he still had many doubts as to the wisdom of this scheme. He could only hope that Ziggy was a wiser man than he was.

CHAPTER 28

2026

Liza pulled hard to finish the interval set. During the winter and early spring, she worked out in the Asphalt Green 50-meter indoor pool on the Upper East Side. It was early February. Sometime in May she'd begin mixing in outdoor swims at Brighton Beach with her indoor workouts. She was on the last lap of an exhausting interval training set—ten 500-meter intervals. The goal of this set was to swim each 500 in 6 minutes and then rest for 2 minutes. The total allotment for each interval was therefore 8 minutes. If she swam slower than 6 minutes in a 500, she would get less than 2 minutes rest. If she swam faster, she'd get more rest.

Liza stretched and rotated, stretched and rotated, stretched and rotated, then breathed on the third stroke, sprinting toward the wall. She hit the wall and looked up at her coach, Sam Forman, who had just hit the stop button on his watch.

"Not bad!," yelled Sam. "You did it!"

Sam was one of the best open water swim coaches in the world, having coached several world champions in various open water distances, including the current women's 10,000-meter champion, Melissa Wells. He intended to have

Liza train with Melissa when they went outdoors in a few months. Liza had hired Sam based on his agreement to facilitate joint training sessions with Melissa, and apparently Melissa liked the idea. She knew who Liza was and was more than willing to help a StrongForce athlete improve her swim. Melissa had completed a few StrongForce competitions herself, although she wasn't a top cyclist or runner, so she stuck with open water swimming as her main competitive emphasis.

"Once you're holding 7:30 in the 500 intervals, we'll begin working on the 1,000 intervals," said Sam, taking in all there was to see as Liza, dripping with water, emerged from the pool. At 30 years old, she was thinner than she'd been in college, and more muscular, but she was still a strikingly beautiful woman.

"Fine," said Liza, breathing deeply while accepting a water bottle and a towel from Sam. She frowned and gave him a hard stare to ward off his wandering eyes, then proceeded to chastise him for not advancing her training more quickly. "But I feel like I should be there already. My first Iconic event is only six weeks away."

Liza was entered in the inaugural Iconic race at Cape Coral, Florida, near Fort Myers. This would be the first Iconic race ever held in the United States. Cape Coral boasted one of the most extensive canal networks in the world, and arrangements had been made with the city to hold an event in a section of saltwater canals close to the Gulf of Mexico. Over an extended period of time, the Iconic organizers had worked with the city, neighborhood associations, and even individual homeowners to block off a race area for the 8 hours needed to stage and run the swim leg of the race.

"It's just that I won't have any time in open water with Melissa before the race," complained Liza. "In fact, I won't have done *any* open water training before the race. I don't like it."

"The race is *part* of your training," said Sam, brushing his long dirty-blond hair out of his eyes. Sam still competed some, but he was no longer as fit as he used to be, concentrating more on his coaching than competing. With clients like Liza in his stable, he was doing quite well financially compared to the meager earnings and sponsorships available in open water swims.

"That's not the way I do it," said Liza, who'd been complaining about this race since Sam added it to her schedule. "I race to win, period."

"You're racing to win the World Championship in September, Liza. This race will let you get your toe in the water, so to speak, at the Iconic distance. It's all part of the plan."

"I don't like it," snapped Liza. "If I'm going to do this race, I want to go down to Cape Coral now and start training there."

"I can't do that," said Sam. "That wasn't part of our agreement, and I have other clients. You know that."

"Then I'll go by myself. No, actually, Billy will go with me."

When Billy had told Liza about his conversation with Michael regarding him coming over to the Iconic for a year, it was a foregone conclusion as to what Billy would do. Liza was ecstatic, and there was no way he could refuse her. Now she could overlap her workout sessions with Billy's and take advantage of training against the best in the world, whenever Billy's schedule permitted him to do so. She needed more work on the swim, and she was pursuing that with the same sheer determination that she pursued everything in her life.

And now that she had Billy in the game with her, her determination increased even further. She pushed him to swim more with her, but Billy refused to swim more than three days a week. Liza was swimming five days a week, and Billy wasn't there that day. The StrongForce swim wasn't a weak spot for him, but he'd increased his yardage in swim practices in deference to the substantially longer swim leg of the Iconic, and on days that he did swim, Liza was in the pool with him. He wasn't worried about the Iconic swim, but he wasn't excited about it either. He'd never loved swimming. Liza felt her idea to relocate to Florida for the next six weeks would appeal to Billy since it offered them the opportunity to train outside and get away from winter, and she had no doubt that Billy would agree to go.

Sam was similar to Billy in one specific area: He capitulated to Liza's demands whenever possible.

"If you say so," he said. "I can do my part with you through Zoom. I'm sure your other coaches can do that as well."

Liza employed four coaches—a swim specialist, a cycling specialist, a run specialist, and an overall triathlon coach who helped with transition techniques and overall fitness and nutrition. The "head" triathlon coach had to approve all of the individual workouts recommended by the specialists.

Billy, on the other hand, just used the triathlon coach. Overall, he did basically what he wanted to do, except in swim training he deferred to Liza's coach to help her as much as possible. Billy had been a triathlete for more than eight years now, and knew as much as most coaches. He also knew what his body was capable of doing. Liza took a different approach. She employed as many experts as she could, but in times like this, when a coach's ideas conflicted with her over-whelming need to win, she overrode them.

"Good," said Liza. "I'll speak to Billy about it tonight. We'll be down in Florida within a week. I'm sure."

After Billy had agreed to dedicate the next year to the Iconic, he *had* insisted that he and Liza enter different Iconic competitions than Michael and Allie, which was not an issue because there were now 21 qualifying events for the world championship race, to be held in Montreal, Canada, in early September 2026. Billy had discussed his idea with Michael, and they'd compared notes of their competition plans for the coming year, made a few changes, then proceeded with their training, which was also done separately. Michael and Allie had their own way of doing things, with their own coach, and both couples were comfortable with the idea of training and competing apart until the world championship race that all of them would undoubtedly qualify for.

So, Liza and Billy went to Florida in mid-February, trained for six weeks down in the Florida sun, then competed in the Cape Coral Iconic event. They both won easily. Billy broke the Iconic world record that Michael had set at the world championships the previous September. He did this with a mediocre swim leg, a blazing bike leg, and a solid marathon. Liza's time was 10 seconds slower than Allie's world record, due entirely to a swim that was a full 10 minutes behind Allie's swim time when she'd set the world record. But Liza had made up eight minutes in the bike and nearly two minutes in the run. There was little doubt that as her swim improved, her times would continue to drop, and they did.

CHAPTER 29

Allie and Michael began their 2026 season in Australia. The Australian people had been triathlon enthusiasts for a long time, so it was relatively easy for the Iconic organizers to secure a race venue Down Under. In fact, they secured two. The Iconic event that Allie and Michael would open their season with in early March was Iconic Penrith. The race venue was the Sydney International Regatta Centre (SIRC). Many athletic competitions were held at SIRC, including a Strong-Force 200 event at the end of March.

March was the beginning of fall in Australia, and the weather was normally outstanding in many areas of the country. Allie and Michael had decided to weave a lengthy vacation around the event. Arriving a week early would allow them to fully integrate their bodies into the time zone and give them an opportunity to train at the race venue a few times before the actual race. They were fully into their taper at that point, but familiarity with the venue was always a plus. Because Penrith was near Sydney, Allie and Michael would spend their week before the race in the Sydney metropolitan area. After the race they would travel to Melbourne in the south, then take a few days to go to New Zealand before traveling home. A few nights before the race they dined out in Sydney and then would be going to a show at the famous Sydney Opera House. They chose to attend a play at the Drama Theatre, one of several venues housed within the Opera House, and one of the more intimate, seating only about 500 people.

They were at dinner at the Quay restaurant, which had a great view of the harbor and the Opera House from its location on the upper level of the Overseas Passenger Terminal. They'd both ordered the eight-course meal, and while they found the food to be delicious, they were struggling somewhat to stay within the dietary guidelines that had been set up by Ziggy. Nevertheless, they were happy to be there and looking forward to the show later that evening.

Allie reached across the table and took Michael's hand. "Thank you for being with me," she said, smiling. "I am *so* happy."

Michael didn't hesitate. "I'm the lucky one," he said.

"We're both lucky, I guess. Do you ever wonder how our lives would have gone if you'd stayed with Liza?"

"Not really. I'm mainly just thankful that we ended on good terms. And I'm glad it worked out for her and Billy."

"Do you really think it worked out for them?" she asked, tilting her head.

"I don't know. Liza *can* be a bit pushy, but Billy doesn't seem to mind."

"A *bit* pushy! That's the understatement of the century!"

"Well, I just want the best for both of them, I guess."

"Does that include them winning the Iconic World Championship? I mean, after all, Liza *does* get what Liza wants, right?"

"That's nearly six months away. I'm not thinking that far ahead."

"Oh, but I am. I'm thinking about it night and day."

"Why is beating her so important that you think about it night and day?"

Allie hesitated, thinking. "You know me well enough to know how competitive I am, don't you?"

"Yes, of course, but how can anyone compete with Liza's headstrong nature?"

"Oh, you don't think I can compete with her?" asked Allie, raising her eyebrows.

"We're talking about competitive nature, not the competitions themselves!"

"Okay," she said. "But do you think I can beat her?"

"Of course, I do. But it's a long season. A lot can happen in a season."

"Meaning what?"

"Meaning injuries, job changes, family problems, who knows what?"

"Well, aren't you 'Mr. Positive.'"

"I'm just saying, no one can predict the future."

"But you can hope for the best, right?" she said, smiling.

"For sure," he said.

"So, if we think positively, then we would say I should be able to beat her, right?"

"Undoubtedly."

"But she nearly broke my world record in her first race, last week!"

"Now who's being negative? Maybe you'll break your record two days from now."

"I doubt it," said Allie. "My bike still has a long way to go."

"So, let's work on it when we get home," he said. "Let's put in an extra day of bike and cut back on the swim a day."

"I don't know about that. Let's ask Two Cool when he arrives."

Iconic Penrith was the first of four Iconic events that Allie and Michael and Ziggy had planned for the year. In May, they would compete in Tokyo, then Vienna, Austria, in July, then they would finish their year at the world championships in Montreal in early September. The Montreal event would be the first time the Iconic World Championship would be held in North America. And since it was only a six-hour drive from New York City, Allie and Michael would drive to the event, the first time they'd ever be able to drive straight from home to an Iconic venue.

Ziggy didn't attend all of their races, but he'd never been to Australia and wanted to check it out. He was due in early the next morning and would probably be so jet-lagged he wouldn't be able to think straight, but they still hung on his every word. He was like a god to them, bringing them from newcomers to the Iconic series to world champions in only six years. They very rarely challenged his advice or training plans and certainly would seek his input on sacrificing a swim session for a bike session.

"Okay, let's talk to Zig about it," said Michael. "What do you think? Maybe we pass on the dessert?"

"We paid for it already, so let's have a spoonful, just to see how good it is."

"Deal," he said.

"I'm sorry I keep harping on the Liza thing. I know it must get old."

"All I want is for you to be happy. If you're happy, I'm happy."

"But we never talk about you going against Billy."

"That's because it's not healthy for me to dwell on that, so I make it unimportant. What *is* important to me, is you."

"Ziggy says you need to get over the 'Billy Hurdle' to reach your full potential."

"Yes, I know," said Michael. "And somewhere deep inside I understand that. I just don't let it rise to the surface very often."

Michael had been able to manage his anxiety related to competing against Billy by telling himself to just train hard, then use his "secret weapon" on race day in Montreal. The secret weapon was the psychological technique he'd used in a few important past competitions where he pretended he was competing against Billy, then made himself angry by letting the pain and suffering from his past competitions against Billy rise to the surface. He was somewhat uncomfortable with this "technique," and he'd never told anyone about it, not even Allie or Ziggy. But his main approach to reducing his anxiety about Billy was simply not to think about Montreal, at all. He stayed in the present and focused on the immediate task at hand, be that a workout, a competition, or a project at work.

"I envy you," said Allie. "But the best thing would be if we both beat them, right?"

"The best thing is for the two of us to give it our best. 'Winning isn't everything, but making the effort to win is.'"

"Well said, Vince Lombardi." Allie raised her glass of Perrier and lime. "A toast then, to people who give their best!" Michael raised his glass and clinked it with Allie's. "And if I might add," she said, "may those who give their best be victorious!"

And for Allie, her wish came true at Iconic Penrith. She won the event, although she didn't beat her world record time. Michael finished third. Danny van Devers hadn't come to Australia, but Vlad Popescu, the Romanian, had found his running legs Down Under and captured first place. An up-and-coming Australian competitor named Len Rogers came in second. But as Michael had said, it would be a long, unpredictable season. It was impossible to know how it would turn out.

CHAPTER 30

In early September 2026, Allie and Michael packed up and got ready for the drive up to Montreal. They put their bikes up on the rack on their new Audi Q7, which they parked in the private lot below their apartment building. They'd moved into a two-bedroom apartment that might one day be occupied by a new arrival, but for now, their plan did not yet include a date for starting to work on expanding their family. The extra bedroom was available to visitors from out of town such as family and friends. Allie's parents had stayed with them a few times, and while Michael's parents had visited several times, they preferred the comfort of luxury hotels like the Waldorf and Park Plaza.

When Michael and Allie finished packing the vehicle—which was large and had more than enough room for their gear, street clothes, and the food they would need for both their meals and the race itself—they jumped in and began the six-hour drive to Montreal. It was a Thursday. The 2026 Iconic World Championship race would be held on Sunday, now only three days away.

The season had produced mixed results for the couple.

Allie had won all of her events, whereas Michael hadn't won any of them. In the last race of the season, near Vienna, Austria, Michael had DNF'd (Did Not Finish) for the first time in his triathlon career. The Vienna course was the most difficult on the Iconic circuit due to the rolling hills in the mountains surrounding the city, where the bike and run legs took place. The couple had entered this event specifically for this reason because the Montreal race, while not quite as hilly as Vienna, was still a challenging course, according to Ziggy.

Unfortunately for Michael, the roads around Vienna had been wet due to a light rain that fell during the race, and he'd crashed on the bike. While suffering road rash and a sprained wrist, he wasn't seriously injured. Soon after the couple returned from Austria, he was able to resume his training, and his intensity and commitment were as robust as ever. By the time the world championship rolled around, however, his ranking sat at number five in the world.

Liza and Billy had won every event they entered. Billy was ranked number one in the world. Surprisingly, Liza was ranked number two, behind Allie. While Liza's swim times had continued to come down, as predicted, Allie's dramatic improvement in the bike had more than offset this and enabled her to squeak ahead of Liza in the rankings after the Vienna race. Nevertheless, the experts considered the matchup between the two women at the upcoming world championships to be a toss-up. They were equals entering the race, but only one would win in the end.

Michael, on the other hand, was not even talked about as a contender anymore. His apparent decline was a mystery to everyone in the sport, except for Ziggy, Allie, and Michael.

By all appearances, he'd handled the pressure of the pending competition against Billy very well. He'd been completely dedicated in his training, albeit without the results he'd hoped for during the season, and with no apparent anxiety about the Montreal race. And in spite of what others might think, Allie, Ziggy, *and* Michael himself were certain that he was in top shape and just needed a little luck to get a good result in Montreal. Another glimmer of hope was that his efforts to help Allie improve her bike leg had ended up helping him in the bike as well. So, a good result for Michael seemed likely to all of them. What was unclear was what a "good result" actually meant. Was second place the best he could hope for this year?

For his part, Billy motored along, winning easily, seemingly bored with the Iconic format. He'd never made any secret of his apathy for swimming, and the length of the Iconic swim simply exacerbated this disdain, elevating Billy's dislike to something approaching abhorrence. But Billy was no quitter, and he'd made a one-year commitment to his best friend, his girlfriend, and his sponsors to compete in the Iconic. So, he did the required training in all three legs, overcoming his negative feelings about the swim.

Billy was regularly a top five finisher in the swim leg at the Iconic but had never come out of the water first. He would normally take the lead in the race during the bike leg, and by the halfway point of the marathon there was rarely anyone even close to his position at the head of the race. Going into the world championship event, Billy was the prohibitive favorite to win.

Michael and Allie had forgone the option of staying in a

hotel in Montreal for two reasons—one, the race venue at Saint-Gabriel was a 1½-hour drive to the northeast from Montreal, and two, they wouldn't have to worry as much about their ineptitude in the French language. While Montreal was the most English-friendly place in all of Quebec Province, about half of the people there spoke only French. And while it was true that the vast majority of hotel and restaurant staff spoke English, and were far more forthcoming in doing so than their counterparts in Paris, neither Michael nor Allie had ever studied the language. So, they packed absolutely everything they would need for the five-day trip into the Q7 and ventured north, with the address of their Airbnb in the town of L'Assomption plugged into their GPS app.

They would have preferred to stay in Saint-Gabriel, which bordered the lake in which the race would begin, but they were forced by dinner obligations to Michael's parents, and to Liza and Billy, to stay about halfway between the race venue and Montreal. Needless to say, both Michael's parents, and Liza and Billy, were staying in luxury hotels downtown. Allie and Michael would dine with his parents that evening, then with Liza and Billy on Friday evening. Saturday evening before the race they'd stay by themselves in their Airbnb, which turned out to be a comfortable little chalet on a river, about an hour's drive from Montreal.

After Michael and Allie settled in, they went for a brisk 5-mile run along a route they had planned out before they arrived. Afterwards, they showered, dressed, and drove downtown to the Four Seasons hotel to meet Michael's parents for dinner. They arrived on time for the 7 p.m. reservation Michael's parents had made in one of the restaurants in the hotel.

Branford Stevens was now in his early sixties and had not aged nearly as well as his wife, Christina, who would turn 60 the following year. Branford had been under quite a bit of stress during the past five or six years. His companies had all struggled during the COVID-19 pandemic and the associated downturn in the economy, and the Alexandria Asphalt Company had closed for good in 2021. His other companies were hanging on, but none of them had ever fully recovered from the COVID recession. Branford knew that the best thing to do was to close all of them and retire, which he would soon do. The family fortune would keep their somewhat extravagant lifestyle going for as long as they needed, with plenty left over for Michael when the time came.

Branford still had a full head of hair, although it was fully gray now. But the dark bags under his eyes and the loose, wrinkled skin of his throat made him look older than his years. He still worked out several days a week, but not with the same enthusiasm as in the past. The silver lining of his recent misfortune was that he appreciated more than ever these rare occasions when he and his wife could spend time with their son and his wonderful wife, Allie, whom they'd grown to adore. All that was missing now was that elusive grandchild.

When Michael and Allie entered the restaurant, Branford and Christina stood. They all embraced, then took their seats.

"I'm so grateful we could be here," said Branford. "Thank you for sharing your mutual success with us."

"No guarantees about that," said Allie. "We still have to do the race!"

They all laughed, most of all Branford. He truly enjoyed Allie's company.

"Ah, yes, the race," he said. "I forgot about that. Well, no matter what happens in the event, your success in my eyes is already a foregone conclusion. You two are building a great life together, in all its aspects, and I'm so proud of you."

"But let's not forget the grandchildren, okay?" chimed in Christina.

More laughs. Michael looked at Allie. "It's up to Allie at this point," he said. "I'm ready." All eyes turned to Allie as her face reddened.

"I'm almost there," she said. "If I win this race, I'm all in."

"Ah, but winning isn't everything, my dear," said Branford. "Family *is*."

"I'll drink to that," said Christina, taking a healthy sip of her wine.

"Wow," said Michael. "How far you two have come." He already knew that his parents were no longer the ultra-competitive, win-at-all costs people they once were, due in large part to the lessons learned from his misfortune back in high school. But it seemed they'd progressed even further now, sharing the wisdom gained from the family tragedy, and their own lives, with others. He was happy that someone other than himself and Ziggy could help to curb Allie's ultra-competitive spirit.

"Indeed," said Branford. "Speaking of the past, there's something I'd like to tell you, son."

"Oh?" said Michael, somewhat alarmed by the serious tone of his father's voice. He raised his index finger to his chin and began rubbing his scar.

"And it's something I'm not proud of. Something I hope that both of you will forgive me for." No one said a word. "You remember your senior year in track, of course. That race with the horrible ending. I'm sure you've told Allie all about it."

"Of course, Dad," said Michael. "Does this have something to do with Billy and his dad, by chance?" Michael had never spoken to his father about the incident Billy had revealed to him the prior year. With help from Ziggy and Allie, he'd been able to process the anger and felt it was something best left buried in the past, especially because his parents had made such strides in their own lives regarding their outlook on competition and the importance of family.

"Why yes, it does," said Branford, raising his eyebrows.

"We know about it, Dad," said Michael. "No need to go into that."

"You do? Well then, I need not go into the details. But, son, if you'll indulge me, please, I'd just like to share my feelings about it with you, and Allie, to help me heal a bit. Can you allow me to do that?"

"Sure." Michael pulled his finger away from his chin and looked his father in the eye. Allie reached over and took his hand in hers, squeezing tightly.

"I'm most sorry about what I did to Bill Dexter. Twenty-five years he worked for me and I just threw him out to an uncertain future. Bill's a good man, and so is his son, and I'm ashamed of myself for what I did. It may be the single most appalling thing I've ever done."

"Have you spoken to Mr. Dexter about it, Dad? Apologized to him?"

"Not yet, but I intend to."

"Billy told me Mr. Dexter's driving up Saturday so he can watch the race on Sunday. Maybe you'll run into him."

"I'll make a point of it," said Branford. "Well, enough of that. Let's take a look at the menu, shall we?"

On the drive home, Allie told Michael she didn't want to drive back to Montreal for dinner with Liza and Billy the following night. Michael felt the same way, so when they got back to their Airbnb, he called Billy and let him know. They would spend Friday night alone together. Ziggy would arrive Saturday in the early afternoon.

CHAPTER 31

On Saturday, they met Ziggy at the beach at Saint-Gabriel, where the swim start would take place the following morning at 8 a.m. The beach was still open to the public, but it was not nearly as crowded as it had been in July and August. Now that the holiday season was over, the number of beachgoers was significantly reduced. Nevertheless, at 4 p.m., the beach would be closed so the Iconic crews could set up the swim course in Lac Maskinongé. It was a beautiful, sunny day in early fall, with blue skies and temperatures around 26 Celsius (80 Fahrenheit).

Ziggy made a special request when they met at the beach at Saint-Gabriel—he asked for a private meeting with Allie, followed by a private meeting with Michael. He normally spoke to them at the same time since they were virtually inseparable anyway. This time, however, Ziggy was taking a different approach, and while they were both a little wary, they agreed to his request. He told them that after the discussions, they'd have a swim in Lac Maskinongé, then drive around to the other side of the lake and go over the bike and run courses together.

Ziggy and Allie moved away from Michael to have their private discussion. Michael looked around and saw a number of athletes he knew mulling around. A registration site was set up near the beach where athletes could get their race numbers, their tracking chips for their ankle, and other paraphernalia that was handed out during registration. They would have to return to that area the following morning to get marked with their race numbers on their upper arms, thighs, and calves.

Not surprisingly, Michael saw Liza and Billy nearby and approached them. Liza was speaking to a race official, in French, even though there was no question the man spoke English, as did all members of the Iconic organization. Michael took the opportunity to pull Billy aside. The conversation he was about to have with Billy was something he'd planned to do, rehearsing what he intended to say many times.

"Hey, bud, you have a minute?" asked Michael.

Billy turned his way, smiled, and said, "Sure. Not much for me to do here, other than listen to a language I don't understand."

Michael started walking away and motioned for Billy to follow him. Billy complied.

When they were a good 10 meters from Liza, Michael began.

"I wanted to have a quick word with you, privately," he said.

"Sure," said Billy. "What's up?"

"First, I hope it didn't cause any problems when Allie and I bailed on dinner last night."

"Well, Liza was kind of bothered, but I was fine with it. I completely understand."

"Anyway, I'm sorry about that. But that's not what I wanted to talk about. I want to talk about the race tomorrow, if that's all right with you?"

"Trying to figure out my strategy or what?" asked Billy, smiling.

"Not at all. Trying to make sure you're going to give it your all tomorrow, basically."

"Why wouldn't I? My sponsors wouldn't be too happy if I didn't."

"You know why."

"Oh, you mean the thing between you and me. The reason we're both here, right?" Michael detected a hint of animosity in Billy's tone.

"Yeah, that's it," he said. "You're still good with the reasons we did it, right?"

"Well, let me put it this way. It's been a long year."

"What do you mean?"

"I mean I can't stand this Iconic format and can't wait to get back to StrongForce."

"I understand. But you want to win, right?"

"Darn right I do. After all the frustration I've experienced doing these long swims and short bikes, the very least I should do is win the thing."

"So, I have your word you're not going to hold back to let me beat you?"

Billy seemed to be a little shaken by Michael's question. "Is everything okay with you? Your health and everything?"

"Absolutely," said Michael. "Just saw the doctor last week. I'm 100 percent fit in every way."

"Then why did your ranking slip to number five?"

"I'd have stayed at number three if I hadn't crashed the bike in Vienna. I went into last year's championship at number three and won the thing. My plan is to do the same thing here."

Billy chuckled. "Okay, if you say so." Michael could see a little fire in Billy's eyes now, which is what he wanted.

"I say so," he said. "So, what do you say? Do you plan to win the race tomorrow?"

"Most definitely. It's time for you and me to get on with our lives and stop handling each other with kid gloves, don't you think?"

"Absolutely. And I thank you for doing this for me. I owe you one."

"No worries. It's almost over."

At the same time Michael and Billy were talking, Allie and Ziggy were having their private discussion. They'd found a few chairs near the snack bar and taken a seat.

"Okay," said Ziggy. "You versus Liza."

"Is that the topic for this discussion?" asked Allie.

"It is, starting with why do you want to beat her so badly?"

"Because I think she's a pompous, spoiled, rich girl who always gets what she wants. Is that what you want me to say?"

"Not sure, dude. I guess I'm just trying to help you understand it so I can help *you* get what *you* want."

"I don't like her. I don't like the way she treated Michael when they were together, I don't like the way she treats Billy, and I don't like the way she treats me."

"Okay," said Ziggy. "Now we're getting somewhere. But let me ask you this. Do you respect her?"

"What do you mean?"

"I mean she trains hard, she competes hard, and she wins."

"So, you think she's gonna beat me?"

"She might. But what I think doesn't matter. What do you think?"

"I think I'll win," said Allie. "Iconic is my territory, not hers."

"True, but she's taken to it pretty well, wouldn't you agree?"

"So, you *do* think she'll beat me," said Allie, frowning.

"Not what I said, dude. You're not getting where I'm going. So, I'll just go there. You don't win a race based on anger. Anger will corrupt your judgment about what to do when. And no matter how much you dislike her, it doesn't change the fact that she's a very accomplished triathlete who can beat you if you let her get into your head, which she clearly has done, probably without even trying to."

Allie sat back in her chair and processed what Ziggy had said. She took a sip from her water bottle and put it on the small table that separated them. "That makes sense," she said. "So how do I control it? My anger."

"You just decide."

"What?"

"You just decide to control it. And when it starts to boil up when she does something on the course that pisses you off, you remember. Remember that you've decided that anger will not win the race for you. Only then will you make the right decision on what tactic is best."

"I think I can do that, maybe."

"Let me give you an example. Let's do this as kind of a multiple-choice question, okay? Let's say you come out of the water first, right, which is what we expect, and Liza comes in a little bit behind you, maybe a minute or two. Then you both get in the bike leg, and she catches you early on and gets up on your back wheel and stays there. She refuses to alternate pulls with you. Then you have three choices—one, you go faster, two, you go slower, three, you stay right at the same pace and let her keep drafting off you. Which one will you choose to do if you're angry?"

"Probably go faster," said Allie.

"Right, and what good would that do you?"

"Probably not much because there'd be a long way to go in the bike. I wouldn't be able to hold that pace for long."

"Okay, so that's an example of how anger can hurt your chances of winning the race. But let's take it a step further. Let's say you want to make *her* angry, and maybe get her to do something stupid. How could you do that?"

"Go slower?"

"Bingo."

"But what if she just slows down with me? What if we stay that way for a long time? Then the other competitors will pass us."

"True, but that's my point. You know Liza, probably better than you know any competitor in the race, except Mikey, of course. You know she won't be able to stand going slow for very long, so all you have to do is wait her out. And what will she do then?"

"She'll pass me, and probably try to lose me."

"Exactly. So, then what do you do?"

"Go after her?"

"Maybe. Depends on how hard she goes out. If she goes out at medium speed, then, yeah, stay with her, and get up on her back wheel and stay there, if you can. If she goes out hard, then let her go. Get back to the pace you want to keep based on your race strategy. But don't let her get too far out of sight if you can help it. Anyway, I think you get the picture. Anger is your enemy."

"Yeah, I got it. Don't know why you waited until now to go over that with me, though."

"I have my reasons."

"Like what?"

"Like I didn't want you to have time to talk yourself out of it!"

Allie laughed. "I hear you, Two Cool. Sometimes I *can* do that, I know. But let me ask you this. What about Michael? What about his anger?"

"His anger is more complicated than yours, dude. But he's up next, so let me take a shot at getting him in the right frame of mind, okay? You two can help each other on the whole anger thing after that. Deal?"

"Deal," she said. "I'll go get him and send him over."

Allie made her way back to where she'd left Michael and saw him talking to Liza and Billy. She came up and said hi to everyone, then whispered to Michael that Ziggy was ready for him. Michael excused himself and went to go find Ziggy. Allie was left with Liza and Billy.

"Sorry about last night, guys," she said. "I just wasn't into it."

"We understand," said Liza, a bit too harshly. "I'm sorry you were so uncomfortable with it."

"I'm just not comfortable with two-plus hours of driving two nights before a race just to have dinner with people I see all the time."

"Perhaps you should have considered that before you accepted our invitation then."

"Michael didn't consult with me before he accepted, but you're right, Liza. I should have shared my feelings right away so we could have given you two more notice. I'm sorry."

"Not a problem," said Liza. "As you said, we see each other regularly in the city."

"How's your Airbnb?" asked Billy.

"Really nice," said Allie. "A quaint little place on the river."

"Ours is very nice as well," said Liza.

"I thought you were at the Ritz-Carlton, downtown?" asked Allie.

"We were, but we reserved a place up here in Saint-Gabriel for tonight and tomorrow night. Perhaps you can stop by when the race is over. It's right over there." Liza pointed toward one of the gentle hills surrounding Lac Maskinongé. There were several homes on it, all of them quite large.

Figures they'd outdo us on the Airbnb as well, thought Allie.

"I'll speak to Michael about it," she said. "See you two at the race tomorrow. Best of luck!"

"I doubt whether luck will have much to do with it, but thank you, Allie," said Liza. "See you tomorrow."

While Allie was having her exasperating conversation with Liza and Billy, Michael sat down for his time with Ziggy.

"What's up, Two Cool?" he asked.

"Yo," said Ziggy. "Did Allie tell you the topic of our discussion today?"

"No, we had company at the time."

"Ah, yes, your best buds."

"Well, at least one of them is."

"And *he* is the topic of our conversation, at least he's part of it."

"I figured he'd be all of it."

"Is all your anger about him, dude?"

"What anger?"

"Your *anger*, dude. That's the real topic to be discussed. Not Billy."

"So, you think I'm angry at Billy."

"Actually, no. I think you're angry at yourself."

Michael considered this. He remembered the races when he really had needed to dig deep, all the way back to the Coney Island race, his first race in his comeback after the long hiatus following his heart attack. There'd been a few others since then, but none so far this year. He was saving that for tomorrow, and this time he wouldn't have to pretend that the competitor he was trying to defeat was Billy, willing himself to get angry, willing himself to defeat the one person who had defeated him when it had mattered most, ignoring the intellectual argument he'd made so many times that it wasn't Billy's fault, deceiving himself into hating Billy for what he'd done to him. The anger would allow Michael to overcome his fear of losing so he could make the supreme effort that would be required to win the race in question. Tomorrow, Billy would *be* the competitor he needed to hate to defeat, in the flesh.

"I'm not sure about that," said Michael. "I'm not sure I'm angry with myself."

"But it's not Billy, right?"

"Not really. I just pretend to be angry with Billy when I

need a boost during the race."

"Oh, I didn't know that. How often do you do that, Mikey?"

"Not often. Haven't done it this year."

"And tomorrow? What's your plan for your anger for tomorrow?"

"Uh, well. I figured it would come pretty naturally tomorrow since Billy's in the race."

"So, you're saying that somehow during the race tomorrow, in the most critical moment, when you have to have it, you'll boil up all this artificial anger toward Billy and voilà, you win the race."

"Kind of." Michael was feeling embarrassed speaking about something he'd never shared with anyone.

"Look, dude. I just got finished telling Allie she can't win the race against Liza if she lets anger dominate her race tactics, and here you are telling me that it's your secret weapon. Something doesn't add up."

"I don't know, man. It's worked for me before."

"You don't get it, dude. But I *do*. And I'm gonna explain it to you."

"Okay, fine. Explain it."

"Those times when you envision it's Billy out there with you, it's not anger you're searching for. You're searching for what *he* has, man."

"And what is that, extraordinary athletic talent?"

"Nope. You've got that too. That's not it."

"What then? What am I looking for that he has?"

"Courage. Unmitigated, unrestrained, go for the gold, courage. That's what Billy has that you want to have. So, when you're thinking you're angry with Billy, you're really angry with yourself for not having what comes so naturally to him. Anger is just your substitute, for courage."

"Are you saying I'm a coward?" asked Michael.

"Hardly, dude. You're the bravest person I know. And that comes from my heart. The PTSD you have is real, man, I didn't make that up. And you overcame it. And that, my friend, took more courage than Billy's ever had to muster. You see, courage is easy for Billy. It comes naturally to him, but he's never taken a fall like you've taken. Maybe he never will."

"So, I can handle the race the way I want to then?" asked Michael.

"Not from my point of view. No, you can't. You can't beat Billy by kidding yourself, dude. You can't beat Superman by pretending you're Superman, too."

"But it's worked for me before!" said Michael.

"Not against Billy it hasn't."

"What do you want me to do then?" asked Michael, desperately confused.

"Stay calm."

"I'm fine. I'm calm."

"Not now, Mikey! Tomorrow! Listen to me and listen to me closely. Courage in my view is not an emotion. It's a decision. It's an intellectual decision. It's a decision to put your *fear*, which is an emotion, to the side. It's a decision to let your training, your intelligence, your talent, and your willpower do all the heavy lifting. Anger has no place in that equation. Fear has no place in that equation. Just courage. Yes, it comes naturally to Billy, but in his case it's not really courage at all, it's the *absence of fear*. In your case, it has to be pure courage, because you have the fear, for good reason mind you, but you have the fear. Only courage can overcome fear, not anger. So, when I say, 'Stay calm,' that's what I mean. Because only when you're calm can you make the intellectual decision to be courageous. Are you diggin' what I'm saying?"

"It's a lot to take in, but I'm starting to get it."

"Let me give you an example then. Let's say you're leading the race halfway through the run and Billy comes whizzing by you, doesn't even say hi. What do you do?"

"Go after him?"

"With 13 miles to go? The guy runs by you at mile 13, blazing at a 5-minute-mile pace, and you're going after him?"

"Yeah, I guess that wouldn't be a good idea."

"Why do you think a guy like Billy would run by the guy leading the race at such a fast pace? Let me answer the question so we can move on. To make the guy do something stupid! Billy knows he can hold that pace for a mile or so and still have enough in the tank to finish strong. But he also knows that nobody, nobody in the triathlon world, except him, can do that. You included. Yes, in our little world of triathlon, Billy *is* Superman. And nobody else is."

"So where does that leave me? Second place? At best?"

"I guess you didn't watch the Superman movies when you were growing up then?"

"No, I watched them."

"Then you are *really* challenging me here, Mikey. Because everyone who's watched Superman knows he has one weakness, right?"

"Kryptonite."

"You got it."

"And what is Billy's kryptonite, Zig?"

"Calm."

"Say again?"

"Billy is a bull in a china shop, man! He knows nothing about staying calm! All he knows is go, go, go! So, he passes you at the halfway point, blazing by at world record speed, and what do you do? Don't even try to answer. I'll tell you. You friggin' smile, man. You smile, because you know you've got a shot at him now. He just fired his best shot, with 13 miles to go, trying to break your will with his unheard of pace. So all you have to do is calmly shake your arms and loosen your legs, getting yourself into a new rhythm, and slowly, very slowly, increase your pace. Then you run the half marathon of your life. And you can bet your bottom dollar that Billy won't be looking back 'cause you told me long ago what his daddy taught him, so he'll keep that 5-minute-mile pace for a short stretch, trying to get out of sight, never looking back. Then he'll slow down. But how much will he slow down? Well, that just depends on what his gas gauge is reading that day, doesn't it? And my read on Billy Dexter is that the swim is gonna take more out of him than he wants it to, either because he swims harder than he should to try to minimize your lead, or because he takes his time in the swim and then has to expend tremendous energy in the bike and run to overcome the big gap you build up in the swim. And that's why he just might be beatable tomorrow. By the man who stays calm. You dig, man?"

"Dig," said Michael. "I think I get it."

CHAPTER 32

The horn went off to start the race, and Allie watched Michael and the other 49 pro men go into the water. It had been an extremely warm summer in Quebec Province, and the water temperature the day of the race was 27.2 Celsius (81 Fahrenheit), so none of the swimmers were wearing wetsuits that day, per Iconic rules. Allie considered that to be a significant advantage for her against most of her competitors because the swim was her strongest leg of the race. It should certainly give her an advantage versus Liza.

Allie spotted Liza nearby, wearing a distinctive red aerosuit that was tight to her body, flattening her front as much as possible to reduce drag in the water. Allie was wearing a sharp-looking aerosuit that was white on the top half and black on the bottom half. It was tight on her as well but just like all aerosuits, it was designed so as not to restrict her ability to use her lungs with maximum efficiency.

When the pro men went in, the pro women moved up to the front and waited for the verbal command to go. At Iconic events, the horn goes off only once. The groups that follow the pro men are sent into the water by a starter using a megaphone. The starter raised the megaphone to her mouth, holding her other arm straight out in front of her. She then raised her arm and said, "Pro women, go!" And off they went.

The swim course was laid out in a three-legged zigzag. The first leg was a 3.5K (2.2 miles) swim from the Saint-Gabriel beach, which was on the western shore of the lake, to the upper, northern end of the lake. The course then turned around and headed down the full 5K (3.1 miles) length of the lake to the southern end. There was a hydration and feeding float along this leg, about 1½ kilometers (.93 mile) from the north shore. Near the south shore was the final turn, which led the swimmers in a northeasterly direction into the final 1½ kilometers (.93 mile). This final stretch went straight to the opposite side of the lake from the public beach at Saint-Gabriel, ending at a small private beach near Magdalene Chapel. A short run up the beach left the swimmers at T1, the transition area from swim to bike.

After a little bumping and shoving, Allie got into the deeper water, established a good rhythm, and found herself in familiar territory, leading the swim leg of the race. She felt good in the water and got into a zone where she wasn't even thinking. Before she knew it, she arrived at the first turnaround, having completed the 3.5K (2.2 miles) first leg. She wound around the buoys and headed south, taking a look to her right to gauge how far behind the other swimmers were. She didn't see anyone even close to the turn, so she figured she had a good lead already.

Allie passed by the hydration and feeding float that marked the 5K (3.1 miles) halfway point of the swim, but she didn't stop, plowing ahead at a strong pace that brought her to the end of the second leg of the swim. After she rounded the second turn at the 8.5K (5.3-mile) mark, she had a good view of the buoys along the second leg of the race. The buoys were spaced approximately 100 meters apart. She counted six buoys before she saw another swimmer. She thought she saw the color red but couldn't be sure. She put her face in the water and pulled hard for the last 1½ kilometers (.93 mile) of the swim, rising up to run as soon as she could feel the bottom of the lake. She surged onto the beach, ran up to T1 and found her bike, dried off her feet, put on her gear, and began running her bike out of T1 to get to the road where the course began.

She saw Ziggy up ahead on her left, a pair of binoculars hanging from his neck.

"You've got a 7-minute lead over the next swimmer," he yelled, jogging along just ahead of her but losing ground due to her speed compared to his.

"Liza?"

"No, she's fifth, around 10 minutes behind you."

Allie ran by, but she had one more question. "Michael?"

Ziggy yelled as strongly as he could, but she couldn't catch all the words. Allie thought she heard the word "strong" but couldn't be sure. She reached the road and used a flying mount to get on her bike, pedaling and getting her shoes fastened seamlessly. It was about a kilometer out to where the bike loop began. Each loop was 33 kilometers (20.5 miles) long, so the riders would make three loops and then end the bike at T2, which she could see straight ahead of her.

Allie turned left onto the loop and began the ride up to Lac Mandeville, about 7K (4.3 miles) to the northeast. From there, the course continued on along the upper shore of Lac

Mandeville in a northeasterly direction and eventually reached the third lake on the course, Lac Deligny, then circled all the way around that lake, traveled back to Lac Mandeville and traversed that lake's southern shoreline, then turned south at the 21K (13-mile) mark. After another 5 kilometers (3.1 miles), the course turned east and followed Route 348 for another 5K (3.1 miles), then turned north and traveled the final 2K (1.2 miles) of the loop.

Allie and Michael had ridden the bike course on Friday. They were both surprised that it wasn't nearly as hilly as the Vienna course. There were some rolling ascents and descents, but the course was much tamer than they'd been led to believe by Ziggy. They figured this was by design because he'd asked them to train in more hilly terrain for this race and wanted to justify the reasoning. In the end, there was no better training on the bike than hills, no matter what racecourse you were preparing for.

Once again, Allie felt the course conditions were to her advantage versus Liza because Liza was used to the typically more rigorous terrain of the StrongForce circuit. A less challenging bike loop should help even the odds between the two riders.

Allie finished the first loop and looked for Ziggy. There were no roads he could travel on to get to spots along the course because this was a rural setting and the only roads were the ones the race was using. But he had the Iconic tracking app on his phone so he could track any racer who hadn't lost his or her ankle chip, which was hard to lose if fastened properly. Ziggy told her that Liza had moved into second place and was now 8 minutes behind her.

Allie was feeling fine, taking on plenty of fluids and eating an energy bar every now and then, interspersed with some of Ziggy's homemade brew. The second loop went by in a blur as she went into another one of those wonderful zones where you weren't thinking, just feeling. She came out of it before she finished the loop, wanting to hear what Ziggy had to report. He yelled out that she now had a 6-minute lead over Liza. She began to get nervous but then remembered what Ziggy had told her and Michael. Stay calm. Michael and Allie had shared all the details of their respective conversations with Ziggy, just as he had encouraged them to do. The lesson that one received was relevant for the other one, and vice versa. So, Allie stayed calm and made up her mind to race her own race as the third loop began.

She checked her power output and saw that she'd been averaging about 235 watts, which was about 85 percent of her FTP (Functional Threshold Power). FTP was a measurement of the maximum power she could produce on average for an hour. Because she was two-thirds of the way through the bike and felt good, she thought she could increase her power output to about 90 percent of FTP without jeopardizing her legs for the run. She sped up and watched the power meter rise to almost 250 watts. With an FTP of 275 and a weight of 59 kilograms (130 pounds), Allie's watts per kilogram at FTP was 4.65, which was as good as or better than most pro men. But she also knew that Liza's FTP and W/kg measurements were probably better than hers, so she had to push her limits in the bike to have a chance in this race. On the other hand, she also had to make sure not to burn herself out in the bike because of the looming marathon. The bike was always a balancing act in endurance triathlons, more so in the StrongForce 200 races, but it was also a factor in Iconic races.

When Allie came into T2 at the end of the bike leg, Ziggy reported that she was now only 4 minutes ahead of Liza. Allie threw her bike into the rack, ripped off her helmet, changed into her running shoes, and got up to run. She fought off the anger she was feeling at hearing the news that Liza was cutting into her lead, shaking her arms and legs to help clear the lactic acid out of her muscles, and began the marathon.

The marathon course was primarily on two small country roads that paralleled each other in an east-west direction. One was named Rang Saint-Pierre and the other was Rang Saint-Louis. The runners would head east on Rang Saint-Pierre (which then changed names into Chemin de la Rivière) for the first 6K (3.7 miles), then turn south for a short stint on Route 348 before turning due west on Rang Saint-Louis. A final turn north brought the course to the end of the 14K (8.7-mile) loop, which they would run three times.

Allie still felt good, as good as she'd ever felt in a race. She made the first loop in 59 minutes, which would project to a sub-three-hour marathon. If she kept this pace, she'd break her personal record of 2:58 in the marathon leg of the Iconic, an exciting possibility. However, when she passed by Ziggy, he shouted to her that her lead over Liza had narrowed to only 2½ minutes, and this did not feel good. But in deference to Ziggy's advice not to get angry, she relaxed and continued to run her own race, hydrating and eating at the appropriate times.

Allie finished the second marathon loop in 58 minutes, another excellent result; however, when she passed by Ziggy, he informed her she now had only a 1-minute lead over Liza. As she began the final loop, Allie looked back and saw her, only a few hundred meters behind.

Doubt crept into Allie's being. What should she do? What *could* she do? The "stay calm" mantra didn't seem to be working. There were 14 kilometers (8.7 miles) left in the race, and Liza was catching her. Suddenly, Allie had an idea. She would keep her pace right where it was. She knew what this meant, and sure enough, after about 5 kilometers (3.1 miles), Liza came up beside her. Allie glanced at Liza to gauge her condition and was both stunned and elated by what she saw. Liza looked horrible. Her face was red, her breath labored. She looked nothing like the beautiful, elegant woman that Allie knew. She appeared to be on the verge of collapse. But the ugly snarl on Liza's face resembled that of a rabid animal, and *that* is what caused Allie to consider that Liza might actually be able to continue on at this pace. She didn't turn her head to look at Allie. She just kept running, staring out into the distance, drawing in ragged breath after ragged breath, obviously deep inside her own mind, concentrating, as if she meant to do what had to be done, no matter what the cost. This frightened Allie, for herself *and* for Liza.

Allie increased her speed to stay beside her rival. That seemed to be the best plan. Just stay with her if she could. They continued on this way for another 5 kilometers (3.1 miles). It was a brutal battle of wills, neither athlete giving an inch. The two women were virtually the same height, and while Liza's bright red aerosuit was easily distinguishable from Allie's black and white suit, their legs moved in unison. Relentlessly, side by side, mile after mile, they duplicated each other's stride and pace. There were now only 4 kilometers left in the race (2.5 miles), and they were still together.

Allie was feeling the pain of the accelerated pace now. It was faster than she'd ever run in a marathon, and the exertion was taking its toll on her. But she stayed with Liza even though Liza showed no sign of slowing down. The pain and exhaustion were overwhelming, but as Allie thought about it, she realized that Liza had to be feeling just as bad as her, maybe even worse. Knowing this, she refused to back down.

Not long after they made the final turn to the north, exactly 1 kilometer (.62 mile) from the finish, Liza broke into a sprint, pulling ahead of Allie. Allie felt the sprint was coming too soon, certainly a lot sooner than she'd expected it. She was stunned and confused, but she tried to respond. She was able to stop the bleeding, but there was now a gap of 5 meters between her and Liza. And no matter how hard she tried, she just couldn't seem to close that gap.

Now it was Allie who was struggling to breathe. She reached deep within herself, calling for anything and everything that was in her to make up that gap! Slowly, ever so slowly, the distance between the two athletes began to close. It went to 4 meters, then 3 meters. She heard the crowd roaring. It was so rare to see a finish this close in such a long race! Now only 2 meters separated them.

Allie heard the announcer calling the race as they approached the finish, but she couldn't hear his words. The crowd was too loud! The roar in her ears was deafening, undulating up and down in volume in a way that made her wonder if it was the crowd or the thunderous beating of her own heart that she heard in her ears. The gap was less than half a meter. But the finish line was right ahead! She literally screamed out loud as the rage built up within her and drove her forward. Allie and Liza crossed the finish line side by side, in a literal photo finish, the first ever such finish in Iconic history. Liza collapsed when they crossed the line. Allie came to her senses and went to her, kneeling down and asking her if she was all right. Liza didn't respond. Liza was curled on her side, crying through labored breaths, her eyes closed.

At that instant, Allie realized that winning that race was far more important to Liza than it was to her. Liza was trying to prove something to herself that Allie didn't need to prove. And Liza had put it all on the line, obviously suffering for a much longer period of time during the race than Allie had, yet somehow lifting herself up until the very end. A grudging respect for Liza found a permanent home inside Allie at that moment. And when the announcement came that Liza had won the race, Allie was . . . fine. Just fine. Calm. For real.

Michael came over, leaned down, and hugged her. Allie saw Billy rush onto the course and kneel beside Liza, who was surrounded by medics from the Iconic staff, still on the ground and still crying. That was the way the race between Allie and Liza ended.

Allie looked up at Michael. "What happened in your race?" she asked, still breathing hard and rapidly. "What happened with you and Billy?"

CHAPTER 33

About 15 minutes before the race started, Branford Stevens saw Bill Dexter standing by himself, off to the side of the start area. The racers were already lining up, so all the goodbyes and good lucks had mostly been said. Bill had aged well. He was in his mid-fifties but was still trim and fit, with short dark hair that had turned a distinguished gray on the sides.

Branford approached Bill and put out his hand. "Hello, Bill. It's been a long time."

Whether it was out of habit or good manners, Bill extended his hand. "Hello, Mr. Stevens," he said.

"Bill, it's been almost 15 years since . . . since our last meeting."

"Yes, sir, it has."

"Please don't call me sir, Bill. I don't deserve it. Please call me Branford."

"Okay."

"Bill, I owe you a long overdue apology. What I asked you to do when the boys were in high school was the most dishonorable thing I've ever done, and the consequences for you were even worse."

Bill didn't respond. His habit of thinking before he spoke

had only become more ingrained as the years went by. He kept his eyes on Branford, thinking. Finally, he responded. "I accept your apology, Branford."

Branford was overcome with emotion, nearly breaking down, tears welling in his eyes. "Thank you, Bill. I really mean that. Thank you."

"Well, in the end, things worked out just fine for me, Branford. The change allowed me to explore my potential a little bit. And I remarried recently, to a lady I met at my job at Home Depot. She couldn't be here today, but she's a good woman. And the boys are fine. You know what Billy's up to, of course. And Richie just graduated college and started work down in Richmond. So, all is well with the Dexter clan. We're doing just fine."

"I'm so happy to hear that, Bill."

"The one thing I still regret is what happened to Michael," said Bill.

"It was a terrible thing, but the doctors say it couldn't have been prevented. It was no one's fault. And Michael's fully recovered and moved on. But thank you, Bill, for your concern."

"I've suffered over what happened to your son, Branford. And I have to admit that I *am* nervous about the race today."

"Why, for heaven's sake? Billy seems unbeatable."

"The boys haven't competed against each other since that awful day."

"I know, Bill. I know."

"I just don't want something like what happened then, to happen today."

Branford was a little shaken by Bill's ominous remark, but

he extended his hand. "Good luck to you and your family," he said.

The two men shook hands, and Branford moved off to find his wife and wait for the start.

The horn went off and the group of 50 pro men ran to the water, rushing in to begin the swim. Michael was happy that Danny van Devers was in the race and was wearing the same orange color aerosuit he always wore when wetsuits were prohibited. That made him easy to find and follow, which Michael did in short order. Michael and Ziggy had agreed before the race that he would either win or lose the race based on his performance in the swim. They knew Billy didn't like the long swim and had not excelled in the swim throughout the season. In fact, in the one race that season when Danny had competed against Billy, Danny had built up a 12-minute lead in the swim. In spite of that big lead, Billy's strength in the bike and run had led him to a 10-minute victory over Danny. Michael was well aware that the provision against wetsuits for today's race could further increase his advantage against Billy, so he got in behind and slightly to the left of Danny, determined to hang with him for the entire swim if he could. Billy had started the race off to the side of the group of pro men, seemingly not worried at all about his start position and with no apparent drafting strategy.

The sky was clear, and the wind was almost nonexistent, so the elements were also conspiring in Michael's favor. Billy was used to the rough seas of many StrongForce events and would have used them to his advantage if he could, but that was not to be the case today. Michael was feeling good and had no trouble staying with Danny for the 3.5K (2.2-mile) leg and for the entire 5K (3.1-mile) second leg. Michael wasn't even looking for Billy after the turns as he was completely enmeshed in his own world, concentrating on his technique and staying with Danny. When Danny made the final turn for the final 1½ kilometers (.93 mile), he increased his stroke count and began to stretch his lead over Michael. Michael dug deep, increased his stroke count, and was able to pull back to Danny's wake. Danny kept up his furious pace for the remainder of the swim, but so did Michael. He came out of the water just behind Danny, breathing hard and hoping he could recover from the extra effort he'd made in the swim compared to his normal swim.

Michael saw Ziggy up ahead. Ziggy pulled down his binoculars and began backpedaling. "He's way back," said Ziggy. "Tenth position. A good 15 minutes behind you!"

"Okay," said Michael, running hard toward T1 and breathing deeply, shaking his arms and legs to loosen up. When he got there, he worked quickly through the equipment changes, ran the bike out, executed the flying mount, and rode onto the road that would take him to the bike circuit. He was breathing hard, but it was flat, which would help him in his recovery from the swim. He used an easy gear that had him using a rapid pedal stroke, forcing blood into his legs to wake them up from their dormancy from the swim. He turned left, noting the location of T2, and switched to a harder gear. His pedal stroke slowed but his speed increased.

Michael passed Danny early in the bike leg.

"Awesome swim!" yelled Danny as Michael went by him. "Keep it up, Mikey! You've got a shot at this thing!"

Michael was a little sad that Danny was throwing in the

towel on his own chances so early in the race, but each of them knew that Michael was now stronger in both the bike and run than Danny, so unless Michael crashed or had some kind of physical issue, which was always possible, he would finish ahead of Danny.

Michael rode hard and skirted the north shores of both Lac Mandeville and Lac Deligny, then came back around and skirted their southern shores. He turned south at the bottom of Lac Mandeville, reached back with his left hand and grabbed the bottle holding Ziggy's "thin" special brew, took a big sip, placed the bottle back in its holder, and then grabbed an energy bar from his integrated storage box. The packaging had been removed from the bars prior to the race so no time and energy were wasted unwrapping them. Michael put the whole bar in his mouth, which in reality was half a bar that had been pre-broken, and resumed his aerodynamic position in the tri bars while he chewed.

When Michael finished the energy bar, he reached down for the water bottle on the front diagonal tube of his bike and washed down the crumbs. After returning the water bottle to its holder, he again resumed his aerodynamic position in the tri bars. He bore down hard and finished the first loop of the bike in what seemed like no time. He looked for Ziggy and spotted him. Ziggy was already running to maximize the time they were in earshot.

"Still a 15-minute lead over Billy," yelled Ziggy.

"Allie?" asked Michael.

"Leading. Liza's second, closing the gap."

And then Ziggy was gone as Michael whizzed by. Michael began to worry about Allie, then calmed himself down and got back into his own race. He remained convinced that his strategy to go out extremely hard in the swim, hold his lead in the bike, and hang on in the run was proving to be viable. So far so good. When he finished his second loop, Ziggy had news.

"Billy pulled into third, but he's still 15 minutes behind you, dude! Keep it going!"

That was absolutely great news for Michael. He didn't understand how this was happening, but then the thought crossed his mind that Billy was sandbagging. That made him angry. Again, he remembered Ziggy's counsel, calming himself down and getting back into his race. He checked his power output. He was currently generating about 340 watts, which was 90 percent of his FTP (Functional Threshold Power). He was taking a chance of wearing out his legs by forcing himself to ride at 90 percent, but it was all part of his strategy, so he continued on through the final leg of the bike with no changes. The scenery went by in a blur, and then he found himself making the final turn of the bike loop and cruising into T2. He quickly dismounted, threw his bike into the rack, and changed from bike gear to run gear. Then he headed out for the marathon. He spotted Ziggy.

"He's 10 minutes down, still in third, about to pass Danny," yelled Ziggy, speaking rapidly to get all the words in before Michael passed by.

"Allie?"

"Still in the lead! Don't worry about Allie!"

Michael knew Ziggy was right, but he couldn't help himself. He wanted Allie to win more than he wanted to win, simply because he knew how badly *she* wanted it. Nevertheless, he had a marathon to run and set out to do it. A 10-minute cushion on Billy wasn't bad at this point in the race, although it was a little concerning that he'd lost a full 5 minutes during the last third of the bike leg, while riding at 90 percent of his FTP. He wondered if Billy had exceeded his own FTP during the final leg of the bike, or if Billy's FTP was so much higher than Michael's that he could gain that much ground without even pressing himself. Michael told himself to stop worrying about Billy and proceeded to get his head and legs into the run.

Michael's goal in the marathon was to hold a pace of 3 minutes 40 seconds per kilometer (5:54/mile) for as long as he could. And while he knew he'd never maintain this pace for the full distance—if he did, he would run a 2:34—the longer he could maintain it, the longer he could hold off Billy. Billy had never run a 2:34, although he'd broken 2:36 in two Iconic races this season, nearly 10 minutes faster than Michael had ever run the marathon leg.

Billy was the current world record holder for the marathon at the full StrongForce distance, logging a time of 3:38:31 in the 2025 world championship. And because the bike leg of the Iconic was 35 percent shorter than the full StrongForce bike leg, Billy was able to improve on his StrongForce marathon time by several minutes when competing in Iconic races. His 10-minute marathon advantage versus Michael would be enough for him to completely erase his 10-minute deficit after T2. Michael knew this, so he continued to hold his planned pace of 3:40/K (5:54/mile) for the first loop of three in the marathon, anxious to hear where things stood from Ziggy, who reported this to Michael in his own unique way.

"He's been doing some Superman stuff, dude! Cut your lead down to 6 minutes. You know what to do!"

"What?" asked Michael, having no idea what to do.

Ziggy cupped his hands around his mouth to create a megaphone as Michael passed by. "Stay calm!"

Michael barely heard him as he was already well past Ziggy's location. He knew Ziggy meant for him to just hold his speed steady, which was easier said than done because this was the fastest pace he'd ever held. And in spite of Michael's extraordinary first loop, Billy was slicing away at his lead. It was demoralizing that anyone could run so fast this far into the race. Michael's only hope was that Billy couldn't hold his blazing tempo. And at least there was no doubt as to whether or not Billy was sandbagging. It was clear that just as Michael had built his race on an exceptional swim, Billy's strategy was obviously to pick up his pace in the final third of the bike and then run an exceptional marathon.

When Michael completed the second loop of three in the marathon, Ziggy updated him, speaking rapidly as he ran along beside the road. "Your lead is down to 3 minutes. If he catches you, it's gonna be in the final 5K. The 'stay calm' mantra goes out the window at that point, dude!"

You're telling me that now? Michael thought, too exhausted to speak as he streaked past Ziggy.

"Better late than never!" screamed Ziggy, as if reading Michael's mind.

Michael understood Ziggy's logic. If Billy caught him with such a short distance remaining in the marathon, Michael would have to stay with him, and that might mean running even faster than he was running at that moment, which didn't seem possible. A more realistic outcome was that he simply couldn't win the race unless Billy somehow faltered. Unfortunately, Billy always won when it mattered most, and he'd been doing that to Michael ever since they were 10 years old.

All I can do is give it my best, Michael thought. *That's all I could ever do, and that's what I'm going to do now.* He considered trying to increase his speed to compensate for Billy's relentless eradication of the time gap between them, but then he decided his best option, perhaps his only option, was to stay calm and see what happened. If Billy could catch him, he definitely was Superman. If Billy didn't catch him, then the "stay calm" mantra would prove to be Billy's kryptonite.

Michael continued running strong for another 5K (3.1 miles), but then his legs began to tighten up. His pace slowed dramatically to 3:55/K (6:19/mile) and continued to slip. With only 8K (5 miles) to go in the race, the cramps in his legs worsened and his pace slowed further to 4:00/K (6:26/mile). He checked his heart rate and saw it was redlining, meaning he dare not try to speed up until his heart rate came down, which would happen with his slower pace. But slowing down was exactly the opposite of what he needed if he was to have any hope of winning the race. Michael feared this predicament would cause him to succumb, once again, to Billy's extraordinary talent and indomitable will, and when he turned his head to look behind him, he saw the inevitable. Superman was on his tail, less than half a kilometer (0.3 mile) back and closing in.

Michael remembered that a few times in training he'd been able to stave off leg-cramping by drinking some of Ziggy's special brew, but he couldn't carry that weight during the marathon, relying instead on the hydration stations for water, and when absolutely necessary, Gatorade. He tried shaking his legs as he ran, which helped a little. He grabbed a Gatorade at the next hydration station and slurped it down. With 5K (3.1 miles) to go in the race, he looked back and saw that Billy had further closed the gap and was now only about 300 meters behind him. He raised his pace back up to 3:55/K (6:19/mile) and tried to hang on, knowing it wouldn't be enough.

With 4K to go in the race, he looked back again. Billy was closer, about 200 meters behind him. As Michael approached another hydration station, he saw something he didn't expect to see—Ziggy. Somehow, he'd made his way over land to get there. He was pointing at a cup on the table. "Take that one!" he yelled.

Michael grabbed the cup and slurped it down. Ziggy's special brew! Michael was too winded to speak, but he raised his right arm straight up and pointed his index finger in the air in a kind of thank-you signal. It was completely legal for Ziggy to put that drink cup onto the hydration table, but it would cost Ziggy dearly. He'd more than likely miss the end of the race, but Michael knew Ziggy well enough to know that all he cared about was helping him in any way he could.

Michael threw the empty cup down onto the road, which was now littered with cups, wrappers, and even a few water bottles. The course was also congested with more and more runners who were in the first or second loop of their marathon leg, but he was used to that and passed them with no disruption to his cadence.

Michael's mind drifted a little. His thoughts centered on

Ziggy, such a talented and thoughtful man who'd shared so much wisdom with him and Allie over the years. At that moment, he experienced a profound feeling of love and appreciation for Ziggy, realizing that he simply could not have gotten this far without his whacky, brilliant coach and friend. He knew how much Ziggy loved the sport of triathlon and the athletes he worked with. He also knew what a special experience it was for anyone who was lucky enough to witness the finish of an endurance race. So many unique stories crossed that finish line, one at a time. Michael wondered what his story would be at the end of this race, and he choked up a little thinking that Ziggy might miss it. All to try to help Michael in any small way he could.

He didn't know if it was Ziggy's special brew or the fact that his mind had stopped thinking about his cramps, but after about a kilometer, the tightness in his legs began to ease. He suspected it wouldn't last, but there were less than 3K (1.9 miles) to go, so it might be enough. He looked back and saw Billy about 100 meters behind him. Ziggy had said the "stay calm" mantra would go out the window if Billy caught him, but Billy had not yet done that, so Michael didn't panic. He checked his watch and saw that his pace had improved to 3:50/K (6:10/mile), which was very encouraging. With 2K (1.24 miles) to go, he looked back again and saw that Billy was only 50 meters behind him and coming hard. When Michael made the final turn onto Chemin Beauparlant, which meant there was only 1K (.62 mile) left in the race, he turned his head to the right and could see that Billy was only 25 meters behind him. The moment of truth had arrived.

Michael knew only one thing at that moment: He wasn't

going to look back again. This was it. He lurched forward and started sprinting. As he surged toward the finish line, he heard the crowd roaring up ahead of him, knowing it meant Billy was still coming. After about 800 meters of sprinting, a wave of hot pain erupted in his legs and his gut. The cramps were back with a vengeance, but he didn't care. Tears streamed out of his eyes, not because he was sad or disappointed about his pending defeat, but because it hurt so much! There were 200 meters to go. Michael's torso began curling over, giving in to the pain, but he forced himself back into the correct upright position, pushing his chest out, his long legs still churning, his arms precisely pumping.

The pain was indescribable. It felt like death was coming. The sun was positioned so that with only 100 meters to go he saw Billy's shadow creeping up on the pavement along his right side. Billy's shadow moved slightly ahead of him. Now Michael could hear Billy's frenzied breaths whispering into his right ear, clearly distinguishable from the deafening roar of the crowd. He was that close! At that instant, with 50 meters to go in the race and Billy edging up beside him, Michael made an intellectual decision. To win.

Michael felt no pain. He felt no fear. He simply ran faster. All of his training, all of his sacrifice, all of his courage crossed the line with him, the one finish that had remained so unreachable for so long. But this time, he reached it, a full meter before Billy did. Michael had finally made it to that distant finish which had eluded him for nearly his entire life—thanks to Ziggy, thanks to Allie, thanks to Billy and Liza, and thanks to his own courage to face his fears and try. He'd fought the good fight—and won.

Michael crossed the line with a marathon time of 2:43:26, his personal best, and a new Iconic "No Wetsuit" world record of 7 hours, 9 minutes, and 5 seconds. Billy's overall time was only a few tenths of a second behind Michael's, and he'd run the marathon in 2:33:29, an Iconic marathon record that would stand for many years. He ran up to Michael and embraced him, speaking loudly into Michael's ear to overcome the wild cheers and applause from the crowd.

"I really didn't think you could do it, bud!" said Billy, breathing fast and hard, his voice choking up a bit. "But you did! And trust me, I gave it everything I had. This makes the past year worth it, much more than if I'd won. I'm so happy for you! And for me!"

Michael broke down in tears, not because he'd won the race but because his friendship with Billy had survived it. Billy and Michael, arm in arm, moved to the side of the finish area to make room for the other competitors who'd be coming in soon. Ziggy joined them.

"What a race, dudes!" he yelled. "You just don't see an endurance race finish like that, period!"

"Did you make it back for the finish?" asked Michael, confused.

"Oh yeah!"

"How?"

"Motor cross, dude! Rented the bike yesterday, just in case. I could tell from the tracking app that you were hurting, and I took a chance that it might be cramps. I rode the bike along an off-road trail that crosses over to the road you were on. They use the trail for snowmobiling in the winter."

"What's in that drink, Two Cool?"

"You'll never know, dude, but let's just say I've spent a lot of years figuring out what natural ingredients work the fastest on cramping, among other things."

"You never cease to amaze me, Two Cool!" said Michael. "You saved my butt today. Thank you!"

"I'll do anything for my people," said Ziggy, choking up a bit, reaching out with both arms and squeezing Michael tightly. Michael held on to his friend for what seemed a long time, feeling kind of light-headed, needing to start hydrating and replenishing soon. But then his parents and Bill Dexter joined them. More hugs were given all around, for a lot of different reasons. They'd all witnessed a special moment, when a magnificent race could be won and friendships strengthened, all at the same time. But the day wasn't over. Another special moment was about to unfold.

Michael, Billy, Ziggy, the Stevenses and Bill Dexter all stood together at the finish area, waiting for Allie and Liza to come in. They knew from Ziggy that the race was tight, that the two had literally been racing side by side for the past 10 kilometers. When they caught sight of the racers, they were about 500 meters from the finish, with Liza in the lead. They were both moving very fast. The crowd was in a frenzy, and even though Ziggy was yelling in his ear, Michael couldn't hear anything he said.

With 200 meters to go, Michael could tell that Allie was closing the gap. He yelled as loud as he could, hoping she'd hear his voice, knowing she wouldn't. With 100 meters to go, about a meter separated the two women. At 50 meters, it was half a meter. At 25 meters, it was about 25 centimeters (10 inches). At 10 meters to go, they were nearly even.

At the finish, Michael couldn't tell who came across first. He watched as Liza collapsed and Allie went to her. He bulled his way into the finish area and ran to his wife, leaning over and hugging her with all his strength, then checked on Liza. Billy was there, too. Michael didn't hear the announcement that Liza had won the race, and he didn't care anyway. He just wanted to be with his wife and to make sure his friend Liza was okay.

The crowd was quieter now, worried about Liza, and he heard Allie's words clearly as she turned toward him and looked directly into his eyes.

"What happened in your race? What happened with you and Billy?" He didn't say a word, just smiled that sheepish, closed-mouth smile of his, one she knew so well. And that was enough for her to understand that Michael had vanquished all of the demons from his past, forever, on that marvelous day. Allie stood and they embraced, tears of joy streaming down their sweat-stained faces.

EPILOGUE

Later that evening, Allie and Michael joined Liza and Billy at their Airbnb in Saint-Gabriel. After the race, Allie and Michael had gone back to their own Airbnb, showered, taken a nap, showered again, then made their way back to Saint-Gabriel for dinner with Liza and Billy.

The home, brilliantly furnished in a modern style, was far larger than any two people needed and had a huge open area, which included a kitchen, a great room, and a dining area. The open area surrounded an outdoor deck on two sides, which had a beautiful view of Lac Maskinongé and the surrounding countryside.

Liza had the meal catered, which hadn't been so difficult for her due to her mastery of the French language and her willingness to pay whatever was necessary to make it happen. The two couples sat out on the deck in comfortable chairs, nibbling at appetizers and sipping wine.

Liza looked better than she had during the race, but she was still pale and a bit stretched for energy, as they all were to some degree. As it turned out, her collapse at the finish area was more about relief than it was about sheer exhaustion, although she was most definitely not back to her normal, energetic self. Nevertheless, she took charge and had some things to say.

"I have a few announcements to make," she said, a big smile on her face. Allie and Michael sat up, wondering what might be coming.

"First, I've decided to retire from competition in triathlon," she said.

Allie raised her eyebrows. "Why, for goodness' sake?" she asked. "You're too good to do that. You're not even in your prime years yet."

"The reason is simple," said Liza. "I've given my all to this sport. And I've proven to myself that even though many things have simply been handed to me in life, I have it within me to accomplish something very challenging, and very difficult, on my own. And while no one can truly be an endurance athlete without help and support, in the end, you have to put in the time, and the miles, on your own. And you have to race the races on your own. I've done that, and I won an event today, which in my mind will always go down as a tie, against the absolute best woman triathlete in the world."

Allie's face reddened, although she didn't speak. She knew there were three or four other women who might have something to say about Liza's statement, including Liza herself.

"And there's another reason I'm retiring," said Liza. "Billy and I are getting married, and we want to start a family."

"Wow!" said Michael. "That's awesome! Congratulations, you two!"

"Congratulations!" said Allie.

"Yes, we're so happy. Thank you!"

"This calls for a toast!" said Michael, standing up. Allie

joined him, and so did Billy and Liza. "To both of you I say, with all my heart, that I wish you happiness forever and ever and ever. And may you be blessed with a healthy, happy baby."

They all clinked glasses and shared some hugs, then found their way back to their seats.

"There's one more thing," said Billy, softly.

"What's that?" asked Michael, sensing something he might not want to hear and instinctively raising his index finger to his chin.

"We're moving to San Diego," said Billy.

Michael's hand came away from his chin as his head tilted an inch or two downward. There was an awkward silence that Allie filled.

"Why?" she asked, her voice conveying concern and disappointment.

"It's really hard to train based in Manhattan," said Billy. "You two, of all people, should know that. You've gotta leave town to get the best bike and run training, and even just going for a swim is an ordeal. And then there's the winter. San Diego's a hotbed for triathlon, and you can train year-round outside. I've hired a new coach out there who's got a stable of top StrongForce competitors. With Liza retiring, I'll need people like that to train with."

"What am I, chopped liver?" asked Michael. "I was hoping all four of us could start doing some training together."

"I would have liked that, too," said Allie, who had already been thinking about asking Liza to train together. Somehow, she felt as if a barrier between them had been broken during the race. A mutual respect had grown to take the place of a somewhat bitter rivalry. But now that Liza and Billy were leaving New York, all of the possibilities for training, and for a better form of socializing, were gone. "I'm kind of in shock."

"Me too," said Michael. "I guess we just took for granted that we'd all always be near each other."

"It's a long way away, for sure," said Billy. "But we're all used to long-distance traveling, right? Maybe you two could switch to StrongForce so we can all meet up at the same events."

Another awkward silence ensued.

"I'm serious, guys," said Billy. "Would you consider making the switch?"

"We'd have to think about that long and hard," said Michael.

"And we'd have to talk it through with Two Cool," added Allie. "I'm not sure he'd agree that the shorter swim and longer bike in StrongForce would match up well with what Michael and I do best."

"I hear you," said Billy. "But StrongForce has so much to offer. You want a short bike, then let's all take a look at StrongForce 100. I'd do some of those during the year if you guys would. And you two could go for the StrongForce 100 World Championship, and I'd keep doing the 200 championship in San Diego. And if you want to take a run at the 200, the more the merrier! Just tell me you'll consider it, please?" asked Billy.

Both Allie and Michael nodded, mildly intrigued. They would never even have to leave the country if they moved over to StrongForce, unless they wanted to. And if they focused on the 100 distance, they could reduce their training hours significantly and maybe get back on track in their careers in wealth management.

"We'll think about it, right, honey?" said Michael.

"Sure," said Allie. "And of course, we have to think about our own family too, right?"

Michael turned toward her, his eyes lighting up. "Are you green-lighting the baby by any chance?"

"I'm green-lighting giving it a darn good try!" she said, smiling.

"I'll toast to that!" said Liza, standing up. They all rose up from their chairs. "May the four of us remain friends forever, and may we be blessed with children who can carry our friendships into the next generation."

They all clinked glasses, shared hugs once again, then plopped back into their chairs.

"I think I'm more exhausted from the news at this dinner party than I am from the race!" said Michael.

"Agreed," said Allie.

"Well, I have to say," said Billy, "if I could've predicted how well this year would turn out, I'd have jumped into the Iconic waters a lot sooner than I did. But I sure am glad it's over!"

"It's only just beginning," said Michael. "For all of us."

The End

About the Author

Steven Decker has traveled throughout the world for most of his adult life, mostly for business, but always with a deep and abiding respect for other cultures. For many years, he was an active triathlete, and in *Distant Finish* he combines his knowledge of the sport with his extensive experiences in many places around the globe. His favorite place is Ireland, which he visits nearly every year to walk cross-country, enjoying the breathtaking scenery and incomparable hospitality of the Irish people. He lives and writes in a small, rural town in the northwest corner of Connecticut, where he lives with his three dogs, and is now working on his next novel.